THE COMPASS POINT

PATTY DUFFY

BOOKS BY PATTY DUFFY

The Compass Point
Song of the Pearl and Oyster
Give or Take

History says, don't hope
On this side of the grave.
But then, once in a lifetime
The longed-for tidal wave
Of justice can rise up,
And hope and history rhyme.

– Sophocles *The Cure at Troy*

CHAPTER 1

2000 New York

A September cold snap had brought early tinges of red and orange to the trees. Past the suspension bridge just short of the steep *Stairway to Heaven* incline, Archie and his nephew found a cluster of ghost apples. Logan looked over the empty, crystalline clusters. Below them, some berry-sized apples had escaped and tumbled to the ground. In a ten-year-old huff, he stomped on them with his hiking boots.

"Okay, are you going to tell me now why I needed to fly here?" Archie said. His impatience was a sham.

"Every time Dad comes home, it's worse," Logan said. "Whatever I do or say, it's wrong. He says not to tell anyone at school that he's home, or they'll come after him. I ask who is coming after him, and he won't answer. 'Why don't you do this' and 'You should do that,' he says." Logan gave his imitation of his father. "He drinks, and then he argues with Mom." He kicked a stone.

Archie waited. Logan closed his eyes and breathed in the cool air. Opening his eyes at Archie, he didn't reveal his usual crap-detecting scowl or glint of anticipation, just sadness.

"He watches me like I'm doing something wrong all the time. I had my history book out for homework, and he grabbed it. He said my book was a bunch of lies and the Civil War wasn't about slavery. He said the slaves were treated great, and it was better for them than dying, that the South had the right idea, and I should tell my teacher. I'm not telling my teacher that shit."

Archie swallowed the words he wanted to say. "There are people who agree with your dad, but your teacher is right. You can make up your own mind." He told his nephew that he did the right thing by calling him instead of running away. Archie told him that there were times he wanted to run away, too.

Logan sighed and kicked the ground. He looked up the steep trail. "Why can't you just stay here? This can be your home base. You fly back and forth anyway."

Archie looked at him with a rueful smile. He ruffled his nephew's hair. "Let's go," he said.

The two followed the circular path for the rest of the day, clearing their steps over stones kind enough not to twist an ankle. Archie listened to Logan's telling of the words that hurt and his dread of the next ones to come until they arrived back at the brownstone late for dinner.

The next day, a secure phone message cut short Archie's visit. He took the stairs two at a time to pack his bag. A shutdown at his university in Hungary had sparked the beginning of a student protest. Archie viewed the forced shutdown as problematic but not unexpected. His surprise was the students' response, and he had to be there in support.

As Archie told his security detail to get tickets for his flight to Budapest and ten boxes of fruit pastries for the protesters, he spotted Logan standing at the bottom of the stairs. Somehow, he'd explain why he had to leave. Logan would have to understand.

A few days earlier, when Archie was in Hungary, Logan had called to ask about hiking the trail.

"I want to try that stairway trail, like the song?"

"Stairway to Heaven? How do you know about that song?

"I heard Dad singing it. He's home. Please, *Dod* Archie. I want to go hiking."

Archie pictured his nephew near the wall phone in the kitchen, twisting the chord as he spoke. He didn't want to force Logan into an uncomfortable explanation, but the timing was odd. All of their prior hikes had been in the spring and summer. Now it was fall, and Logan was back in school. He'd have to pick up some warmer gear.

Logan spoke so quietly on the other end of the line that Archie could barely hear him. "*Dod* Archie, if you can't come, I think I'll run away again."

Archie recalled his sister's wailing phone call last year when Logan had been missing for fourteen hours. Uncounted blocks away, a homeless man had listened to Logan's story and walked him back to the brownstone. "I'll clear my calendar and catch a flight from Budapest tomorrow," Archie said.

"The earliest one?" Logan asked.

A tug on Archie's raincoat brought him back to the present. The SUV was quiet on the ride to JFK. Everyone seemed as lost in thought as Archie was. He felt his nephew lean into him as the SUV turned a sharp corner, and he watched as Logan's finger traced the tiny black monogram beside the buttons on his frayed shirt cuff: a six-pointed star, bars, and a bird in flight.

"What's that?" Logan asked.

"I'll tell you." Archie rechecked his watch. "These are reminders to me. That's the Star of David." He pointed to his cuff. "It means harmony. The lines are a *mitzvah*, to do what we can to help level the playing field. Like your mother needs a prosthetic foot. Sometimes, we forget she has it because she gets around like we do, but doctors needed to fit the foot and help her learn to use it so she could walk again. A *mitzvah* is like that, making things fair. The bird means a release from fear and hope for the future."

Archie looked down at the wayward waves of his nephew's hair and worried about him.

"*Dod* Archie, Mom said it was just your fancy shirt," Logan said.

"*Dod* Archie, *Dod* Archie, call him your uncle like a normal kid," his father said, turning to them from the front seat.

Archie caught his sister's frown in the rearview mirror as she drove toward the airport, the SUV's windshield wipers working against the Midtown rain. "It's what he wants. *Dod* is the language of our people," she said.

"Yeah, well, this is not the land of *your* people," Logan's dad replied as he fiddled with his phone. He turned and looked down his nose at Archie. "What time ya need to be there?"

"If I'm there in forty-five, that should do it." Archie's baritone voice cut through the echoes of street noise outside. He hoped their hike, that time away to vent, would be enough to keep Logan from cutting loose.

CHAPTER 2

1967 Israel

Archie and Rivka hadn't been on the kibbutz for a year yet when the taunting started. Rivka was only four but made friends easily in the children's house. For most of the day, she could forget that they had no parents to visit at 4:00 each day like the other children whose parents came to collect them. For Archie, it was more difficult. The boys made fun of his Hungarian birth, his accent, his skinny legs, and his poor health. It wasn't as bad as the first years after the war when they moved to Israel with his mother.

Walking the streets of Haifa, a man shook his fist at them, calling them traitors. He claimed to be a resistance fighter and called Archie's father a coward. When Archie yelled back, his mother yanked his arm "Shh. It's not safe."

Back at the house, his mother locked the door. Shortly before they had fled Hungary, because of the threats, and fear of something worse, she said. But the anger seemed to follow them here.

At home, his mother had a way with words, telling him the truth about his dad and the Hungarian resistance so that he would never forget. Jews worked hard for Hungary before the war, and they thought that the government would protect them like any citizen. Instead, the government handed them over.

A tip from a neighbor revealed that his father was working for the resistance, making weapons from broken guns. Rather than kill him, the Germans made him repair weapons for them, threatening to kill his parents if he refused. At the end of the war, he learned that they took his parents to Auschwitz anyway. The years he spent in the resistance never mattered. He was an honorable man, but neighbors knew him as a collaborator, a pariah. After the war, he married and had a family, hoping that times would change and that they wouldn't have to suffer. One day when Archie was small, his father was gunned down by another resistance fighter, a veteran. It was hard for Archie and his sister either to act ashamed about their father or to risk violence.

After their mother's death from random crossfire in front of their home in Haifa, the children were sent to a kibbutz near the border. Early on, the older neighborhood boys blindfolded ten-year-old Archie and dragged him far away to disorient him, removing the blindfold in a place in the kibbutz he'd never been in the hope that he'd get lost and never return. After a few of these episodes, he considered these kidnappings to be little adventures. He'd listen to the sounds of goat's bells, echoes of cantors through open synagogue doors, the smell of the baker's bread or the mechanic's oil, and trace his way back by sound and smell. When the boys discovered that he didn't mind these excursions, they gave up. But not Archie.

Although he was supposed to stay in the Children's House, he found it easy to escape and to wander around the kibbutz during the parent visits. He was a curious child and enjoyed the freedom to go where he pleased. From time to time, he often ended up at the mechanic's shop. The grandfatherly man would stop what he was doing and tell Archie stories about places he'd visited – Sharm al-Sheikh, Istanbul, and Rome. On one visit, he pulled a battered compass from his pocket and showed Archie how it worked. "Here is true north," he said. "You know there is only one true north. People may try to tell you something different, but a compass reminds you to depend on yourself. Any time you're lost, it will remind you to find your way." Archie thanked the man and pushed the compass deep into his pocket, holding it tight. Like a soldier with a gun, he felt in charge.

He returned to the Children's House and Rivka shortly after. With Rivka came her friend Adi who had just returned from Adi's parents. Adi's parents were happy to have Rivka join them as their daughter was an only child. Time with their quiet child was more pleasant with bubbly Rivka nearby.

Archie showed the girls his compass and told them about True North. He told Rivka the compass would always help him find the best way to care for her.

The next day, Archie was in the grove, raking olives from the tarp and putting them in boxes. The sun was hot, and Archie was tired. Jacob, Adi's brother, who was big for his age, approached.

"Give it to me."

"What?"

"That compass. I'm gonna tell. You can't have anything that you can't share. Give it to me, or I'll turn you in, and you'll be in big trouble."

Archie clenched his fists, but Jacob pushed his shoulders and knocked Archie off balance. He landed on the olive tarp.

"C'mon. It's old. It has dents in it." Archie's hand slipped into his pocket, and he held tight to the compass.

"Give it to me now," Jacob said. He kicked Archie's ribs and pulled his hand open. He grabbed the compass and ran off.

That night in the cafeteria line, Archie had an idea. He saw Jacob leaning over a bowl of hummus and left the line to talk to a cook. "I saw Jacob spit in the hummus," he said, pointing to the bowl.

The cook went to the line, batting away a child who tried to pick up the serving spoon. She grabbed the bowl and took it to the kitchen. "Jacob Klein, come here."

Archie watched from his table as the cook called out Jacob, gesturing and pointing to the dinner line and then the door. Jacob left for the Children's House.

The next night, Archie got in line behind Jacob. He watched Jacob pull the ponytail of the girl in front of him. She turned to scowl at him, and he did it again.

Archie left his place in line and found the cook. "Jacob pulled Leah's hair twice. Then he put hair in the salad."

"Stop with this tattling," she said. Mind your own business," She walked around the salad and decided to remove it. "Jacob," she called once more.

The next day, Archie found Jacob in the olive groves. "Give me back my compass."

"What are you gonna do if I don't?"

"I'll tell Cook that you shit in our food."

"Get outta here," Jacob said.

That night, at the bottom of his toothbrush mug, Archie found the compass.

The following week, he sought out the grandfatherly mechanic who appreciated a good story. But the mechanic was gone. He returned and asked around, but no one knew where he had gone. Archie missed him.

CHAPTER 3

2000 Hungary

Students at Archie's University Europe Central had been protesting in the streets for over 30 hours. His journalists walked with the protesters in Budapest's Szechenyi Square and refused to leave. "All they want is relief from blisters on their feet," Zolt told Archie.

"Betadine, Zolt. Send someone for Betadine cream and new socks. And ten more boxes of those layered fruit pastries from the Bottega di Finestra on Platnerska 11."

Archie walked down the line of protesters, shaking hands and hugging them, ignoring the shouts from counter-protesters on the other side of the street.

"The Russian government subsidizes their protesters. We do not." Nicoletta told Kristof. Nicoletta edited her story as they walked, but she wanted it out of her notebook and into the world. "So many signs – about freedom to make the films we want, books chosen by professors not – " Nicoletta stopped in mid-sentence. Three young men in black t-shirts, arms linked, goose-stepped next to them singing the Russian national anthem loudly enough that the hairs on the back of her neck stood up. Kristof linked his arm in hers and tugged her away to another part of the crowd.

"The protesters started as a few hundred, and now the crowds have grown to include townspeople by the thousands," Nicoletta said, "with no shots fired."

"We deserve free access to our history and culture with nothing left out. If this is a test of strength, we will win!" Kristof's voice was ebullient, unusual for him. "Look at the rooftops with soldiers pointing guns - chilling, but they can't suppress our will. Like the protests in 1848 and the 1956 uprising, this is the power of a free press."

"Think of Genevieve Marx's poem. We cannot tolerate this to be woven into forgetting," Nicoletta said. She pointed and read more banners: *We want no red terror. No police state. We want our school. Let us learn freely.* Nicoletta added to her notes.

That night, they carried torches to Buda Castle. Young and old, college employees, farmers, shopkeepers, and families stood with the students. "I heard some older people talking about the 1956 uprising. I need to interview them," Nicoletta said.

Police had positioned water cannons nearby, but they remained unused. Nicoletta was not diminished by them but felt invigorated to consider the strength of a sea of protesters compared to the purview of the Russian gaze.

CHAPTER 4

1978 Austria

In high school, on the kibbutz, Archie waited after class to share a few words with Mr. Friedman, his history teacher. Then, he'd race to the next class to dodge the jeers from other students. They didn't appreciate his detailed knowledge or how he corrected their answers. At lunch, he'd sit alone working on his Rubik's cube, solving the corners first. If anyone stopped to look at the curious block of squares, he'd tell them that a Hungarian architecture professor invented it, and they'd walk away. Rivka's friends were even less appreciative of his comments, especially boys who tried to take her on dates.

By graduation, Archie had shown promise in economics and languages, English, Czech, Hungarian, and Hebrew, but mainly in German. An international banker in Vienna offered him a scholarship to major in finance, and he accepted. Rivka was more excited than he was. She would be free of his meddling in her life during her last two years of high school.

The reality of three years of compulsory military service loomed over Archie. Rivka was secretly anxious to get him out of her life, so she encouraged him to take the scholarship and find a way to escape the country. Once he left, he would never be able to go back. Guilt weighed on him along with his compulsion not to mark time waiting for his life to begin. He wanted to change worldviews, not carry a rifle.

They were close to the border, after all. He didn't take much convincing. The night before Archie was to report for service, he hopped into the back of a flatbed truck, hid under dusty canvas tarps, and made it across the border into Jordan. From there, he hitchhiked to Syria, where he picked fruit. He passed through Turkey and Greece; and then Serbia, where he worked on a farm; and Hungary, where he tutored in languages. After several weeks he finally arrived in Vienna.

His host, Max Bauer, was astounded that Archie had hitchhiked across several countries, living on the odd jobs he'd picked up along the way. On second look, he noticed how thin Archie was and decided that he and his wife needed to feed him before he began his course of study. Archie wasn't used to the attention but was happy to regale them with stories of his journey. Through it all, he had discovered that he loved to travel.

As part of his scholarship, Archie worked a few hours a week in the offices of Max Bauer and his son Elias, who was also Archie's classmate. Max was impressed with the quality and speed of Archie's work and hoped that some of this work ethic would rub off on his son. Although Elias didn't aspire to Archie's grades and his meticulous attention to the details of finance, Elias was lighthearted and tried to teach Archie how to joke. Life was about living, not working. Archie's journey to that conclusion was long and hard-fought. With Elias, he didn't feel as if he was expecting a punch or a humiliating comment. He now understood what friendship meant when Rivka's letters from Israel lamented her friend's woes and celebrated their happiness.

Archie needed to find something worth his time in Vienna. Economics and banking made logical career sense, but he longed to make sense of his life. *Vater* Bauer, as Archie called him, opened his library, and Archie, always a quick reader, discovered biographies. He read about Ben Franklin, Alexander Hamilton, Rene Descartes, Hannah Arendt, and Albert Camus. But, one adage that justified his worldview – an affirmation, was from Aristotle in his *Rhetoric*: everything in moderation, nothing in excess. Even America's Ben Franklin and Mark Twain had their versions of this.

He was ready to share Aristotle in a letter to Rivka when he came across a biography of Teddy Roosevelt. The Trust Buster had even named one of his five children Archibald. Archie didn't ride horses like Roosevelt, but when he read about Roosevelt's having overcome childhood asthma with a strenuous lifestyle, he began working out at the university gym and running before morning classes. He convinced Elias to join him on the Lünersee trail outside Vienna. It was six kilometers long and could be reached by gondola. The trail wound around lakes and through dense forests. By the end, Archie had a new passion for hiking, and Elias told him never to suggest hiking to him again. When Archie wrote all of this to Rivka in a lengthy letter, he ended with a Roosevelt quote: "Knowing what's right doesn't mean much unless you do what's right."

After that letter, Rivka decided to accept a scholarship as far from Archie as possible: in New York City.

CHAPTER 5

1980 Austria

Max Bauer wasn't just a banker; he knew a talent when he saw one. After Archie's summer internships and his university MBA in finance, the world of Klimpt art, opera, Viennese coffee, tortes, and mountain climbing opened up to him. Archie worked and played hard but lived differently from his childhood kibbutz life, where everyone had the same: enough. Social housing in Vienna helped, but the homeless people he found in the subway ate away at him.

Archie talked freely with bankers who recognized his financial insight. Bauer's cohorts encouraged him to give Archie control of his own small fund, unheard of at his young age. He took calculated risks and poured his private money into the fund, dutifully disclosing his contributions. It became wildly successful, but once he'd succeeded, he felt restless to do more than make money.

On a trip to Africa, he saw the poverty, the men who were off fighting, and the women who were resourceful enough to keep their children alive with no support. Imagining what they could do if they could afford school for their children, he set up a fund to offer microloans to the women left behind. With a goat for milk and cheese or chickens for eggs, the women could pay for school and uniforms for their children. And with few exceptions, they always paid him back. As much as he aimed toward balancing the scale with this type of loan, autocrats worldwide saw his growing power as a threat to established society and spread rumors about his motives.

CHAPTER 6

1988 Austria

Despite the indignant anger among European and US investors toward Archie's success, they flocked to his lectures on investing. Embarrassed by his growing wealth, he started a free international university in Budapest, Hungary –, University Europe Central –, hiring lecturers he'd met from around the world and guest lecturing there himself. The university garnered a reputation for diversity from a growing number of cultures and also openness to truth-seeking debate. Multiple threats to Archie's safety required security forces wherever he traveled. His fame left him in physical danger, feeling isolated and alone.

It was the evening of another of Max Bauer's dinner parties. Archie was still on good terms with the Bauers despite working for himself in Europe and abroad, but he balked at the invitation. Elias told him he had to come to this dinner. There was someone he wanted his friend to meet.

At the table, he looked past Elias to the polymaths, economists, and philosophy professors from the University of Vienna, and the bastions of the Vienna Securities Exchange engaged in civilized but bracing arguments. After the wars, Vienna's artists, architects, and designers, who saw art, science, and economics as puzzle pieces of philosophy, fled west in a diaspora to Britain and the US. Austria's Arnold Schwarzenegger was now governor of California, applying Austrian influences in his adopted country – working hard and gathering a variety of perspectives in support of environmental issues and a push toward universal health care. From Schwarzenegger's life during the war, he knew that everyone had to contribute. A state-run economy was impossible. An Austrian native son inspired and influenced Americans in the American state that Europeans loved best.

Vienna's vibrancy, beauty, and stability made Archie feel grateful. Even now, it remained a city of ideas, thinkers, and doers centuries after Florence, Italy, and decades before California's Silicon Valley existed. Instead of tormenting and using brute force to point fingers of blame around a cause, the Viennese disposition was to embrace new ideas, draw on traditional civilization, and protect the rule of law. As often as he declined these dinner invitations, he blamed himself and his hubris. Vienna's economics professors were some of the best in Europe, and his successful application of their knowledge made him the scourge of polite society in Vienna.

The stock market crash in '87, the year before, forced selling that triggered what was now known as Black Monday. Archie had been alarmed by what he had heard from his European financial friends in the months before. They spoke of portfolio insurance and how it would protect them, but Archie had predicted danger and told them so. They laughed at his caution when he broke ties and sold trusts. He bought gold with some of the proceeds and sold real estate before the flat real estate market fell further. Hong Kong crashed first before the spread to European markets. When the British FTSE dropped 23% in two days, Archie was one of the few left standing.

On that infamous Monday, October 19th, British brokers, in

particular, were eager to unload loans to him. When the loans appreciated within days, he packaged them as securities to sell at a premium, as British law allowed. Stocks in 19 countries lost a year's gains, and Archie's canny moves gave him cash to buy them up. With the selling frenzy, liquidity vanished, and everyone from CEOs to homeowners was stunned.

When Archie profited, British newspapers painted him as a villain and called him reckless. Editorial cartoons in Europe caricatured him as a grotesque puppet master with a Star of David on his lapel. In America, Wall Street claimed that Archie was partly to blame for his packaging of securities. Ignoring the backlash, he quietly bought up bargain bin stocks that he found most resilient – a call center company and a meat packer, on the New York Stock Exchange. Another American company he had been watching, Apple Computers, looked like a bargain at $14 a share. He liked the inventor Steve Jobs' idea to make computer design intuitive and easier to use. Archie hadn't broken the law, but he had used the trajectory of the market to his advantage. His rocketing wealth had made him a scapegoat for everything that was wrong with capitalism.

Archie sat next to Max at the head of the table with Elias on the opposite side. Elias's mother had set the table with particular care this evening, it seemed. The candelabras seemed brighter, the flatware newly polished.

"Archie, this is Jean Marc Arbogast." Max said.

"*Ravi de te rencontrer* Archie - real estate and finance from Strasbourg."

"Arbogast – "

"Yes, from south Germany. The Arbogast name means foreign warrior. Our family has been in Strasbourg since the 7th century." He puffed his chest when he spoke. "Maybe you've heard of our organization – "

"I remember that German billiard table salesman with the same name in prison for – "

"Archie, I'd like you to meet Layla," Elias interrupted, and Arbogast fell silent.

Archie turned his attention to the woman on Arbogast's right, a striking presence. Elias spoke to introduce them, but Archie interrupted with his own introduction. She met his eyes, angling her head slightly, tucking a wave of dark hair behind her bare shoulder. Layla revealed her name and said that she was working on a project requiring his expertise. Archie decided in an instant that whatever project she wanted his help with, sewers in Bangladesh, flack protection for Tibetan Buddhists, he would be her expert.

"Now, no more talk of business," Max waved away her comment. "Layla, tell us what you think of our city of Vienna?"

Archie knew that she was speaking, but his eyes held hers, so lovely it felt as if he was looking into a still mountain pond after an all-day climb. He forgot where he was. She paused. Had she asked him a question?

"What was that again?" he asked.

"*Der Haberer* – " Elias guessed that his friend had no regrets over his mother's seating arrangement. "She heard you were going hiking and asked where."

Archie was ready to leave on a long-planned vacation, but he knew better than to say so with so many people listening. Instead, he spoke of another hiking trip in Spain, the Camino de Santiago.

Layla's face lit up. "I've covered various lengths of it with my *Tia* Gabriella but never the whole trail. Maybe someday."

Their conversation turned to pitons, hiking boots, and trail food. Dinner guests around them seemed nonexistent until after dessert when the *Fakir* was served. The waitstaff placed strong black coffee with sugar and rum before them, and at last, they paused their conversation to look at the others.

"*Mutter* Bauer, the meal was superb," Archie said. Other than the coffee, he couldn't recall one thing he had eaten.

"I can't remember when I've had a more pleasant dinner conversation," Layla told her.

At the end of the evening, Archie drew Elias aside. "*Oida*, you didn't tell me about Layla. This woman! Why haven't I met her – "

"We have been friends for a while. I thought you'd hit it off, but step back, my friend. You'll scare her off with your tactics!"

"Tactics, nothing. I'm going to ask her to go on the hike with me. Two weeks. I'm taking a holiday."

"What woman would agree to that – mud, dust, twenty miles a day? You saw her, impeccably dressed in every detail." Elias shook his head. "Prepare to be disappointed."

"All she can do is say is no."

As they were saying their goodbyes at the door, Archie asked her in blunt terms if she would go on a two-week hike with him.

He saw a trace of a smile. "I think that it would be a wonderful opportunity for us to talk about foreign relations, and we are hiking," she said. "No stuffy boardroom."

CHAPTER 7

1988 Corsica

Archie lowered his expectations when she mentioned getting away from a boardroom, but he was hopeful. He explained that this was his holiday and that he didn't take many vacations. They flew to the island of Corsica and spent the night at a local inn before their hut-to-hut hike, the Tour de Mont Blanc.

After a light meal of local food, the two sat shoulder to shoulder on the ground before a campfire. Archie felt a charged pulse. He knew so little about her, but the anticipation was palpable as they watched the last tinges of orange sky escape between the Corsican mountains.

"So – what's your story?" Layla asked.

"I guess – " Archie didn't want to scare her off. "My sister and I grew up on a kibbutz in Israel, where we moved after my father died in Hungary. Our mother was killed in Haifa, crossfire during a random dispute, and we were sent to a kibbutz that looked after us. I came to Vienna for college and met Elias. After graduation, Elias' dad gave me my first fund to manage. My sister is married to a New Yorker and teaches international relations and history at CUNY."

Without comment, Layla began with her own story in a strangely dull voice. "I grew up in Palestinian territory next to the West Bank, land that was stolen from us. My parents were activists who planted hundreds of land mines."

"Terrorists."

"Activists. We want our state back. I grew up living with the sound of Israeli shells exploding, never feeling safe. When I was old enough, *Tia* Gabriella invited me to join her in Spain. She sent me to college." Layla stared into his eyes.

"My sister lost her foot from land mines." Archie snapped. "I took off before my compulsory three years of service and never went back. She said her mandatory service in the military was for both of us. It wasn't long before she became an expert in anti-personnel mines. They assigned her to de-mining duty during the last six months." He tried to keep his voice steady. "She was so good at it that she trained other soldiers to find IEDs." Archie stood. "It should have been me." He gave her a look. "That land you mentioned had been Israeli land since 2 BCE." He left the campfire and returned to the room. In a corner chair, as far from the bed as possible, he tried to sleep.

Layla watched the embers die and returned to the darkened room, covering herself in the only bed. From the corner of her eye, she could barely make out the shadow of his figure slumped in the chair and wondered why she had agreed to two weeks with this man.

When they woke the next day, Archie spoke only of necessary things. Layla inquired and found that neither had been able to sleep deeply. Archie asked if she wanted to spend two weeks with him after their prickly night. She blinked and nodded, not a resounding declaration of agreement. By the time they stopped for the cheese, baguette, and dried fruit that had been packed for them at the inn, they had trotted out a few safe subjects. The mountain views and bracing trails had lightened their moods. "I've only hiked alone, so you must tell me if I'm not considering what you need," he said.

"I think our pace is sustainable," Layla agreed. "I can pick up the pace if we need to."

Since Archie had walked this trail before, he pointed out the most picturesque places on the afternoon hike. "The last leg to the hut is pretty steep. Wait until you see it. But it looks worse than it is. The hut for tonight is one of the more rustic ones we'll stay in. They're all a bit different."

Layla had experience hiking, but Archie's heads-up of the "pretty steep" last leg of the hike was an understatement. By the time they spied the first hut, reachable by one last precarious balancing act down a craggy hill and into a valley, Layla felt ready to collapse. When they arrived, Archie used a key to open the padlock. Layla walked to the back, where she found an outhouse and a metal showerhead hung from the wall. She grabbed the soap from her backpack, tossed the pack to the side with her clothing, and turned on the cold water. It felt delicious.

By late afternoon, the sun had dropped behind the mountains. Layla washed her clothes and dried them on a fence post in front of the hut.

"I'll make dinner," Archie called out to her. Each hut contained simple camp food provisions for one night and backpack food to get them to the next evening's hut. "We're in luck. This one has a bottle of wine."

The sun left them in darkness within a short time, except for one kerosene lamp. Archie brought their dinner on two plates and served the wine in coffee mugs. They sat on a bench with the kerosene lamp between them, using their laps as tables. The amount of food was generous: canned vegetables and fish. They attacked their food with ravenous gusto.

After dinner, Layla sipped her wine. "I think of what we just ate, and then I think of the women of Kenya." She picked up the bottle and read the winery label - Corsica and the grape was Nielluccio. "I have a message for you from a woman I met there."

Archie looked up from the small wooden puzzle he was working on. "What message?"

"Your microloan allowed her to get a goat. She sold some of the milk and learned to make cheese with the rest. Your loan allowed her to send her little boy to school. She was incredibly grateful."

Curious, he put down the puzzle. "Tell me about her."

Layla gave the details of the mother, Elida, and little Juma's progress, surprised that Archie was still listening.

"I've given more of these loans than I can count. African leaders have denounced me for upsetting society by the power it gives to women. But this is what I want to do. He hugged Layla. "That's the best thing I've heard since we came on this trip. The best thing I've heard in a month." He stood up and began pacing. "I see the spreadsheets and hear the quarterly reports, but think of what this boy might do someday. It's worth all the tabloid headlines that I'm a Jewish Nazi, even though I was born 17 years after World War II. Russia claims I've sworn to destroy them. Poland claims I'm a sexual predator who kills children because I promoted family planning organizations. And in Hungary, where I was born – well, you get the idea." He sipped the wine. "Your story of Juma is worth it all." He looked at her and raised an eyebrow. "Could you put me in contact with his mother? I'd like to arrange for his college if his mother agrees."

Layla was skeptical of his offer; her feelings were prickly and complex. "It's part of my job – locating and recording stories of local women who have been abused, archiving the evidence, and showing it to the country's government so that they will do something instead of nothing."

"You do that?"

"Every day. I learn the laws of a country to know what questions to ask the victims for their relief."

"The poverty, the struggle, the disconnect – " He checked the kerosene lamp. "So, tell me a story about you."

She thought of one that was too personal and opted for a safer topic. "My aunt loves to drive. On weekends, we'd get in the car and just go. Once we were on the back roads far from Madrid and– "

"Is that where you lived, Madrid? Beautiful city."

"Yes, well, my *Tia* Gabriella was involved in telling a story. I hadn't been in Spain that long. The story was about her neighbor fighting with a Basque neighbor, and as the story unfolded, she drove faster and faster until the police caught up with her."

"Did they ticket her?"

"That's the thing. When Palestine police pulled us over, we just paid them off. The rule of law didn't mean anything. I asked *Tia* Gabriella, "Why didn't you pay him instead of letting him give you a ticket?"

"She looked at me like I had shocked her with an electric cord. 'Pay him? That would be illegal, *mi niña*. We don't pay off our police. We obey the law. Who told you otherwise?' That's when I realized."

"That you didn't want to return to Palestine?"

"I will always love Palestine." She frowned. " I realized I wanted to live where people followed the rule of law. If people and politicians and business owners aren't accountable, bad things happen, especially to poor people."

"You have your memories of Palestine, and I have mine of Israel. Even though there are people who don't believe our countries should exist, the souls of our countries are in us."

The evening grew suddenly cool. Inside the hut was one double bed and a cooler with the next day's food. There was no fireplace, but the bed had two heavy blankets. They took off their boots and fell into bed, spooning in a shivering embrace.

CHAPTER 8

1988 Corsica

On the fourth day, it rained. They had an established routine: get an early start, break for lunch at midday (usually a baguette, dried fish, and cheese) and reach the next hut in late afternoon before nightfall. That changed on the fifth day. Heavy rain that had begun the night before continued to pour down, deepening ruts at every turn of the trail. By midday, mudslides were common. After their midday meal, Layla slipped on a downward trail, her knee smashing into a pointed rock face. She swore and sat in the mire, searing pain in her knee.

Archie doubled back. "Are you all right?"

She swore a string of epithets that included him and what he could do with his compassion.

He ignored her words. "Let's take a look."

The blood was already seeping through her pant leg. Underneath was a kneecap left of center with a gash along the side. Archie unlaced her boot and gently took it off. The rain soaked her sock. "Put your hands back behind you. Now take your leg and hold it straight out in front of you."

"Do you know what this feels like?" Her voice had gravel in it.

"I'll help." With rain running off his nose and chin, he gently guided her leg to a straighter position. "Now, we're going to raise it as high as you can."

"I'd rather chew off my leg."

She held her breath, and the two of them lifted her leg.

"Now comes the hard part. Bend the knee in and out from your body. Listen for a pop."

"It's not working."

"Keep going."

She bent her knee two more painful times as the rain puddled more mud around Archie's boots and Layla's hands. At last, they heard a pop. She lay back on the rocks with a relieved sigh.

Archie took off his pack and found the first-aid kit. He treated the gash, and wound a tremendous wad of Ace bandaging around her knee beneath her rolled-up pant leg.

He searched the kit. "It looks like aspirin is the strongest painkiller we have. Want some?"

The last three miles felt interminable. Archie carried all of their equipment. Where it was possible to walk two abreast, Layla put her arm over Archie's shoulders, hopping to keep weight off her knee. At other points, he grabbed her arm and pulled her along. As they made slow progress, the last hour of the hike ended in darkness. At last, their flashlights reflected their hut's white A-frame walls and dark windows. The rain stopped, leaving a dense stillness.

CHAPTER 9

1989 Corsica

At the end of the seventh day, they approached a brick cottage, bigger than the previous huts. There was no evidence of habitation, but something made Layla hold back.

"What's wrong?" Archie said.

"I've not been candid with you," she said.

"What does that mean?"

"I don't think you'll mind, but I've invited an acquaintance who wants to meet you."

Hers was far from the first betrayal Archie had experienced. Someone he had begun to trust was only attentive because of his influence or philanthropy. But never had someone gone to such lengths to gain his trust as Layla – he had to give her that. "You got me. I didn't expect this from you," he said.

"I don't think you understand. He's in the cottage now waiting for us. I couldn't tell you because his whereabouts have to be kept secret. There are threats against his life." She looked at the cottage, and then her eyes pleaded with Archie. "Please just keep an open mind and hear him out."

Archie turned away from her and stalked toward the door. It opened before he reached it.

"You must be Archie."

"Vaclav Havel." Archie blinked to see if his eyes were deceiving him.

"And in the middle of your vacation, too. I have important news, or I wouldn't have interrupted." Havel's furtive glance darted around the surrounding rocks and pine trees. Archie followed his line of sight. Without a sound, two snipers had appeared at his back. At a nod from Havel, they tossed their rifles over their shoulders and retreated to the trees.

Havel greeted Layla with a ready hug like an old friend. "Some refreshment. How was your hiking today?" He traveled light, one backpack hanging from a nail in the wall. This cottage had a small kitchen, and Havel brought a pitcher from an ice box and poured drinks.

"Layla dropped her gear and rushed to Havel. "Did you bring it?"

"Yes, yes…there is time. Sit down. I want to know more before we talk of business."

Archie glanced at Havel's Frank Zappa t-shirt. He looked like an ordinary tourist, not like someone who was trying to win the first free election in Czechoslovakia.

"I read your *Power of the Powerless*, how citizens are repressed into silence and marked by prejudice to accept living a lie," Archie said. "You moved people to action like Thomas Paine's *Common Sense* did for the American Revolution."

"You are too kind," Havel said, surprised that Archie had read his book.

"And Poland's Solidarity movement in 1980. Power cannot be effective if people are not willing to submit to it."

"That's why I'm here talking to you," Havel said.

"This whole situation – " Archie paced in front of them. "I have no experience with politics. I consult financial conglomerates, mergers, and futures markets and give the profits in microloans to poor people. I started a university – "

"I know these things. I looked you up. But the people you know are the ones I must convince that Czech democracy can work. I'm a poet, not a politician. But I can't run a country by touching the hearts of the people."

"Vaclav is saying that he needs practical advice for choosing capable people to run the day-to-day workings. People who cannot be corrupted or bought off." She looked at Archie. "I told him you know such people."

"I've seen the books of some Czech legislators, some judges," Archie said.

"Yes, yes. The ones who have not yet been tempted with bribes or those seductive words which have been deprived of their meaning, the words that never benefit the people. Those are the ones I want."

"Remember, your ideas are foreign to the everyday people who are so used to the Communist yoke. You have to compromise to sell your idea, build a consensus. That kind of trust won't be easy," Archie said.

"We don't have time. The election is at the end of December. What can you give me before the end of the year?"

"Now you sound like an American. Everything's fast. Do it now." Archie drank deeply from the glass Vaclav had poured for him. "Besides, I've heard there is some apathy among your people."

"Apathy!" Havel stood. "My people are tired and oppressed. The totalitarians tried to destroy justice, but they couldn't do it. My people are not apathetic. To hell with apathy. We will live in truth."

"Say you win. What do you see happening first?"

"I see walking into Prague Castle to work, secret police cameras ripped from walls, people pouring into the streets cheering and dancing, taking back our country – "

Archie watched Havel look past them, seeing something else as he spoke. Such idealism was doomed, but he wouldn't say that to him. He slapped him on the back. "Good man. You'll need independent media. An independent judiciary. Let's get to work."

Havel brought out a zippered notebook, and the two men

hovered over it, pointing, turning pages, disagreeing, then nodding. Layla busied herself, making the best dinner they'd had since the hike began – roasted duck, vegetables, and fruits. Hours passed, and she noticed how well Archie had adapted to Havel's poetic notions, providing the concrete underpinnings that he needed to create this brave, new government. One of them would call out a legal question, and she'd reply with a caveat of her knowledge of Spanish, French, and British law, but she admitted to having a limited understanding of the Czech legal system. She would contact an expert when they returned.

Aromas filled the cottage, and the three enjoyed a hearty duck dinner. Archie praised Layla for her resourceful cooking in a strange kitchen.

"It was well stocked, actually," she said. "We have some left. I'll offer it to your security men outside if that's all right?" Layla turned to Havel.

"They're hardened outdoorsmen. But I'm sure they wouldn't object," he smiled.

Layla prepared two plates and left the men alone.

"I have to tell you about my imprisonment in '82," Havel told Archie. "It was decided that my poetry was subversive and fomented anti-government passion. It's the highest praise I can think of for my poetry. In one letter to my wife Olga, I wrote about the need to begin:

I am neither the only one,
nor the first,
nor the most important one
to have set out
upon that road.
Whether all is really lost
or not depends entirely on
whether or not I am lost.

"I tell you, Archie, I am not lost. With your help, I know what I'm doing." His face grew yet more serious. "The French have a saying; *Cherchez la femme.*"

"Yeah, look for the woman who caused the situation," Archie said.

"But that's not the case," Havel said. "I see it as the woman who is the partner, who stands side by side, equally important."

"What do you mean?" Archie said.

"We have to look for her because our culture is not used to equality. My Olga is my equal. I don't have to look for her." He nodded at Archie.

Archie was uncomfortable. He prided himself on understanding people and situations, pivoting to find common ground. Havel was out somewhere beyond his reach.

Havel thought his meaning was clear. "You understand, Layla is such a woman. Olga and I have known her for a few years now, since we met at a human rights rally in Prague. She bakes. When she visits us, she brings her Austrian raspberry shortbread. It is – aah!" Havel lifted his fingers to the ceiling. "But believe me, her heart is strong. We never thought she would find someone, you know, *rovnoprávní muži a ženy* an equal, but now there is you."

Layla opened the door. "Havel, are you sure these men had something to eat? Look!" She held up two plates scraped clean of food.

Archie took the plates from her. "You and Havel catch up," he said. Under the sink was a dish pan. He heated water on the propane stove, soaped and rinsed the dishes, then set them on a towel. Meanwhile, he half listened as they reviewed more pages in Havel's notebook. Layla was advising him about her area of expertise, international law. After the last week of hiking, Archie wasn't sure how he felt about Layla.

Because of her, he had met Vaclav Havel, and it was possible that they could continue to have a fruitful working friendship. Both Havel and Layla didn't just talk about *kompromat* but worked every day to defang powerful totalitarians and call them out. But a Palestinian woman! He looked at his past as well as his sister Rivka's.

How could he justify a relationship with this woman? Why was he even thinking along those lines?

When he called his sister, she was surprised that he had taken a vacation. He wasn't surprised that her comments were rude – rude by accident, he was sure, as some people's comments are. He mentioned only the good points, the views, a few benign conversations with Layla, and nothing about Havel. The following week, Rivka wrote to him:

My Dear Brother,

I'm pleased to hear your hiking vacation worked out for you. You never stop working, and you needed the rest. This woman, I'm not so sure about. I thought Layla would be a momentary distraction like the others, but you seem taken with her. If she wasn't Palestinian, I might like her – but Archie, how can I endure a woman whose people planted the land mine that blew off my foot? If you choose her, you will wound me to the quick.

I'm preparing my fall classes for NYU and have found more jarring evidence that continues to change my teaching and worldview. I'll tell you when I see you, but I can't tell you in a letter. You live a dangerous life, Archie. Be careful.

More news — Wilson and I are trying to become pregnant. You'll have to come and see us once the baby is born.

Rivka

CHAPTER 10

1989 Dubai

Archie ran his fingers inside the collar of his crisp tux shirt. After two weeks in hiking gear, the opulence of this floating palace, the *Sea Eagle*, seemed absurd. When he stepped onboard, a uniformed waiter offered champagne from a tray. He walked to the back of the ship to gather his thoughts and look at the remarkable view of the Dubai skyline. What did Koslov want from him? It couldn't be about a donation to his favorite projects. He was sure of that. He only agreed to the invitation because to decline it would have been more dangerous.

The Italian word *sprezzatura* means that eye-catching, effortless ease in Layla that made people turn as she passed. It is so different from the way she looked at him when her Achilles was in searing pain. There she stood at the rail before him, her scarf swept by the breeze — this woman would never belong to anyone, but he stood straighter and smoothed his jacket as he approached her.

"How's the knee?"

She turned to face him, and her knee peeked out of the slit in her gauzy white gown. She knew now why she had been invited. It wasn't about *her* work, but *his*. She looked up at him with a raised eyebrow. "Fine, thanks. I'm not surprised to see you here."

"You look – " He paused. What could he say to this vision of a woman when there was so much to say?

"Layla and Archie, you accepted my hospitality." Koslov grabbed their shoulders and pinched a bit too hard. "Please enjoy the party. I have a treat for you later in my private dining room – just the three of us."

The two of them nodded and turned to Elias. Layla spoke first. "Archie, I believe you know my plus-one and protector," she said.

"Are we here for a new foundation? A new private equity fund?" Archie greeted his friend and then spoke close to his ear. "Small talk only."

"Oh, this and that," Elias said. "You know, I've heard that meals in the private dining room are beautiful, but – "

"I feel that way as well." Archie understood. He looked at Layla, and her eyes widened. "Layla, I don't believe Elias has heard about our hiking adventure. Tell him why you decided never to hike with me again."

A waiter came by with canapes, and Layla tucked into them. Archie admired her appetite.

"I haven't had lunch," she said.

Archie noticed a smirk from the rangy-looking waiter, instead of the predictable lionizing smile. Maybe it was just naked self-interest. When he caught Archie watching, he backed away.

The three of them walked around the two-hundred-foot deck of the *Sea Eagle*.

"I heard it was designed and built in Italy. Their prices are better than the builders from the Netherlands," said Elias.

"I'll stick to Marek's barge, thanks," Archie said.

"You know there's a submarine marina in the back, and that helipad up there will be the performance space for the *Velvet Constellations*." Elias pointed to the circular disc over their heads, half the size of a football field. "They're playing after dinner."

Layla looked up. "I like their music."

"Did you ever collect music as a kid?" Archie asked Layla. "I collected vinyl records, especially The Dead."

"The Grateful Dead? You were a Deadhead?"

"That's how I learned English." Archie smiled at the thought. "Elias and I finally got to see them in Bremen, outside of Hamburg in 1981. We hitchhiked for nine hours. We'd seen them on TV on *Rockpalast,* and we brought a bootleg tape from Grugahalle in Essen, Germany, to listen to along the way. Most of the drivers didn't mind."

"Yeah, then we waited in line overnight on the sidewalk for tickets," Elias said. "But they'd sold out."

"So that night, we climbed the two-story building across the street and listened from the roof," Archie said.

They played "Feel Like a Stranger" and "Saint of Circumstance." Elias said. "Phil and Bob were hard to hear, but the sound was legend. Even across the street, there was fire in Jerry's vocals."

"The concert was almost over by the time the police found us. We'd heard most of it," Archie said.

"They fired shots into the air and scared the shit out of us. So we took off," Elias said.

"Those years were crazy. Remember, we thought about following them to Barcelona." Archie held up his champagne glass to toast with the two of them.

Layla told him about her Mercato collection and the song *"No es serio este cementerio."* "Looking back, I don't know why I loved a song about death, but it had some humor, too. I'll play it for you sometime."

"Make myself a bed by the waterside…" Archie sang.

"I think I've heard that one," Layla said.

He hummed more of the tune.

Archie returned to their present situation, the floating grandeur that surrounded them. It was all so foreign. "Elias, you do financial work for this guy, but you're not impressed by all this." It was a statement, not an accusation.

"We all have to feel we're important. We want others to feel our presence, and we buy things that say something about us. You're here, aren't you?"

"It's business."

"Have you noticed how every waiter is young and attractive with perfect teeth?" Layla marveled.

"They've all signed non-disclosure agreements," Elias added.

CHAPTER 11

1989 Dubai

Dubai settled into night as they walked the deck, discussing the guests they'd seen previously only on news pages. The horizon blinked with skyline lights. Elias left, and Archie danced with Layla, relaxing into the music of a jazz ensemble until the two of them were summoned to the private dining room.

"Notice instead of overlook, listen instead of ignore," he whispered.

"I'll deal with you later," Layla gave him a look that told the waitstaff that he had said something more intimate. They waited alone with an array of exotic foods, which the head waiter described and invited them to eat.

"Lovely painting," Layla nodded to the Renaissance painting of Roman ruins on the wood-paneled wall across from them.

"Erm," Archie chafed. Only someone like Koslov would risk the safety of a centuries-old painting to the wild swings of humidity on a boat. He pivoted to a safer subject. "Layla, you're a superb dancer."

"You should tango with me. *Tia* Gabriella taught me. She believed that every Spanish woman should learn to be a *bailaora*. It's a very passionate dance."

"I'd like to meet your *Tia* Gabriella someday." Archie tried to continue the small talk while they waited for their host, unsure if the room was bugged. Neither one trusted eating the food.

The air conditioning made Layla hug her arms. The smirking waiter rushed in. "May I offer you a scarf?" He held a pashmina drape in his hands. She nodded, and he placed it delicately round her shoulders before disappearing once more.

"Here you are," Koslov rushed in through the door. He checked the table. "You haven't eaten. Is this not to your liking? I can order something else."

"You're more than kind, but I have a slight upset this evening," Layla said. "I hope your chef will not be offended that we didn't eat."

Koslov ignored her. "So Archie," he settled himself in a white leather chair across the table from them. "I have an idea." Koslov steepled his hands and laid out a scheme where Archie could make millions of rubles, or Viennese schillings, his choice. All he had to do was to assist Havel in a way that would ensure he would lose the election. Once Havel had lost, there would be more rubles or schillings for supporting Moscow's version of the truth about him. "The Czechs and the Russians are brothers with a common history, one history. The Czechs can leave their illegitimate Nazi government and join with us as brothers." Koslov's arms reached out as if to embrace his guests.

"I have no evidence of a Nazi government, do you, Layla?"

"No evidence."

Koslov smiled. "Archie, you think President Reagan's missile defense system and the free world propaganda you throw about is going to overpower us? All your talk of political justice and human rights is nothing in the presence of our KGB."

A waiter came to Koslov with an urgent phone call. He stood and then turned away from them, his voice barely audible. "Get closer, Orlov."

Koslov returned to the table and savored a slow drink from his wine glass before continuing. "Intelligence leaders are now in official positions of governmental power. In league with intelligence, political might, and now *Glasnost,* our *Bratva* is free. We have Russian groups around the world. With the help of the new oligarchs, opposition to our power is more limited than ever." He looked at Layla. "You know a wise man once said there is your side, my side, and the truth. There are no lies." His eyes widened, then narrowed. "You can trust me when I say it's for the people."

"Koslov, I heard a story at a gathering in the States once when the writer Joseph Heller claimed he had something that a billionaire fund manager would never have. You know what that was?"

"You tell me."

"Enough. He said he had enough. I don't need your rubles or schillings. I have enough."

Koslov replied, "The Soviets know how to create an enemy of the people. Suppression by business and government together needs only one authoritative figure. They give the people a focus for their hate. If this authority tells the people often enough that this enemy is evil, they'll believe it, even if it's the neighbor they've known for years. Words like *corrupt, disgrace, failure, liberal, lie, steal, traitor* are words of control and power. It's not propaganda anymore. It's a new reality." His glistening eyes bore into Archie as if to drive his point home. "If the enemy fights back with evidence, the authoritarian claims it's political sabotage. The bigger the new reality, the more likely it will be believed. Keep the people in a constant state of anger and anxiety. An authoritarian is never to blame, especially when proof of his wrongdoing exists. Loyalty to the new reality must be respected above all else."

"You're talking about the Third Reich," Archie's voice growled.

Koslov smiled. "Not at all. This is our present leadership. How could you mistake a despicable Nazi playbook for our brilliant leader's plans?"

Koslov stood and walked toward the only exit. "I have a room for you here on the ship. Perhaps some time here will help you understand reality." Koslov's voice changed to one far from that of a welcoming host.

Koslov ramped up his threats to a ball-breaking pace until, at last, his phone interrupted, a call arranged by Archie from the Austrian consulate to Koslov. Arrangements had been made beforehand should he not check into his hotel room by midnight.

"I see you understand that we have other obligations," Layla said. "Our home governments of Spain and Austria have laws about keeping citizens against their will."

After the call, Koslov tried one last tactic. "Allow my driver to give you a ride back to your hotel." He was not smiling.

But Layla offered to drive Archie to his hotel in her rental car. "I'm surprised they aren't following us," she said over the engine hum.

"Don't be so sure they're not." Archie checked the rearview mirror. Between streetlights, he saw the glint of a single silver chain rise and fall on her collarbone. They stopped at the *Al Shorfa* for a quick bite.

"He mentioned *Bratva*. I don't understand," Layla said.

"It's the Russian *mafiya*, and it's getting bigger, one of the world's most powerful organized crime associations. They're involved in arms, drugs, money laundering, real estate, extortion – "

"What about Havel? He was talking about *Bratva* in Czechoslovakia."

He knows. They bribe legal businesses. Companies that need help with debt collection use them because they settle things quickly, if not legally. It would take years if business owners went to the courts to settle debts. It's one of the first things Havel wants to change, and that would mean *Bratva* would lose income. *Bratva* supports charities and soccer fields to look legitimate, but everyone knows they're a deadly outfit."

"And who is Orlov?"

"You heard that too. There must be some connection to *Bratva*. And who is he supposed to get closer to?"

After their meal, they returned to the car. Layla grew quiet before starting the engine.

"Don't you want directions to my hotel? Archie asked.

"I'm taking you to my room," Layla said. "I'd feel safer if I wasn't alone. What if my knee goes out again?"

"Agreed." Archie felt that the evening was looking up.

CHAPTER 12

1989 Czechoslovakia

Archie and Layla traveled to Prague to meet Havel and his wife, Olga, before the election. Archie wanted to warn Havel personally about Koslov, not that he believed that either he or Layla could influence the national agenda, but he couldn't forgive himself if something happened.

The leisurely morning they had planned was interrupted by last-minute political meetings, so Havel suggested that Archie and Layla become tourists for the morning. He gave them a few suggestions and promised that they would get together with Olga in the afternoon.

Layla brought a guidebook and began their tour with a Kafka quote: "Prague doesn't let go, either of you or me. This little mother has claws."

With raised eyebrows, Archie looked at her book and found the Staropramen Brewery. "If we head over there now, we should make the next tour," he said. At the end of the tour, they tasted a glass of the brewery's famed golden lager. Layla liked its light flavor, but Archie preferred something deeper and more roasty.

With the time they had left, Layla checked the guidebook and suggested a different kind of tour, *Speculum Alchemiae,* located in one of the oldest buildings in Prague. Once there, they arranged for a tour and browsed through the tidy shop's bookcases of tinctures, potions, woodcuts of cackling occultists, and *grimoires.* Alchemists wrote potion recipes in their own secret codes. On the floor was a black bear's hide.

With others on the tour, they watched the guide put her hand on a small statue, twist it, and open the bookcase to reveal a landing with railings. They followed her down a once-secret stairway to an underground dungeon-like laboratory where ancient alchemists had labored. The laboratory had been recently discovered after having been lost for hundreds of years, yet much of it was preserved as it had been. The labyrinth of square stone rooms and arched ceilings was far more spacious than the shop above. The guide told them that Sir Isaac Newton had studied alchemy and the British alchemist Edward Kelly, known to "speak to the angels," had worked here in the 1500s, trying to turn lead into gold. Among the dried herbs, crucibles, ancient glass containers of all shapes, scrolls, and bellows for fireplaces they were startled by a mummified hanging crocodile.

"So the Czechs had an interest in the occult," Archie said, fascinated by the dark feel of the place. "Vienna has its haunted furniture museum. I prefer the Esperanto Museum with its history of the language."

"Can you speak Esperanto?"

"It's kind of like Romanian. I know a few phrases. *Kio estas via profesio?* is, What do you do for a living? Then there's *Kie estas la necesejo?*"

"Meaning?"

"Where is the bathroom," Archie said.

"Ah – *la necesejo.*"

"I love hearing you say that." His hand hugged her waist, and she laughed.

A tour member turned around and loudly shushed the two of them.

The guide told them of experiments conducted in secret, hidden away to protect alchemists from the Inquisition. One elaborate tunnel system connected the laboratory to a safe exit into the woods and another to Prague Castle. "Besides alchemy, the chemists worked on an elixir of love and another for memory. They were quite popular, and some of the alchemists took teaspoons of their own creations every day."

When Archie and Layla met with Havel and Olga that afternoon, Archie could tell that the hectic days before the election had drained them. They sat together in the living room of Havel's cozy apartment. "The Alchemist Museum is a good one for tourists, no?" Havel asked.

Olga brought a tray of Heinekens for everyone.

"We have nothing like it in Madrid," Layla said.

"Vienna, either. I was wondering if Central Europeans are more open to misinformation if they are believers in the occult?"

"I haven't read any studies like that," Havel said. "I know that those who follow the strictest orthodox religious practices tend to be more comfortable with authoritarian leadership than with democracy. Atheists tend to support democracy, and we have many of them – so they may even out."

As the afternoon continued, Archie delivered his warning about Koslov. Olga brought out more beers until Archie gave up counting, and at last Havel seemed to relax.

In the middle of the night, Layla woke, thinking about the election. She noticed the empty bed and padded out barefoot to find Archie in the adjoining room sitting under a dim corner lamp with papers spread over the coffee table in front of him.

"Why are you up?" She pushed her hair back from her face.

"You couldn't sleep either?" he asked. "Take a look. I'll show you what I have." What Archie had were the preliminary plans for Havel's blind trust. "When he's elected, he'll require transparency for every investment. I'll organize everything and invest for him during his term. He'll have no information about the investments, and no one can say he's showing favoritism. When he leaves office, he gets it all back."

From the window, she saw the night lights of the Old Town's *Malà Strana* neighborhood with its medieval merchant shops and church spires sitting snugly below Prague Castle. Layla sat close to him on the sofa while he pointed out some of the companies he had chosen – stable world-renowned corporations with strong balance sheets and solid prospects. Layla also recognized some of them as ones he had recommended to her.

"The trust papers will be complete the day Havel takes office. My associates can take them to *Brno*, their Supreme Court, and the Senate of Parliament."

"I like it that you said *when* he's elected, not *if*. But blind trusts aren't legal entities in Czechoslovakia."

Archie hadn't considered that. "I don't think that anything else can be done to communicate transparency. What do you think?"

"If you present it, they have to keep it on record. It's still the best thing you can do within Czech laws." She rested her head on his shoulder. "Thank you for helping my friend."

"Now he's our friend," Archie said.

CHAPTER 13

Czechoslovakia

After taking the Presidential oath at Vladislav Hall in Prague Castle, Havel headed past the secretary's antiroom with its antique manual typewriter, into the gloomy office of the president – his quarters. It was in disarray and nearly empty, detritus from its former occupant on the floor and around the wastebasket. Outside the tall window on Wenceslas Square, as far as he could see, the streets were filled with people cheering for freedom, hundreds of hands in the air with fingers in V-signs for peace. Eighty percent of the votes had gone to Havel.

Alexander Dubček, a formidable competitor in the presidential race for his outstanding role in the Prague Spring of 1968, was now Chairman of Parliament. Vaclav was blessedly alone for the first time today without the noisy, smoke-filled cacophony he'd experienced for most of the morning's meetings with the cheering crowds, only a muffled undertone. Could he live up to their trust?

Layla had called earlier to congratulate him. "Remember the women, Vaclav," she said over the phone, as he and Olga packed for their move to the palace after the election. "They are agents of peace, and they vote. Reference them in your speeches, and remind them what you will do for them. Use your poetry to make the truth more exciting than those appalling lies against you. Feed the hope of women. Give it some spectacle – show them what independence would look like, feel like – a vote for a referendum that would change over time to fit the needs of the people, no longer one leader's whims."

"Layla, your poet's heart is showing." Vaclav chuckled. "You've been talking to Olga, haven't you?"

Deep in thought, he walked the perimeter of his cavernous office, the many doors leading out to various rooms, sealed by heavy locks. Electric wiring reached from walls like raven's claws where hidden cameras and listening devices had been cut away. He winced at the memory of his four-year imprisonment from 1979, for his stand on human rights and for refusing to cave under daily surveillance from the secret police. He pulled open the President's desk drawers, looking for keys, paper, and pens, but found none. The bridge over the yawning Soviet gap was about to take shape using a receipt and pencil from his pocket. He was a dissident, a writer, not a politician. Here was his desk and his chair, so he began to write.

- Human rights
- Paint gray buildings in color
- Call foreign friends to visit, ask for donations - car? desks?
- Ask Americans for Safe Room and call it the fridge, ha
- Release political prisoners
- Rip out all spy cameras, add news wire services, press room
- Bring in my paintings for bare walls

He paused and thought about more minor details that would make the people hopeful. The marching music of the dull-uniformed military band was uninspiring. He chose the tune *Sinfonietta*, remembering the avant-garde rock band Emerson, Lake, and Palmer. Their version of the song was the one he enjoyed. The military band uniform colors would be smartened up to a brilliant sky blue. The castle must return to being a symbol of cultural history and recreate an atmosphere of respect for humanity.

He imagined a concert, a nationally televised celebration with bands and singers from all over Europe. The American group Yes would play. Chumbawamba, Rammstein, and the Spice Girls would perform, and young people would fill Puskás Stadium.

That first week, people lined up to see him – even Barbara Walters, the American newscaster. He spoke to her about the mess in his office, the absence of anything of value, and the absence of clocks. Not one was to be found. The meaning of this absence came from the Communists' lack of need for clocks. Time and history stood still here in the castle and in the whole country. Now freed from the handcuffs of the totalitarian system, history would barrel forward, he decided – pushing on and making up for lost time.

CHAPTER 14

1990 Austria

Layla, how about mountain climbing this weekend?" Archie left a brief message on her voicemail, hoping she would see it. It had been a year since they had shared beers with Havel and Olga, and months since Havel had won his election. She moved around Europe nearly as much as he did, but he heard through Elias that she was in Vienna on business.

Within an hour, she returned his voicemail. "Archie, what a surprise to hear from you. I had nothing planned but a stuffy awards ceremony tomorrow. I'd love to go climbing."

On Saturday morning, they stood at the base of Raxalpe mountain. "Show me your pitons," Archie said.

Layla laughed at him, recalling the conversation from their first meeting over dinner. Raxalpe was a good day's hike with breathtaking snowcapped views, but she found that many of the steep routes weren't much more challenging than their hike the year before.

Near the top, it began to rain. "Believe me, I checked, and this wasn't supposed to happen," he said. Their rain gear was packed, and the drop in temperature added to the discomfort of their rain-soaked clothing. Archie took extra care and hammered four pitons with safety lines into the granite – or quartz – he wasn't sure which. Shiny with rain, the two portaledges for their night's lodging looked secure on the mountainside.

They positioned their feet together to see each other's faces in the opening of the ripstop nylon windbreak. The rain passed, and the setting sun melted down the mountain in a plum blush. The two of them split open their nylon garb like pea pods, and their upper bodies felt the mountain air once more.

"This look on your face – you wear it well," Layla said.

"It's the mountains that feel like home more than anything. They don't judge Palestinian from Jew, Hungarian from Russian, and they'll outlast all of us." Archie moved himself around and retrieved a small cube puzzle from his vest pocket. "You never asked me why I do this."

"You've never asked me either." Layla inched herself snugly into the hammock, hoping that her body heat would dry her soaked climbing gear. "I love the earthy smell of the air after the rain." The scale of the chasm below dwarfed them and she shivered at the thought.

"That's petrichor. It's the Greek word for stone and the fluid that runs through the veins of Greek gods." He worked the puzzle as he talked. "I bought a country home once outside of Vienna. I had horses, goats, and even a trout pond. It took a small army of caretakers to staff it. Parts of it were over two centuries old and in need of constant repair, with the fireplaces and the tall leaded windows with their family crests. The heavy oak doors hand-carved with generational stories were worth preserving. The staff and I learned a lot about respecting its historic tradition." He completed the puzzle and tossed it to Layla. "Would you mix it up again?" he asked. "Neighbors who had known about the place helped, too."

"So what happened?"

"I was away for a few weeks on a consulting assignment. When

I returned, my detractors had ransacked the place. They'd poisoned the caretakers." He bowed his head while he collected his thoughts. "I told myself never again. I'll never own a home. I lease offices in cities where I work, but I choose not to own anything of value that they could use as leverage to get to me. I have political enemies, even more so now that Havel is in power. I'll always carry with me the fact that those fine people died because of me."

"*El pasado es el pasado*. Some things are too heavy to carry," Layla said. "So hiking like this is a mental reset?"

"I don't want anything to happen to you because of me," Archie said.

Layla tossed the mixed-up cube back and looked around. "No one has ever pitoned a portaledge to a mountain before so that I could spend the night with him." She blew him a kiss.

In less than a minute, he had the cube's patterns arranged again, and he put it back into his vest pocket. "So where were you when Havel walked into the Prague Palace?"

"Visiting my aunt. Her health has not been the best, and doctors can't figure out why."

Thoughts raced through Archie's head, but he didn't want to alarm her. He would have his people check her aunt's surroundings for anything unusual, substances left on a mailbox, or on a car door handle.

"It's a miracle, isn't it? Havel takes power with a free press, free judiciary, elected parliament members – the works, all without a shot fired. The Velvet Revolution."

"Were you there afterwards? Did you see him go into the palace?" Layla asked.

"I went the next day and couldn't get near him – and that's okay. I got carried away by the crowds in the streets, people pouring out of their houses in Prague, people shouting from the balconies *Svoboda! Svoboda!* Freedom!" Archie raised his hand high. "They held up their fingers with the V-for-victory sign. What a day."

Layla was reminded of her trip to West Berlin nine days before

Havel was elected. She had hand-delivered papers that she and her interpreter, Bibi, had completed. November 9, 1989, was the day the wall fell. But that was a story for another day. "It won't be easy. The Jenga tower we helped build for Havel – if you remove a piece – "

"I used to think that way, but he's a man of the people. He'll make it work, and there are no problems with the blind trust I created for him – so far." Archie pulled a piece of baguette from his pack and chewed thoughtfully. "After everything quieted down in Prague, I biked to the glass factory. Have you seen the Bohemian art glass?"

Layla broke off a piece of cheese and shook her head.

"Czechs are true artists with glass – have been for centuries. Now, they aren't limited to utilitarian Soviet glass anymore. I had tea with Jaroslava Brychtova and her husband Stanislav in the factory. They took me around and pointed out their latest projects."

"Should I know that name?"

"They are among the finest artists in glass. Their newest project is a glass obelisk to celebrate the day everyone in the street was making victory signs. The glass is clear but it reflects like a prism. It has V marks cut in the sides, and when it's finished, it will reflect and refract light in multiple ways however you turn to look at it. They are originals, those two." He drank from his Camelback pack. "They could never have made such a piece under Soviet rule. They are like enslaved people freed from chains. Freedom has a ripple effect. We don't know how far it reaches." From his cocooned hammock, he studied her face, the high cheekbones, and the curve of her chin. He wanted to caress that cheek.

"A glass obelisk," Layla said. "I'd like to meet Jaroslava sometime."

"I'm going to Hungary in a few weeks." He looked to the side and pointed between two mountaintops. "See that space right there? It looks a darker gray than the mountaintops on either side. That's Hungary."

Layla reached forward with a fist-sized chunk of cheese. "It's too much and I don't want to carry it back down tomorrow. Here."

She reached forward, and Archie took it from her hand.

"The authoritarians are attempting to oust the open university I'm supporting there. They claim it's dangerously broad-minded." His eyebrow shot up as he took a bite of cheese. "But I know a barge owner trying to get his tourist business off the ground. He sails down the Danube. We could hire his barge for a few days and see how Jaroslava's obelisk is shaping up. How about it? Think of it as helping a citizen in a new free-market economy."

"Archie, how could I refuse such a sweet and sentimental offer," Layla chided.

He felt his ears turn hot. Hoping that the darkening sky obscured him, he admitted, "Well, I'd like to see you again before waiting for months."

"Give me the dates, and I'll be there," Layla said. "One more question, and then I'm going to sleep – or will try to." She stole a quick look down the side of the mountain and shuddered. "Why is your university in Hungary?" Layla asked.

"It is my birth country." His voice was emphatic. "It's the country where they killed my father even though he worked to support the Allies. He was labeled a traitor because of ingrained beliefs. My free university had to be in Hungary. Truth won't return my father, but it's how I fight back." He thought before he spoke again. "Am I that different from you, gathering testimony from people without voices so that someday they might see justice?" He tore off the heel of the baguette. He waited with the sound of the breeze watching the first evening stars above them.

She stretched the toes of her hiking boots to touch his soles, the only physical contact available from their pinioned portaledges. "Being up here like this makes me *feel*. I get numb listening to the horror of depositions. I have to numb myself, or I'd go crazy listening to the atrocity. But here, I can feel fear. I try to do things that scare me so I don't go through my life numb."

Archie didn't know how to respond. Layla was the least numb human being he had ever met. "Last time I talked to Havel, he said that half the developed world is middle class, and the Czech middle class is growing. That's the best change in our lifetimes. Before the 20th century, there was no middle class at all. But things have changed in the eighties. Now, growth has been funneled more to the rich than ever before. Besides, you are anything but numb." He couldn't read her expression in the dark. "Are you still awake, or did I bore you to sleep?"

"No, go on," she said.

"I want to use what I have to help those who are doomed to poverty by those who want to take everything they can get."

"Like the Soviets."

"And their satellites. The Czech Velvet Revolution wasn't the first, but it was peaceful. Remember, besides taxes that helped make the middle class, there's property. Property brings wealth. More property means more political clout and more wealth. I lease my offices around the world. Property's a great investment to be sure, but I'd rather give away the little power I have. I pay more taxes, I give more away, and still, the wealth grows. He shrugged. It's my *mitzvah*, my mission to give it away."

"Archie, you still feel responsible for what happened to your sister. Is that what lies at the bottom of all this?" Layla said.

"That was a long time ago!" Archie shot back before his voice tempered. "I look at what I've done and it's nothing compared to what's left, what needs to be done. Nothing I can do will help her walk on her own two legs again." He swallowed hard.

"Have you told her about me?"

"She thinks we're just friends," Archie said.

"So are you telling me I'm more to you than just a friend?"

"I don't know what we are, Layla. I can never call a place home. I just store things in various places in Europe and in my sister's place in Brooklyn. In each office, I have three items: a socket wrench, headphones, and a roll of duct tape. A change of clothes is a given, but more often than not, a comfortable hotel room in a major city has a wobbly chair, loud neighbors, or mismatched draperies that let blinding light in way too early. I'm a citizen of Austria and a foreigner to the world. How's that?"

"Not enough for me." Her voice had an edge. She looked up at the dazzling constellations but couldn't appreciate them. "It sounded like you were opening up, but all you were doing was explaining your nomadic citizenship."

"Layla – "

She waited, but he paused long enough so that she nearly dozed off.

Were they having an argument? He thought he heard it in her voice, but he wasn't sure. "It's *torchlusspanik*. Do you know what that is?"

Layla gave a loud sigh. "Never heard of it."

"It's the feeling of panic, that I'm getting old and will never find a mate. Time goes by, and my life shrinks away."

"You're thirty-five."

"I'm afraid, Layla. I can't bring children into this world. I'd put them in danger wherever they went. I put you in danger just because I can't stay away from you." His was a messy, complicated business. "But I want a family. My desire for you is a constant, but there are too many variables."

Layla shivered. "I want you too."

"Besides, I must be young enough to teach my child how to hike and climb."

"Goodnight, Archie."

The following morning, he listened to her gentle breathing and watched the cloud ballet overhead. He waited for Layla to wake so that he could tell her about them. "*Boker-tov*," he pointed up as he saw her stir. "See how the upper ones are more tenacious? The lower ones slip below in a slow skate with the breeze."

"*Merhaba*," Layla greeted him in her language. "That's beautiful, Archie. You may take to poetry yet." She shifted as much as she dared, taking stock of her stiff muscles, skin sticking to the cool, damp hiking gear. "I don't think I've ever been this close to them before. It's almost as if I can touch them." She looked down and wiggled her boots.

"I've been hiking high enough before where I could hike through them." He motioned to one cloud. "In the center, you can't see too far other than a fogginess. It feels damp, but not very. But when they're below you, and the sky is clear, they look solid like you could walk right out on them – more like cotton."

Archie caught her smile.

'Why wait any longer for the one you love when he's standing in front of you – ' That's from the Nashville Skyline album," Layla said.

"I try my best to be just like I am…The man in me will hide sometimes to keep from bein' seen – "Archie sang.

"I know that one," Layla said. "Trust yourself to do the things that only you know best."

"I can't help it if you might think I'm odd –" Archie sang.

"I have one," Layla said, "It only goes to show that while life's pleasures be few, the only one I know is when I'm alone with you."

The last crumbs of their breakfast bread and cheese were gone. Layla contemplated the beauty of their perch with a pastel peach morning sky and Dylan on her mind. Now, how was Archie going to get these portaledges down?

CHAPTER 15

1991 Hungary

There's the issue of the personal rights versus the right of the state," Archie continued, comfortable as a guest lecturer at his university in Budapest. The students in *Ethics and Beliefs 300* took notes.

Layla had slipped into the back row of the 250-student wood-paneled lecture hall, hoping that he wouldn't see her. Walking across the back of the room, she found no empty seats, so she sat in the aisle with students. "If we look at Ireland and its majority of Catholics, we can understand why the government supports a no-abortion policy." Archie spoke without notes, pacing before the students and holding their gazes from random rows of the lecture hall. "But in the states where hundreds of religious denominations are supposed to be considered equal and separate from the government, abortion is accepted in more than half of the denominations, and it's legal. If Ireland treated religions equally, what about equal treatment for Jainism?"

"When I visited India, practitioners taught me about their belief in not causing the death of any living thing – chicken, cow, or insect," Archie accentuated the words. "Doctors are working to rid Africa of malaria mosquitoes, but Jains believe the rights of the mosquito are just as important as human rights. What happens when belief systems conflict with the majority rights of people?" He looked for raised hands, but no one questioned him. He'd hoped that they would, but he gave a shrug and continued.

"You've heard of Occam's Razor?" Some students nodded. "It's a Scottish philosophy meant to solve problems with the smallest set of elements. Start with what is known to trim the complex issues down to the gist. Simplest is best. In reality, simpler is easier, but not always best. Doctors start with it - eliminate the most obvious causes of disease first before looking for more complex issues. Car mechanics use it. So doctors and mechanics shave away unnecessary assumptions or cut apart two similar deductions. As with Jainism, simple and ethical are not always compatible." Archie looked at the clock at the back of the lecture hall. "Your professor wants you to read Chapter 16 for next week."

Layla dodged the exodus of students on her way down to the podium. She waited as he organized his papers into his briefcase, clarifying a few points for a handful of students who waited to talk to him. When he saw her, he left the students and wrapped his arms around her in a bear hug.

"You command quite an audience. Were all of these students from this class?" Layla said.

"I'm just a guest speaker. I didn't take attendance." He grabbed his case. "Are you ready to see the barge?"

"Lead the way," Layla said. Her deck shoes, jeans, and white shirt rolled up at the sleeves looked more suitable for sailing than Archie's crisp blue button-down and dress pants.

"Let's walk. It's just a mile to the dock," he said. A driver had arrived at her hotel that morning to take Layla's luggage to the barge. It would be unpacked for her by the time she stepped on board. She squeezed his hand, and rather than let go, Archie guided her away and stepped forward into a puddle in his Oxfords so Layla's deck shoes could have the dry part of the path.

CHAPTER 16

1991 Hungary

Twenty minutes later, they spied the barge from the dock. "It looks – practical," Layla said.

"It's very unassuming. It doesn't draw your attention, and others like it are all along the river. Wait until you see inside." Archie squeezed her hand as they crossed the gangway.

"*Vitejte*…welcome to *Fortuna*!" The captain met them on deck. "Here she is, Archie. What do you think?" His Czech accent was slight.

"I'm impressed, Marek. After only a few months, you've done a lot of work."

' "*Děkuji*, thank you. Let me show you your room, and we'll be off. The chef suggests dinner at seven unless you would prefer another hour."

"Seven is just right," Layla said.

Marek led them through a cozy salon with windows on three sides. Comfortable white upholstered sofas and chaises with colorful geometrically patterned pillows invited conversation. In the back was a teak-paneled hallway that led to their cabin. Marek opened the door to a spacious room. Sheer curtains billowed from open sliding doors that led to deck chairs outside.

"Your wardrobe has been placed in the dressing room for you, Madame."

Marek motioned to a square room – bigger than her kitchen, she thought. A doorway at the end of an entire mirrored wall led to the bathroom which featured a marble-walled shower and a marble bathtub. Over the tub, a chandelier sparkled with tear drop prisms.

"Oh, Marek, it's beautiful." Layla walked to the end of the tub to see the light changing color in the angles of glass.

"Ah, yes, the *lustr*." He shook his head. "We just finished the installation yesterday. I won't tell you the difficulty. It would spoil your cruise," he laughed. "Champagne is by your bed. Have a pleasant afternoon, and I'll see you at dinner."

"Wait, Marek," Archie disappeared into the dressing room and came out with a pineapple. "This is for you and the crew. It's a traditional good-luck gift for your new boat."

Marek was spellbound, holding the fruit like a fine plate of caviar. "I've never seen one except in a can." He looked it over and felt the spiky leaves on top. "Chef Dobo will love this." He closed the door quietly behind him.

"Archie, I had no idea." Layla looked at him.

He held her hands. "We're helping out a new entrepreneur, that's all," he said. "I thought about what you said in your hammock on the mountain. We'll be more relaxed here."

"Let's talk in the bath," Layla said. She turned on the taps, unbuttoned her blouse, and as it fell to the floor, she tapped her shoulder. "Deal-breaker?" She pointed to a small blue tattoo of the scales of justice. The word *familia* was written in script below it.

Archie worked to focus his eyes on the tattoo. "Not a deal breaker at all," he said.

Pulling the tie out of her long, wavy hair, she flipped her hair to the front and with a grab and twist, piled it high atop her head to tie it again.

Archie returned with the chilled champagne and two glasses.

He had removed his shirt. She swallowed hard at the jagged scar from his shoulder to his rib cage.

"*Preciosa,*" Archie said to her as he twisted the cork to a satisfying pop.

They entered the tub and set their champagne glasses on the marble edge. The warmth of the water relaxed them, and Archie tapped his glass to hers with a resonating ring. "Here's to us and Havel's leadership of the new Czech Republic."

Layla rested her head and looked up at the chandelier. "I'm happy to be here. Just you and me and this work of art hanging over our heads. The design is striking." She took a sip. "Marek has good taste."

"You can tell Jaroslava tomorrow when you meet her at the glass factory," Archie said. "She designed it for the barge."

"Did you – "

"I had nothing to do with the design. I only paid for it and a little extra to help with the cost of the Prague obelisk. No one tells Jaroslava how to design anymore. Well, her husband Stanislav and their team collaborate. You'll meet him tomorrow, too." He sipped from his glass. "Hear that?" He refilled their glasses. The barge engine shuddered and came to life with a low rumble. "We're underway."

Layla wanted to ask Archie about the scar, but they were having too pleasant a time to be serious. What could be more pleasurable than soaking in a marble tub and drinking champagne with a handsome, big-hearted man who thought that she was *preciosa?*

CHAPTER 17

1991 Hungary

Captain Marek kept them entertained over a leisurely dinner of local delights. His years in the Merchant Marine provided colorful stories that he clearly enjoyed telling. Archie and Layla hadn't laughed so much in a long while. By the time dessert arrived, the mood was light.

"This is the chef's special *Trdelnik*, the specialty of Prague. There is cinnamon in the whipped cream, and Nutella in the pastry." He waited while they took a bite. "So what do you think?"

"Oh," Layla took another bite. "Do you think we could have the recipe?"

"You cook more than roast duck?" Archie looked at her.

"Not so much, but I love to bake," Layla said. "I'll get the recipe, and you can be my assistant baker," she winked.

Marek's expression was unreadable.

After dinner, Archie led Layla to the deck, where they walked the perimeter admiring the night lights and the illuminated bridges of Prague. "This one's the Charles Bridge, the oldest bridge in Prague." Their eyes traced the ancient gate, the bridge tower on one end, and the arches dotted with lights that reflected like scalloped shapes in the river. "It was the only way to get from the Prague Castle over the Vltava River and into the town."

"How old?"

"They started it in 1357."

As they passed under, they heard a violinist on the bridge playing a soulful Eastern European melody, unlike anything they would have heard in Vienna.

From their bed that night, they glanced through the filmy curtains at the occasional light on the shore. Layla's hand found its way across Archie's chest to trace the scar from his shoulder across his torso. He tensed. She lifted her head from his chest. "I'm sorry. Did I upset you? I want to know what happened."

"It's an old scar. The only hurt left is in my mind. It is always there."

"Can you tell me about it?

"It will drive us apart. I can't argue with you."

"I don't believe that." She returned her head to his chest.

He released a long breath. "It was near the end of the Six-Day War in Israel. It was night, but there was a sliver of moonlight for vision. It was just outside the Kinnutz Cabri kibbutz where my sister and I lived. The soldiers were looking for *sabras*. We were prickly-pear *sabras* willing to fight for freedom. Back then, I saw it as something more exciting than working in the olive groves. The Israeli military is formidable."

"I know." She felt his voice rumble in her ear.

"So our kibbutz had secret contacts inside Jordan, and the border tension was palpable – you understand."

Layla felt the muscles in his arm tense as he spoke. "They made you fight when you were just a child? How old were you in 1967?"

"They didn't make me do anything. I had no parents to forbid it." Archie felt confrontational but tried to keep his voice calm. "Palestinian guerillas had broken through a border. We had to hit back for that and a land mine attack. Then there were the Soviets who claimed that we were attacking Syria – which wasn't true but added to the chaos.

"I was a small, skinny twelve-year-old, and Rivka was two years younger. They told me what they needed – they would sew a secret message in my pocket. All I had to do was walk across the border and deliver the message because who would suspect a kid? Didn't I want to be a brave little soldier and keep my sister safe? That's all I could think of: I was the only one who could keep her safe. So, I volunteered. Again and again, I got out of working in the olive groves. June was hot in the groves and with the sun and the heat, it was like I couldn't get enough breath.

"So the last time I delivered a message, the sliver of moonlight was getting smaller. I struggled to see and stumbled, scraping my knee on a rock. The guns went off around me, and I howled. I tried to stand, but a guerilla fighter on the Jordan side caught me and sliced me with his knife. He yelled, *Aleaduu aleaduu!"* – for enemy! When I stood up and landed a punch to his chest, he saw I was an unarmed kid. I made it back through the break in the border fence. One of the soldiers cursed me for not delivering the message. He threw me over his shoulder and took me to the medical tent.

"He tossed me on a gurney, and I got a good look at him," Archie said. "I wondered why he was covered in blood. Then I must've passed out. I don't remember."

Layla rested her head over the scar and held him close. She heard only their tandem breathing and the soft rumble of the engine. Her hand tightened around his arm as she thought of the hundreds of thousands of Palestinians displaced from the West Bank because of that war. She and her family were forced from their apartment to live in a refugee camp. She grew up with stories of Palestinian bravery during the war, but slicing a child across the chest would not be one of them. "You thought you were protecting Rivka."

"They let her see me the next day. She was scared of all the bandages. I told her I was protecting her, that I'd never let anything happen to her."

Layla had to think before she spoke. "The war had not only been a disaster for Palestinians. Jordan lost 6,000 people. So many refugees came under Israeli control. Losses were crippling, and a two-state solution looked further away than ever." Here was an emotional wound for someone whose life she cared about as much as her own. "It was a bloody battle," she said, turning away from him.

Archie turned and gently wrapped her in his arms, his cheek on her shoulder. The boat rocked peacefully. Her skin was warm. He heard the shudder in her sigh before his own and felt the closeness of her. "You know, misinformation made it worse." His beard scratched her shoulder, and she pulled away. "Layla, it was a long time ago. *Hasbara** manipulated both of us. They burned both sides."

** Hasbara: A communicative strategy that explains actions, whether or not they are justified.*

CHAPTER 18

1991 Hungary

The next morning, Marek's Chef Dobo served them a hearty breakfast of cheese, ham, and fresh pineapple. Layla noticed the croissant first. She stripped off the tail, holding it up to examine the shine of an obscene amount of butter before dangling it into her mouth.

Archie watched, entranced by her focus. A drop of butter lingered at the corner of her mouth. He picked up his own croissant, hoping for the same effect.

"Who makes croissants in Hungary?" she asked.

"It's a local baker," Marek said. "She studied in Paris and returned to open her own shop. Croissants and baguettes are the only things she makes. Sometimes the line is down the block, but it's a small shop. Cook got there early this morning as soon as they opened. She said she uses 50 kilos of butter a week."

"I can believe it," Layla said. She examined the center of the croissant, its layers resembling the whorl of a nautilus shell, and took a big bite. "Umm… paradise," she said. Archie agreed.

After they had docked, Marek readied the bikes that were

roped to the back of the barge. The trail that hugged the side of the Vltava would lead them to the Libensky's workshop. They wove their way along the tree-lined trail past early morning joggers, rollerbladers, and parents with strollers until Archie turned off on a deeply wooded trail lined with tree roots and rocks. As he bounced along, he wasn't watching Layla balancing with her feet off the pedals, falling behind.

Archie stopped at the clearing, a small parking lot next to a factory that could have been left from the Industrial Revolution. Looking to see how far behind she was, he remembered her knee and admired her endurance all over again. "You're almost there," he called.

Together they found spaces in a rusty rack packed with bicycles. Before Archie could knock, Jaroslava opened the thick metal door.

"I see you found space in the bike rack. We'll wait here for Stanislav." She motioned them into a cramped office which had small windows on two side, overlooking the factory floor. The clanking sound of machinery softened as she closed the door behind her. "I have water heating for tea." Jeroslava busied herself, floating around the desk, moving papers, and placing tea cups and embroidered napkins in front of them.

Archie looked at Layla and she understood that this was a tradition that could not be passed over.

"How is the barge?" Jaroslava asked.

Layla looked at this woman of indeterminate age. She seemed to be curious about the barge, not just making small talk. "It's lovely," Layla said, "down to every detail. And your glass chandelier – the *lustr*? It's breathtaking from every angle." She winked at Archie.

"*Ano ano* – the *lustr*. I received many phone calls from Marek on that one. Was it short enough for the low ceiling? Were the fasteners strong enough for waves on the river – though we rarely have waves on the river. Ah! Here is Stanislav now." Jaroslava introduced her husband and excused herself to get the tea.

"You're here to see the obelisk, yes?" He smiled through bespectacled eyes that turned down at the corners. "It's nearly finished. Now the glass is different. The *lustr* Jaroslava talked about was Bohemian crystal - high lead content, very reflective, and heavy! Archie, the obelisk is a different glass because of its height and weight. We cut it so that when you move around it you see new angles and perspectives reflected back at you like in our new country." He chuckled and rubbed his bald head. "Archie, we feel like kids again, Jaroslava and me, free with our ideas, not looking over our shoulders to see who will report us, who will turn us in."

The Soviet troops are slow in leaving. Most are gone, but some stayed back. Good riddance to the occupation! So aggressive! So arrogant! We found door locks smashed and our glass factory is missing crystal lamps. We've filled out the forms for damages, but we don't trust that those occupiers will ever pay. They live by their own rules.

Jaroslava returned with a pot of tea and began pouring, her gauzy white cotton shirt moving with every motion. They spoke of glass and of the dramatic changes they'd observed in Prague since Havel had come to power, the entrepreneurship of Marek, the opening of art-filled coffee rooms, and colorful flower shops in bright contrast to the dismal Soviet gray.

"The biggest concern is corruption," Archie warned. "With all the sudden change, those hoping to make fast money will say whatever they can to skirt laws and make it hard for honest people to raise their families. We can't have people blaming Havel when there are those who promote corruption to encourage the state to fail."

Stanislav nodded his head. "Right you are. But here we are together, drinking tea. Let's talk of other things. Jaroslava, should we take them to see the obelisk now?"

Layla drank the last of her fruit-flavored tea and stood.

Jaroslava opened the door, and the clanging metal made Layla cover her ears. Jeroslava and Stanislav seemed used to it.

The rough-hewn obelisk didn't look as close to being finished as Layla had imagined, but it towered over their heads. Maybe Jaroslava's artist's eye could already see the carved Vs for victory. Layla peered into the multi-faceted prism-like dimensions in the polished blocks of lead crystal, its angles changing with the light and every step she took. Afterwards, Jaroslava treated them to lunch and spoke with pride about the clarity of the crystal, like the clarity of Prague's new journalists – free to tell the truth without fear.

CHAPTER 19

1991 Hungary

Another ten kilometers along the Vltava was Petrin Park. They secured their bikes at the statue of Macha, the poet of love. As they touched the feet of the statue of the dreamy poet, a photographer snapped their picture. After the click, Archie grabbed the camera and stuffed money in the man's hand. "Buy a new camera," Archie said.

"Was that really necessary?" Layla said.

"We don't know where that picture could end up," Archie said. "Besides, the money I gave him will allow him to buy a much better camera." He showed her the old Flexaret before pulling its roll of film from the back.

They caught up with Marek and the *Fortuna* in the afternoon and tied the bikes to the back of the barge.

"I had Marek dock here, hoping we'd have time to explore this old abbey before dinner."

Layla looked at the Vyšší Brod Abbey on the shore. "Let's go."

They walked across the path and joined other tourists waiting to pay the admission. Layla admired the courtyard gardens and water lily pond, wondering about the monks who'd lived in this meditative paradise. Walkways surrounded them, probably areas for the priests to wander in prayer. Their guide told them about the Gothic-style abbey, first opened in 1259, with its colorful rose window. But as the guide began detailing its history, Archie grasped her arm and led her down a narrow hallway far from the group.

"We're a bit late and we need to step it up," he said. Around a corner, two steps down, then up a narrow spiral staircase probably used by choir members or servants, then down a dark passageway they went. Archie lifted a latch and pushed open a heavy door to reveal the second monastery library.

"We're making our own tour," he said. Archie left her side to check between the twelve shelves of books separating the windows. Lighting was unnecessary when the windows allowed afternoon light to flood the room.

Layla wondered what Archie was doing. No velvet ropes cordoned off a path on the patterned travertine floor, and the marble columns gilded with gold leaf had no plexiglass protectors. The upstairs balcony held more books than the shelves below, its carved balustrade lined with statues of great classical writers. Twelve gilt-framed murals were painted on the ceiling with religious themes around a sweeping mural in the center. Mary visited by angels, perhaps? Hundreds of books lined the walls and balcony, all covered in the same coveted 18th-century vellum, tempting her to pluck one from their shelves. She breathed in the faint, animal-like scent of the vellum. Reaching for the *Zuniga Book of Hours*, she drew back, fearing that the moisture from her hand could cause a print that the pounce, the centuries-old cuttlefish bone powder that dusted the vellum, might not absorb.

Layla heard a door open at the opposite end of the library, and three men approached. Archie reached them first, and she saw him pass a note to the man on the left. He motioned for Layla to join them and gave introductions in Czech. "This is Lonna, my – lawyer," he said in English. The men nodded.

Their remaining conversation was entirely in Czech. Layla could make out only a few words: Havel, tunneling, and pistol, but without any context, she was lost. The men stopped talking, gave curt nods, and left the way they had come.

"*Muj drahy*, I think we have time for a drink before dinner," Archie said.

Layla read his face, and although the Czech words he used were probably endearments, she knew that the conversation had been troubling.

Their last dinner with Marek filled in the answers to Layla's puzzling questions. Not only Marek but also Jaroslava and Stanislav were gatherers of information crucial to the success of Havel's fledgling administration. Soviet loyalists did their best to find corruption in local economies or fabricate it if it didn't exist. With outside efforts, they planned to bring doubt and instability to the new administration and usher it back under the apron of Mother Russia.

"What about journalists and the news sources?" Layla asked.

"The Czechs aren't used to evidence-based news free of state interference," Archie said. "Vienna has seven daily newspapers, all protected by free speech laws, but Prague is just developing a free press. It takes time. I'm working out how to pay them." He knew that would be Layla's next question.

"The *Prague Post* will break the story before the loyalists can smear Havel's work. That's the plan." Archie sat back in his chair. "The journalists' pay has to come from a commercial Czech source, not from me; otherwise, they'll claim that I paid for fake news in support of Havel."

"When Vaclav and I were talking about meeting with you, we discussed the rural people. Not all rural people read the news. We can't forget the rural issues." Layla saw his look and got her answer.

At the end of their cruise, Layla assured Marek that his new business would be a success. She worked with people who would love to take a similar cruise and planned to recommend it. As she gathered the few things that the staff hadn't efficiently folded into her bag, she picked up Archie's blue Oxfordcloth from the day they'd come. The sleeve brushed her arm, producing a faint scent of his lime cologne. With one last look at the beautiful *lustr* over the marble tub, she told him, "Archie, we can't go so long without seeing each other. I'm in Syria taking depositions next week. How about meeting me in Spain after that? I want you to meet my aunt."

Archie crossed his arms. "I'd love to meet your aunt. But will she make us sleep in separate rooms?"

Layla laughed. "You know, I'm not sure. I'll have to ask."

Archie decided to have his security people available to protect Layla in Syria. The risks she took to join him seemed to concern him most. After he'd met her aunt, he'd have to get Layla to New York to meet Rivka. Thinking of it, he'd almost rather face that Jordanian sniper instead.

"Hold me," she said.

CHAPTER 20

1991 Hungary

At the bottom of Gellért Hill, Archie met Havel. Gellért was one of many baths in Budapest known for its thermal springs. Archie had invited Havel to be a guest lecturer at the university, and the baths seemed like an excellent place to talk afterward. Together, they walked the ornate mosaic-tiled hallways, past Art Nouveau metalwork and stained glass, experimental for its time. As long as they kept walking around the complex, their conversation was masked by the voices of so many bathers.

"The *agitprop* against you is building, Archie." Vaclav shook his head. "Now they say you worship Moloch, the Canaanite god of child sacrifice. Parents believe they shouldn't send their children to your university because you may sacrifice them by fire. These parents don't know that their corner market was once required to collect information on them."

"The manipulation is sneaky and slow so that if people aren't aware, it seems like a crazy scheme that will pass. The more outrageous it is, the more rational people want to wait." Archie said.

"They feel that the believers will come to their senses and the *agitprop*, or *kompromat*, or propaganda will fall away. But the more it's repeated, the more ingrained it becomes, the more impossible it is to refute. They have lots of time for denials and excuses."

"I had coffee with one of your university students and his father, a friend of mine. He said it was a thrill for people, this forbidden knowledge of Moloch," Havel said.

"Zolt has said as much." Archie agreed.

"Did you know you're also in the news for campaign money you've invested? It seems you support candidates for prosecutor in areas that are most often accused of jailing political prisoners. Stories are splashed across front pages in Hungary and the Czech Republic."

"Nothing secret about it. I'm proud to do so. People of all backgrounds need fair sentencing when they disagree with leaders. They deserve real representation, not kangaroo courts," Archie said.

Havel lowered his voice. "I have proof of meddling within our courts to protect that oligarch Chertok. His so-called news conglomerate is a tool of the Kremlin. He's smearing a legitimate Czech builder of apartments and pushing a contract from an indicted Russian builder. Now that we have jobs, we need housing and transportation nearby, Archie. Now, this maniac Chertok is trying to strong-arm the judiciary so he can escape indictment for bribery and get the contract for his friend. I'm sure this is only the beginning of what he wants."

"Nakita Chertok, is it? Archie asked. Chertok had his hands on much more than his Reynard news media empire. I know a journalist from the *Guardian* working on it."

They passed a second pool and walked under an arched marble promenade. Archie lowered his voice, concerned about the echo. "It takes months for investigators to follow the trail of corruption back to the Kremlin. Checks on power stop when they install friendly judges. Those judges look the other way when budget increases give oligarchs more and the workers less." Archie noticed one of his security detail to their left and wondered about his visibility.

"Some of these guys studied at your university, Archie. Now they're organizing youth resistance groups denouncing you." Close to their bath, Vaclav tapped Archie's back. "You have the courage of a journalist. Hungary will feel the impact. It takes time."

They stepped into the warm spring bath that was surrounded by ancient columns from Roman times. Overhead, the sun shone through a skylight spanning the length of the pool. Here, they spoke only of fishing, hiking, and poetry, not the agenda for their upcoming talk with the Club of Rome. The quiet echo of the pool made for easy eavesdropping.

"Vaclav, we've been avoiding Olga. How are you holding up? Talk to me."

"No. It's too soon. If I allow myself to think of her, I will fall apart. I bury myself in work. Thank you for your concern, but no. Maybe someday, but now, if I allow myself to think of that monster cancer that took her life, I will crumble. My Olga. It's too much, so no."

"I just – " Archie began.

Vaclav gave him a look that stopped him cold. Instead, Archie launched into his latest acquisition of a Grateful Dead bootleg until he felt a growing heat in the bath water.

"Feel that?" he asked Havel.

"They've reduced the cold water that makes the heat bearable," Havel whispered. "No sudden moves." Havel's discomfort showed on his face.

Archie looked at him, anguishing pain shooting up his legs and heat seizing his testicles. He nodded to security, and the two exited the bath as if the temperature had not reached unbearable levels. Towels covered the redness and prickly itch, until they dressed without showering. Archie's security team located a private back exit for them.

CHAPTER 21

1991 Hungary

The two men walked quickly away from the baths. "They are making life increasingly difficult for our journalists, pressuring them to ignore the corruption," Archie said.

"The bank transfers you sent to buy protection for me and my staff were 'freed' by the bank."

"I heard." Archie was hoping for answers, but Havel gave him something different. "They used the money to buy guns to harass my people at the border.

Here's what we will do," Archie said. "We'll have couriers and safer transfers next time. Zolt is looking into it."

"Their *agitprop* claims that you stole dirty money and used it to turn your university students against the Hungarian people. They want the university out of town," Havel said.

"And truth with it. One of the Czech student journalists got a bank teller to talk about the illegal transfer. They threatened the teller's family if he refused to release the money."

"That's the family with new names and documents that my judicial system fast-tracked. They should arrive in their new country by tomorrow," Havel said.

"Your judges worked quickly. Let's hope that it doesn't backfire on the judicial system," Archie said. "This student's bravery will keep the university open a while longer."

"You have doubts of the university's future?" Havel asked.

"It's only a matter of time. I'm considering contingency plans with Estonia."

"A loss for Hungary would be a win for Estonia. Have you heard about their folk high schools?" Havel asked.

"Isn't that adult education for jobs – with community engagement thrown in?" Archie asked.

"It might be a source for your journalists."

Archie nodded. "Now tell me what you know about village newspapers."

Suddenly hungry, they decided to find a bite to eat. They passed by some young backpackers who reminded Archie of Elias and himself in college, exploring Europe and finding welcome in this beautiful city of bridges and castles. He wondered what the city meant to these young people, coming from all parts of the continent, bringing their ideas to his university.

They ducked into the VakVendiglo for lamb stew. Two young travelers stopped at their table. Havel shook hands with them and answered their questions.

"Do you worry that so many young visitors will change Hungary?" Havel said.

"Worry? That's a vibrancy that makes Budapest come to life. Bring them here with their imaginings and dreams. They become part of our transition to the future. Surely your influence was part of the change now that you are president of Czechoslovakia," Archie said.

"Archie, I'm not Hungarian, but it started long before! The Magyar resistance in 1790 after the French Revolution made the idea attractive. The agricultural depression after 1815 made Prince Metternich squash revolutionary ideas.

"The nobility ignored the trouble thanks to their wealth and power, and a monstrous class difference. The rivals for power were the *bene possessionati,* average families who held local offices. The nobles were far removed from them, and they feared a change of status. When the toll bridge joined Buda and Pest, the nobles refused to pay the toll that everyone else paid."

"I know about Szechenyi, the founder of the Hungarian Academy of Sciences who opened education to everyone, including the Jews," Archie said. "In the 1830s, he proposed infrastructure for the towns and private investment for entrepreneurs – important steps."

"In 1841, Kossuth started his political and civil rights newspaper," Vaclav said.

"The freedom fighter? He wanted freedom from the Habsburgs and the Austrian Empire, and freedom of the press. Even the nobles weren't above the law," said Archie.

"Then, in 1849, Russia came to the Habsburg's aid, and Kossuth fled to Turkey. But the embers of democracy in Europe continued to glow, even when the Habsburgs ruled with absolute power."

Havel was recognized again by more well-wishers. Archie finished his stew and left his friend. Walking through a residential area by his hotel, Archie stopped to look at an alleyway between two mid-century homes. Wrought-iron trellises climbed the bricks of one time-worn house. The walkway led to a garden seat surrounded by a shock of orange poppies. A boy sat on the garden seat, playing with a toy.

CHAPTER 22

1991 Austria

In Vienna the following week, a messenger from Havel sat opposite Archie in a dark wood-paneled *viennoiserie*. Archie admitted that he was unsure about the success of this meeting Havel had asked him to take. He repeated the points he would make to Georg, his old Schönbrunn Palace acquaintance. Together, they left the shop, the messenger walking in one direction and Archie in a black-windowed car traveling in another. The driver dropped him at the tourist entrance of the Palace. Ambassador Habsburg was not a supporter but was sometimes known to lean toward reality over propaganda. Archie opened the one unlocked double door and remembered the last time he'd walked these halls, years ago at a state function. His footsteps echoed on his minimally heated walk through the Great Gallery, its Rococo ceilings once echoing with dignitaries' cheer and laughter.

It was a costume party, and he had worn a *Phantom of the Opera* mask and a Goethe-like hat. Elias wore a court jester's colorful cap and bells. Now, the only sound was the echoing tap of his footsteps. He passed by a few of the 1400 rooms, including Marie Theresa's

Balcony Room, with portraits of her many children. It seemed most Habsburgs – including Georg — had big families, in the Roman Catholic tradition. He passed by the ornate black lacquer-paneled Chinese Room and continued through the tall doorway of the Audience Room with its multi-faceted chandelier, round-topped windows, red carpet, and velvet tufted chairs. He felt the warmth from the fireplace, and its glow was reflected in the walnut-paneled walls – conducive to good conversation.

He wasn't alone for long. "Good to see you, Archie." He turned back to see Georg at the end of a jog, wiping his brow with the towel around his neck. Georg dried his hand on the towel before reaching out with a solid handshake. "With all these rooms, I get in a good run and check up on the place to boot." In his running shorts and t-shirt, he sank into the chair behind the desk. Archie sat in one of the velvet-tufted chairs at the side. Georg was experienced in putting his guests at ease and engaged Archie in a conversation about hiking destinations in the area. Once he ran out of questions, he rose. "I know it's not winter, but I'm in the mood for *Jaegartee*. Will you join me?"

After Archie agreed, Georg approached a spot in the wall where a hidden door opened to a closet. A bright light glowed within, and Georg brought out two glasses of black tea and rum. He sipped one and placed the other on Archie's side of the desk.

"I was visiting with the Pope at *Santa Maria Dell'Anima* last week," he said. "We agreed that we are both optimistic and cautious in the case of Havel's leadership." He chuckled. "You know, Havel sent the Pope a Czech dictionary and a collection of his poems. He claimed that the meaning was lost in translation and wanted His Holiness to understand them as the people would."

Archie sipped the drink, which was strong in both tea and rum flavor. He admired the fragile lead crystal glass with its intricate centuries-old etching, and placed it back on the desk. He planned to wait, say as little as possible, and encourage Georg to reveal his loyalties.

Georg looked upon Archie with regret. "My father couldn't

have done this, run around the palace," he said. "He was raised in exile in Paris to preserve democracy, like many exiled royals in Europe. We share an age-old community. My family ancestry – Maria Theresa – is passed on to my children," he said. "Empires come and go, but they're not all bad. Look around you." He motioned his hands to the beauty of the room. True, thousands of tourists visit this palace each year.

"Your ancestors had an eye for beauty and supporting the arts," Archie admitted. "Havel would be the first to agree that the art of words is powerful, although it doesn't fill an empty belly."

Georg ignored him. "I talked with the Pope about our historic connection. My family roots go back to 950 in Switzerland, supporters of the church even then. That painting," he nodded at the wall beside Archie. "One of the 14th-century battles of Morgarten and Sempach in the courtyard of the Swiss Guards." His shoulders leaned forward. "They ushered my family out of Switzerland."

Archie wasn't impressed. He considered sharing his very different take on family history but thought better of it, opting to appeal to Georg's sense of compromise. "So you can agree with the Pope about the importance of protecting workers' families as Havel wants to do," he said. "I told Havel that you had a way of weaving mercurial world leaders onto your side." He watched Georg sip his *Jaegartee*. "How about your son Albert? Does he feel entitled? A birthright to power through coercion?"

Georg gave a strained laugh. "If you're talking about politics, Albert has a future before him if he wants it. He can be an ambassador to France or the Vatican. But politics is a dirty business."

"Ambassadors sometimes remain isolated from the people they represent. They're surrounded by those who tell them what they want to hear, and that... detachment... could lead to unsound decisions." Archie wanted to say deadly decisions, but that would have ended the conversation.

"Albert can marry a commoner for that. My cousin Heinrich did. People love that sort of thing, like Charles and Princess Diana. That reminds me." He laughed at the thought of another of his stories. "When Queen Elizabeth came for the State Banquet in 1969, I indulged in a bit of youthful recklessness, I'm afraid." He snickered. "I was young, and I filched a bulb of garlic from the cooks and told the staff to tack it above the doorway for the Queen's entrance. She's a descendant of Vlad the Impaler, you see."

"Are you the confessor who admits sins or the confessor who listens to them?" Archie asked. He thought the Queen's heart was in a better place than Georg's and imagined her driving a wooden stake through Georg's chest. But of course, she was too kind.

"This place was Maria Theresa's summer palace. So much of my ancestors' history took place here. She was a contemporary of George Washington, but she preserved the peace by marrying off her sixteen children to other royals. Her army was formidable. The rebel colonists' Revolutionary Army was a ragtag bunch despite Ben Franklin's warning – after observing the five tribes in the Iroquois League – that they should hang together or hang separately, you know. Years later, Kennedy and Khrushchev met in the room where you attended the costume party – the Great Gallery, like the Hall of Mirrors in Versailles. Even Napoleon once stayed in Marie Antoinette's room." Georg seemed to be enjoying his boast.

"Our Habsburg Holy Roman Spanish Emperor Potosi – you know him as Charles V – discovered a fortune in silver in the Andes." Georg opened a drawer and withdrew a large coin. "Here's a souvenir." He slid the silver replica to Archie. Emblazoned on the piece of eight was the strong-jawed family image.

Archie turned the coin over, a reminder from a colonialist past when enslaved silver miners toiled for the Habsburg family fortune. "Next thing, you'll say your family was kind to their slaves." It was a relic to pass along sometime with an explanation. He slipped the coin into his pocket. "Where is your Catholic guilt? Is there any greater internal conflict?"

"Think this through, Georg. You'd be surprised at how this could play out. Even the plague was an equal-opportunity killer: the wealthy came to a stark realization of the importance of laborers to keep up their estates, and that was the end of their feudal system."

"Habsburg rule suffered in the Netherlands from the Protestant Reformation in 1579," Georg said. "With all their land reclaiming and windmills, they needed the workers to survive. The idea of one controlling Habsburg leader didn't stick with those freethinkers. Humph. What did they know?"

Archie had so much to say but he waited for the end of the historical puffery in the hope that Georg would reveal more.

Georg continued, "You have your ideas about independent journalists making the truth clear, but you don't take into account how many people want to believe the *agitprop*. They want to believe that there are less worthy people and they are the more worthy, not the "All men are created equal" claptrap of the States. When the propaganda paints the unworthy as cheaters and frauds, they eat it up, and countrymen are pitted against one another, weakening the whole population. It's worked time and time again in Africa, and it used to work in Central and Eastern European countries, too, but now they're becoming wise to it. That doesn't mean Moscow is giving up on it. Their ministry of propaganda is a pillar of impossibilities propped up with malicious threats grounded by modern communications. Once they create a big enough division in the population, they can claim savior status, swoop in, and establish absolute control. Populations would rather be told what to do."

Archie corrected him. "They understand the need to fall in line with the strongman to survive, but there has to be more than survival. People can thrive knowing that their work improves their families' lives."

"For my children, yes. But if that is the way for everyone's children, then it is at the cost of my children. Mine shall not suffer." Georg blotted his brow with the towel.

"You're playing your ancestor's song in a different key if you promote suffering for the people, so that you can feel above them. You're asking for a return to feudal times! You can't govern a country based on a false reality. It won't last," Archie argued.

"The Soviets didn't invent nation-blaming," Georg shot back.

"Seventeenth-century tribes in Africa were set against one another and gave each other over to slave-traders. Warring American native tribes sided with the French or British against each other and decimated thousands." He laughed. "Then, in the 1950s, the Red Scare brought about the McCarthy witch hunt, jailing Hollywood actors and Broadway musicians for un-American activities. But before the conservatives could drive the country from Cold War to repression, even the crazies realized the limits of loyalty oaths."

"Your cavalcade of history impresses me, Georg, but consolidating power and wealth breeds resentment. Havel's Czech democracy has new businesses everywhere you look. People with hope aren't likely to start an uprising. Their pride and unity is a strength you can't imagine."

"Don't be naive, Archie. What do you think keeps all this going? The neighborhood *viennoiserie*? I have no throne, no power, but we Habsburgs make our way. It takes wars to make money. Look what happened to the US during World War II. Sure, we all lost lives, but the Yanks have GM, Lockheed, and Remington, and they made a fortune from tanks, ships, and guns – not just their own, but lend-lease. Then, there was Dupont for the atomic bomb. They hung back until near the end and swooped in all *Deus ex Machina*, and now the world looks to them to call the shots."

"Where FDR got it wrong was that it takes time to win over election votes." Georg's voice rose. "Most of our citizens don't want to bother with politics. Just give them a man who will tell them the way things are. He declares war, he says, to protect the people and flavors the news to make the other side into an enemy worse than a filthy animal, despised and loathed. The people will fight for that. Companies then make money quicker than by this nonsensical globalization scheme." He stood with his hands on the desk. "A controlled burn keeps the forest healthy. Remember that." He finished his *Jaegartee* and left the room.

So much for optimism and caution, Archie thought. He had hoped at least for a neutral partner for Havel but had succeeded only in maddening Georg.

CHAPTER 23

1992 Vienna

Layla told him she'd be in Vienna for a few days. Archie wanted to free up his schedule and asked Zolt to plan for it.

"You know the consequences for getting too close to anyone. You told me if you ever got too close – "

"I know, but this is different. Layla knows all about what this is like. She's been through everything I've been through and more."

"You'd never forgive yourself if you put her at risk," Zolt said.

Archie glared at him.

"The best thing you can do is try to forget her. Ignore her, and she'll lose interest over time," Zolt said.

"I can't do that."

"All the more reason to let her go. It's the only way to protect her."

"This feeling… I don't know how to deal with it."

He reached into his pocket and pulled out an orange ear plug. "I found this in bed. She says I snore, and I don't snore." He shook the squishy earplug at Zolt. "It was Sunday morning, and we were at the hotel here in Vienna. We were reading the *Sunday Krone* together, papers tossed everywhere. I must've fallen asleep, and when I woke, there was this earplug in her ear. She took it out and smiled her *'ce n'est rien'* smile." He looked at it in the palm of his hand. "Who does that?"

"Get out of here. Far away. I'll get the tickets. Where will you go?"

With a sinking feeling, Archie returned the earplug to his pocket. "For all the financial transactions, the microloans, and the journalists I try to protect, this little vulnerability of human affinity outweighs it all." He recalled their Danube cruise on the *Fortuna*, imagining scenes in Viewmaster clicks. If he left, he would save her. How much love hurt when it risked her life.

"I need to talk to Chertok. Make the arrangements." After the meeting, he would return to Vienna and an empty hotel room.

The Habsburg cousin Georg proved to be less helpful than Archie had hoped. But he promised Havel that he'd find out what he could about news mogul Chertok's latest attempts to control the Czech judicial system. Flying to Tallinn, Estonia, took longer than he thought, despite Zolt's best efforts. Archie wearily sat down on the opposite side of the empty desk, fully aware that Chertok was nearby but was making him wait. The silence was oppressive in Chertok's office as in the rest of the building: sleek and gray. One decorative exception hung behind Chertok's empty chair: the Estonian coat of arms with three blue lions and twin trees on either side.

His thoughts returned to Layla and how he had gone without seeing her for weeks and sometimes months. But this was different. Without the expectation of her, there came a desolation. The actions he took – the investments, conversations, and journeys – held the knowledge that he would tell her about them once they met again, watch her eyes light up, her brows furrow, or her laugh break loose. What defined him when he no longer heard the lilt of her voice as she talked about the child who had wandered into the office or the herd of goats that blocked traffic in the street? Going forward appeared to be a dead question, nothing more than an endless expanse of time alone.

Chertok, the chairman of the Reynard News Corporation, walked in. Chertok, with his growing control over the global news narrative, was eating from a bowl of trail mix and held up a finger to stop Archie from saying anything until he had finished chewing. With deliberation, he placed the bowl on the glass desk top, where it clattered, breaking the silence. True to his punctilious ways, his fingers pressed the nut crumbles on the desk and rubbed together over the bowl, leaving a scrupulously clean work surface before he sat down to face Archie.

"I shape perceptions as I wish. I influence the political landscape, by decisions aligned with my interests." He stared down at Archie with his chiseled-rock face. "If there is competition, I arrange the buyout or put the insurgents in jail. Nothing is so revered that it cannot be destroyed for profit. It makes the next competitor think again before crossing me. I have access to the judges. I know what governments will do before they know they will do it, so I can tell my viewers what side to take. This leverage can ramp up support or anger, and governments know it." He picked up more trail mix with a flourish of his hand. "I guess you could call it my destiny."

"Manipulating the judiciary and limiting perspective is – productive journalism, would you say?" Chertok asked. "Listeners need to be guided. Propaganda is merely a shared experience or public relations like an ad campaign for a prize fight. We do their thinking for them. You want peace, don't you?"

"Peace. What we used to think were natural laws we now know are dictated by humans." Archie said. "If I had millions of years to perfect the world… I don't know about you, but I could have done better than the so-called peace of the Holocaust. I wouldn't consider faith in the idea that produced extreme cruelty as an advantage."

"So what you're saying is that truth doesn't matter. It's about how useful the belief is." Chertok's voice was a warning shot.

Archie tried to calm the anger in his head from Chertok's twist of words. "How convenient that the being you worship shares your prejudices. Panic produces the worst cruelty. For progress, people need hope. My university journalists and my microloans give hope. Like Mephistopheles in Dr. Faustus, these dictators you support bask in the joy of being worshiped by those they torture. Their followers feel that raw power alone is worthy of their loyalty, even if that power is used against them."

"The world was not made for bleeding hearts like you. Your prying is unsophisticated, Archie. You'll never understand how one well-crafted lie can entrance the populace with a power and strength that your thousand reasoned, insightful facts never will. My advice for you: trust in the fabricated reality."

"Moscow domination traumatizes," Archie said. "I can't tell your epidermis from Koslov's. Moscow demands subordination to restore itself to greatness in the fear of Western influence. Tolstoy said real Russians distrust all things foreign. Do you distrust Western influence, Chertok?"

Chertok's derisive laughter was sharp. "You trust and you trust, and when someone betrays, you trust more. It keeps the loneliness at bay. Unlike yours, my soul is thick, and my Russia is patient. Moscow is the city shining on a hill, and Archie, you are standing on a crumbling precipice. We control the most powerful nuclear force and the ability to decide whether humanity continues or ceases to exist. We will win in the end."

"Only the soul of a madman wants such destruction," Archie said.

"The West needs to understand that cooperation with Russia is the only way forward. Otherwise, China and North Korea will support us, and you will be weaker for it." Chertok's lip curled into the hint of a smile. "When you fight back over our taking of borders, it's your actions, not ours, that strengthen Russia. It is not Russia's fault that we enlist our courts to take back what has been ours for all of history. We do this for the people. Your press independence is weak, and ours has the government's strong backing."

"Our narrative becomes the will of the people, and your journalists are the enemies of the people." Chertok paused. "We can tell our networks to say that your news is false, we can imprison your journalists as spies, we can harass them to create fear, and we can question your sources to erode trust and divide groups of people. You can do none of that! Your free journalists will never stand up to a government-controlled media. The sooner the West realizes that, the better for all of us. You do realize that Russia loves your Vienna, yes? We have more diplomats there than anywhere, and many of them spy for us."

Archie had had enough. "You claim that falsifying history lifts a nation? Where is the ladder up from the hell of their worst impulses? Chertok, expertise and authority are not the same. You may be willing to slam the door of human rights on the fingers of your people, but I will use every resource I have to pry it open," he said.

"Archie, those windmills you're chasing – "

"We can admit that we need each other or keep losing lives to anger over our differences." Archie's impatience made him speak faster. "Ordinary people have the right to prosper, not to play slave to the strongman's alchemy when he whips them into a rage against an imagined foe. Then, he falls into the fantasy of needing to take back the country. Successful factories and growing companies are swallowed, their owners imprisoned, and their ownership gifted to young Kremlin oligarchs. When the oligarchs gain power and take everything, how does the nation grow? The oligarchs claim that the business builders were interfering with prosperity, that only their revolution will restore things to their pure, ordered place. Your radical news revolution takes things back to their starting point, with the only gains going to those who already have more than they will ever need."

"Look at the growth of small businesses under Havel's watch." Archie looked at Chertok, who was picking cashews from the trail mix. "Men and women reinvest because they know that their businesses and those of their neighbors aren't at risk. They don't have to look over their shoulders for wolves ready to take them over. That kind of model splinters and stagnates a country. There is no incentive to grow if you know the government will steal your business as soon as you prosper."

Chertok countered, "Why shouldn't we have all the seats at the best schools, all the homes in the best neighborhoods, take over the best businesses, and buy the best judges in the courts? We can afford to ignore the so-called sovereignty of pitiful nations with our influence. As Caligula said, let them hate as long as they fear."

"Wasn't he murdered by his closest guards? It's hate that tears apart – "

"Ah, but Caligula didn't go far enough. Our truth teaches that resistance is immoral. Only loyalty deserves reward." Chertok smiled as if it pained him. "Archie, these sovereign nations have stronger backbones than yours. Don't believe that they will fall so easily. You look too closely, and reality will change on you like a magician's trick, your truth hidden under a cloak, and *voila!* It disappears."

"Like the books your university students are denied. Their limited access to knowledge will come back to haunt you," Archie said.

"You're talking about something bigger than we are. There's no stopping it; and why should I try? Compared to the impotence of your journalists' words, it pays handsomely." He smiled. The look in his eyes defied understanding.

After his dispiriting talk with Chertok, Archie couldn't face the walk to his hotel room, and its solitary quiet. He'd wait until tomorrow to call Havel and tell him there was no support from Chertok for fair judges. A block past the hotel was Devil's Absinth. He pushed at the stuck door until it opened and found a seat at the bar. The stained-glass lampshade over his head cast a yellow glow on the wooden bartop. Archie watched as the bartender took the glass with absinth, placed a strainer spoon over the glass, and dripped water over a sugar cube until it dissolved. Without a word, he tapped, stirred, and pushed the greenish drink over the sticky counter to Archie. Besides the flavors of licorice and fennel, Archie felt the intense burn in his throat. A man at the opposite end of the bar sat hunched over his drink, still as a diner in an Edward Hopper painting.

"Hey, Erik, you know this guy?" said the man, lifting his chin in the bartender's direction. He fiddled with a frayed green scarf around his neck with some party insignia that Archie couldn't make out, an oddment left from a political campaign.

"You one of those spies?" His voice rumbled at Archie.

"Not me," Archie said. "I'm the one they'll be looking for."

The gravel-voiced man leaned back and laughed. "I'll buy that drink," he said.

The man, who wouldn't give his name, said that he ran a tourism company, training young people as guides and cruise boat workers. Archie told him he sold newsprint wholesale, and turned the conversation to his reason for being there. "Women. Why are they so confounded difficult?"

"Right that," the man said.

"You know where you're headed, and then they come into your life, messing everything up. Nothing is the same."

"You know it."

"They're a distraction, a trap, impossible to break free from. Make you want to quit it all."

"Got one like that myself. Can't shake her," the man agreed.

Drink after drink, the men talked themselves further into a muddle of lonely, moping pity.

"Then I have this nephew – " Archie stopped. At that moment, he hated his life. Why not quit trying to protect Havel, quit the university journalists, quit helping village newspapers, quit microloans for African women, quit it all? He could retire peacefully by holding the hands of nervous millionaires and steering them toward sound financial advice.

And when the Kremlin declared war on Hungary, Estonia, Ukraine, the Czech Republic, and their imagined Nazi leaders, where would Logan be? He'd be the first to sign up to fight them, the first to be killed.

Archie finished his last glass and nodded to his companion. He'd lost count of the drinks, but his mind still stopped him from speaking Logan's name. A whoosh of cold air hit him when the door opened. Absinth didn't work. Not for one night could he forget. He'd do this for Logan and to hell with leaving Layla. After he and Zolt's team had met with Vienna's parliament about surveillance and the Russian diplomat spies, he'd take her to New York to meet the only family he had left.

CHAPTER 24

1992 Vienna

Layla was in Vienna just for an afternoon. She would not accept Archie's attempts to break things off with her, but at the same time, she let Archie know that her schedule wouldn't allow them time together. Indifference be damned, Archie thought. As soon as he'd read her refusal to break up with him, he cleared his schedule and headed for the Altstadt.

The innkeeper had performed many favors for Archie in the past and used his *passe-partout* to let Archie into the room where Layla was staying. He checked the chilling champagne and from his pocket, drew a package of *stroopwafels* he'd picked up, just because he knew she loved them. The last time he'd bought some to take to New York, she'd found them first and eaten them all.

He wandered to the bedroom and felt alarm and pleasure at the wallet-sized photo of them together on the nightstand by the bed. He had no photos of Layla, as much as he wanted one. It was too dangerous. He picked it up and recognized Marek's boat on the Danube in the background. Maybe he could get a copy made, just one picture they shared when they were apart. She had only a few hours here before leaving for work. Looking down from the height of the second-floor window, he saw Layla approaching at a fast clip. A thin, unkempt man was at a safe distance behind her, puffing a cigarette, shuffling in baggy pants that covered his shoes. Archie lost sight of her entering the building, and shortly after, the man followed.

He heard her key in the lock. Her eyes grew wide. "Ar – nold, how wonderful to see you!" The disheveled man entered behind her and she pushed him toward her closet. He slipped inside and closed the door.

Layla put her finger to her lips, then threw her arms around Archie. "May be bugged. May be cameras," she whispered in his ear.

"Heart thief," Archie said.

"Blockhead"

"Mesmerizer"

"Pirate, bandit: kidnap me now," Layla said.

"I could force you to dine with me in the room," Archie said.

"I thought you'd never ask." She stood back and looked at him. "Oh, Arnold." She smiled her most genuine smile and hugged him again. In another embrace, she whispered, "I'll explain."

Layla found glasses, and Archie popped the champagne, trying to ignore the man hiding in the closet. They appeared to be conversing and sipping on the sofa, in full view from the window. Layla brought paper and a pen to tell Archie what to expect. She reached for his hand, and he felt the crumpled note. *In one-half-hour two men take the witness to safe house. Trial in six days.* "So tell me how is Momo?" she asked.

"Oh, you know," Archie recognized that the name was made up. He paused as he read her note. "Momo tells stories and Leopold corrects whatever he says." Archie wrote back, *Okay, small talk. I can contact Zolt.*

An hour passed, and the champagne was gone. Layla's eyes darted to the door. Archie put the paper in his pocket and excused himself to the bathroom where he took a call from Zolt. When he returned, he reached for her hand and slipped her the paper: *5 minutes*. At that time, the two stood before the window in an embrace. Behind them, the door barely opened and two men belly-crawled to the closet to retrieve the witness. Archie swung Layla sideways to see the man exit in a different shirt and slacks like a hundred other male workers on the street. With thick-rimmed glasses, he was unrecognizable. In less than a minute they were gone. Layla and Archie withdrew to the bedroom. "You make quite an entrance," he said.

"You couldn't have timed your surprise visit any better." She hugged him with a sigh of relief. He tried to talk about his attempt to leave her but she wouldn't let him finish. "I'm not concerned with when or how we will end. We can't agree on a two-state solution, so how could we live our everyday lives together?"

Archie gave an involuntary snort. "My feelings for you go beyond a ring. But the thought of never seeing you again is unthinkable."

Archie grabbed her in a hug so powerful that it disguised the shaking in his arms.

An hour later, they gathered their clothes and Layla returned to the closet to collect the witness's rumpled pants. She tucked them in the bottom of her suitcase for her flight.

"Can I have Zolt arrange a later flight, say tomorrow? Max is having a dinner party, and I need someone there who won't talk about bond futures all night."

"Is that why you want me there? I don't know if I can refuse such a charming invitation."

"Let me try that again," Archie said. "I would move heaven and earth, and Lufthansa, to breathe the air next to you for a few more hours."

"That's more like it! Let me see what I can do." Layla called her office and postponed a day's worth of appointments.

CHAPTER 25

1992 Vienna

As Archie had predicted, the ten men at the dinner table bantered, lamented, hailed, and lugubriously mourned the state of the bond market while many of the women gave sideways glances and feigned interest. But after dinner, Archie asked if anyone would like to see the library, particularly Layla. Men ignored him, brought out their cigars, and *Mutter* Bauer forbade the bitter, lingering smell in her house, shooing them to the covered porch.

In the library, among floor-to-ceiling books with the soft light from one library table lamp, Archie steered her to the window overlooking a leafy backyard basking in full moonlight. He missed her already. He should have tried to get one more day instead of asking Zolt to get her a ticket for tomorrow morning.

"I see you're showing Layla where you spent most of your time with us." Max walked up behind them. "We had more than a few good talks in this room." He walked to the wall beside them, and his fingers traced titles on a row of books. He pulled down Nietzsche's *The Birth of Tragedy* and handed it to Archie.

"You'd get so animated telling me about the Greek gods and how drama revealed human fears and desires."

"And you'd argue back about the Apollonian idealism and how the Greeks couldn't compare with their chaotic human will."

"But that's the thing about tragedy," Layla said. "The tragedy of death and excess in Dionysian drama is what allows rebirth to occur."

Archie nudged his shoulder to hers and smiled at Max. With her quick riposte, they stood united in opposing Max's idealism.

Layla pulled away and scanned the walls for titles. "Marx's *Communist Manifesto,* Descartes' *Meditations on First Philosophy*… here's one - Spinoza's Ethics."

With arms folded in front of him, Max shook his head. "This is really my father's library. Archie has read more of these books than I have."

"My aunt loved Spinoza," Layla said. "In my teen years, she was all about virtue and controlling passionate impulses. She would read me excerpts before bed, and it would put me to sleep."

Archie and Max laughed.

"Solzhenitsyn's *Day in the Life of Ivan Denisovich,*" Layla drew the thin volume from the shelf. "So much secrecy. Everything must be hidden to trade for the smallest extra crust of bread."

"Bread is everything," said Archie. "That and a belief system that gets you through." With great care, he opened the cover of the battered copy. "This one was smuggled out after the ban in 1966." On the time-tinted page, he pointed out a list of penciled words. "Look at the names - codes of people and places where it was to be safely carried and passed on." His finger ran down the list of names. "When the Communist Party fought against intellectual rebellions, dissidents smoked the air blue in Prague's pubs to discuss and smuggle their banned works. They had a person-to-person network. I bet Havel was involved with them."

"Ah," Archie reached up for a history book. "Remember Segur's *Napoleon's Expedition to Russia?*"

"I heard you marvel over the campaign, and voice your disgust over the loss of life," Max said.

"A million soldiers," Archie said.

"You couldn't sleep for days," Max said.

"You brought me warm milk in the middle of the night."

"Yes, well…" Max checked the buttons on his jacket. "On one of those days you had an important exam the next morning and needed your sleep."

Layla grabbed a book to fill the awkward silence. "*Les Miserables*," she held out the well-worn book to him. "Archie, I bet you've read this one."

"*Don Quixote,* too," he said. It's up there nearby. There it is." He pulled it down.

Layla sneezed. The library didn't get much use now that Archie was gone. The two sat down to pore over the books on the table. In their own rarefied existence, they didn't notice Max quietly close the door behind him. Max wondered if Layla knew that one way to that man's heart was through his library.

CHAPTER 26

1992 Spain

How were your depositions?" Archie asked.

Their flights into Madrid were a few hours apart. Before she had arrived at the Barajas airport, he had time to visit the shops to find a gift for her aunt.

"The depositions were productive – and troubling." Layla shook her head. "There are so many women, and we could only talk to a small number of them. I'm going back at the beginning of the week."

"You need a break." Archie embraced her in the busy concourse, forcing travelers to walk around them. He admired the progress she had made recording pages of war crimes from victims of atrocities, archiving them. A war tribunal would someday bring justice to the survivors. Her knowledge of Syrian law was instrumental in the wording of the documents. A tribunal could connect the offenses using her carefully chosen keywords.

"I found a *Palava*." Archie held up a Czech wine he had selected. "It's like a *Gewürztraminer*."

"She prefers reds, but I bet she'll appreciate the thought," Layla said. "If not, I'll enjoy it."

"What did you do this week?" Layla kept up with Archie's long stride to the rental car concourse.

"Oh, you know, I had that small group of investors, and we brainstormed about the strength of some new start-ups I'd researched with my team."

"Let's hear it, Archie. Give me a stock tip." Layla had invested in a few of Archie's researched stock ideas in the past, and the start-ups had increased their value beyond anything she'd had before.

"Well, we talked about the Eurozone economy now, inflation, profitability, competition from Asia – "

"Just the name, Archie. What's it called?"

"You have to hear the story, Layla. It's about this guy, Steve Jobs, who liked type fonts and wanted to make a computer accessible for everyday people to use. He lost his parents. He's an American, but his birth father was Syrian, and his mother was from Germany. He built his first computer in his adoptive parents' garage."

Layla waited while he picked up the car keys at the rental desk. "So what's the stock name?"

"Imagine, Layla, people will use these computers to explore the World Wide Web. They can leave messages for free at any time of the day. They can research the best libraries in the world. Have you seen the Austrian National Library in Vienna?"

She shook her head.

"Next time we're both in Vienna, I'll take you there. Remember the *Vyšší*

Brod Abbey library? Wait until you see the National Library. People in Asia and America will use personal computers to conduct library research from home. It will change my work. Yours too. I'm investing in the creator's brain, a dream with fundamentals. The inventor believes in autonomous computers that will organize our communication and free people up to be more creative. Apple computers will change the way people understand reality."

"Wouldn't that be dangerous? Computers that make their own decisions?"

"Not at all. The programs will have guardrails."

"You're not going to tell me the name, are you?"

"Wait until we meet your *Tia* Gabriella," he said.

"You are in the neighborhood of Malasaña, good for young people and foreign visitors," *Tia* Gabriella wanted to give Archie an idea of her Madrid neighborhood. They sat together on her arched porch with a leafy courtyard view, relaxing and private. Overhead were solid wooden beams. She looked at Archie, then at Layla, and back to Archie again. "Our square, *Plaza Dos de Mayo,* is famous for a place where our soldiers conquered Napoleon's forces," she said with pride. She reached for a pitcher and served them tall glasses of *Tinto de Verano* – cool, but without ice.

"You have colorful flowers." Archie looked around the courtyard of riotous flowering plants twined round with rambunctious weeds. "Do you enjoy gardening?" Archie was struggling to make small talk.

The two women laughed conspiratorially. " *Tia* Gabriella loves flowers, but hates gardening," Layla explained. "She would rather lobby City Hall for single mothers' rights or foster parent funding."

"That is true," Gabriella nodded. "They know me by name over there. And I know which ones listen and which pretend to listen."

Archie found himself more at ease as they explained the local issues. *Tia* Gabriella's explanations, which included hand gestures that made her look more like a dancer than a lobbyist, reminded him of Layla's passionate stories about the Syrian people. Gabriella's mature beauty made him imagine what Layla would look like in years to come.

"Enough," Gabriella announced. "Has he had enough *Verano* to drink, Layla?"

Layla stood up and clasped her hands, pulling Archie from the patio chair. "Now it's time for your tango lesson," she said.

"I don't tango," Archie sat back down.

Tia Gabriella returned from the house, having slid a CD into the player. Around her neck was a sheer red scarf, which she tossed over her shoulder. She stood before Archie, pointing her index fingers at him and tapping her heels on the patio tiles in a fast, rhythmic beat. She spun around, her eyes riveted on him, demanding his attention. Swaying with the intensity of the music, she began to move around the patio in a sensual arc.

Before he knew what was happening, Layla placed his right hand in hers and the left around her waist. *Tia* Gabriella gave him an impulsive hug. "Watch her *duende*, her playful spirit," she said softly and backed away.

Archie found himself moving to the rounded guitar melody, first sounding like a shimmer, then pounding in a percussive beat. Guiding his steps in line with Layla's, their cheeks touched, radiating the early afternoon heat. When they reached the end of the patio, she turned abruptly to hold his face in her hands and gaze into his eyes. It was at that point that he decided he loved the tango. Her waist pivoted back and he instinctively knew to dance back the way they had come, matching her steps, sensing the movement of her waist.

The song ended with a flourish of guitar string sound, but Archie continued. He held her close, and Layla leaned back with her arms overhead. Archie kissed her, tasting the salt on her skin. Was there ever a time when he felt so tuned to his body? For him, the dance with Layla felt like scaling a cliff and reaching the top. He looked at the women in amazement. "What's next?" he asked.

Tia laughed, a sound just as fluid as her dancing, a natural part of her.

Layla and her aunt steered the conversation in a comfortable round-robin of flights and dives, hovering, soaring, with an occasional flap between them.

After dinner, they walked around the *Plaza Dos de Mayo*. *Tia* Gabriella held one of Archie's hands, and Layla, the other. Gabriella played tour guide and stopped at spots where famous Spaniards had risked their lives to speak out during the Franco years, or in a narrow alleyway that had become a lively secret night spot during the dry Franco crackdown.

"Here in Madrid, we call ourselves *Gatos*."

"Yes," Archie said, "your soldiers from the Middle Ages were known for scaling the castle walls like cats. How about the Basques?"

Gabriella turned to Layla. "He knows his history, this one! We are not bothered by the Basques. Yes, some call the Basques terrorists as evil as Tolkien's Mordor." She shooed away the thought with her hand. "They are a strong, resilient people. Many are in the military protecting all of Spain."

"So not all Spanish agree," Archie said.

"*Etxerat* means homeward in the Basque language. It's a group of Basque relatives that march for their friends and family who were jailed or killed as political dissidents. I saw one of their marches right over there." She pointed to a plaza near the town hall down the street. "Basque political prisoners fought to protect natural resources and have a say in Spain's land use. There were thousands of supporters. They held posters of their family members' faces and chanted, 'Independence!' The separatists are an indigenous group treated no better than Native Americans in the US. They have been here longer than any of us, and their language is the oldest in Europe."

"Basque women have come to *Tia* Gabriella for help," Layla said.

The three approached a towering, airy structure. The doorway's monumental pillars on strong granite posts opened into the bustling, hundred-year-old farm market, the *Marcato de San Miguel*. Its high central hallway ceiling crisscrossed by a cast iron skeleton made it cool and comfortable.

Shopkeepers called out their wares in echoing voices. *Tia* Gabriella stopped at her favorite olive vendor, and Archie stood back. "I've picked enough of those to last a lifetime. No olives for me."

Tia laughed and chose a variety of olives for only herself and Layla. The lively crowd forced the three of them to shout to hear one another. A few vendors down, Layla found spices in open bins. Archie watched Layla's back-and-forth negotiation with the shopkeeper and then marveled at the giant scoops of seasonings the vendor sealed in paper bags for her.

"I thought you didn't cook," he said.

With hands full of packages, she gave him a playful elbowing to his chest. "I didn't say that. I don't *like* to cook, just bake. But I have to eat, so why not make it tasty?" She gathered the seasonings in her net shopping bag, and they moved on to a tapas stand.

Archie selected a bottle of wine, making sure that it was red, and saw *Tia* and Layla watching a vendor advertising his crab tapas. As tempting as they looked, no one had an appetite after *Tia's* generous dinner. They admired the display case with its crab, tuna and potatoes, manchego, and more, then spotted a table in a corner where they could enjoy the wine and watch people from all over the world experiencing the *marcato*.

It was after midnight when they returned, much later than *Tia* Gabriella was used to. Archie noticed Gabriella's face had turned gray. Maybe she was tired. Then he saw her trembling hand reach for her forehead as she said goodnight and made her way to her room on the opposite side of the house. He caught Layla's eye, but she frowned and looked away. This was not the time to discuss her aunt's health.

This was your room growing up," Archie looked around.

Layla closed the door. "*Tia* has turned it into a guest room, but yes," Layla said.

Archie noticed a change in her voice as they got into bed. "What's wrong?"

"What do you mean? Nothing's wrong!" Layla got out of bed and walked to the window. She turned and climbed back into bed, sitting with her legs tucked under her. "It might be wrong. I don't know. It doesn't feel wrong. I told you I used protection."

"I did, too." Archie was puzzled.

"Spain has strict abortion laws, but I don't want that anyway." She squared her shoulders. "I'm going to have the baby. I've decided."

Archie looked at her, but no words came.

"Archie, you don't need to do anything. I've thought about it and decided – yes, I will forever have my heart walking around outside my body."

"A baby – "

"I know that we must be careful about foreign interference in our situations. I can do that."

"Are you sure?"

"Without a doubt," Layla answered immediately in her lawyer voice.

Suddenly, Archie's heart felt unbearably light, as if something that had been dormant in him was wide awake. A father. First hike, where? First investment, what? First listen to Grateful Dead, which? First picture book, Dr. Seuss's star-bellied *Sneeches*? He assured himself that his son would never bore him, and not in his lifetime would the boy need to impress his dad. But what if it was a girl? Even better.

He placed his hand gently on her belly, as if he might break her. "I – this is so good. *Three* of us. Layla, this is better than so good."

"I won't tell anyone until I need to. It's for the best."

"I want to tell the world, Layla."

"Then you want to be a part of it all?"

"Every midnight feeding, every soccer game, piano recital, visit to the head teacher's office – the works."

"Now I can tell you," she sighed. "This was such a hard secret to keep. Before we left the barge, Marek took me aside to tell me something I needed to hear."

"Oh?" Archie's face ached from smiling.

"He said something like, "*Snesl bite ti modré z nivi.* It means – "

"*Snesl bych ti modré z nebe.* I'll give you the blue from the sky," Archie said.

"Yes, that's it. Marek said it meant you'd do anything in the world for me, so I shouldn't hurt you, or I'd have to answer to him."

"Well –Archie was at a loss. His chest tightened as he thought of Layla's vulnerability dancing on a razor's edge for her work or his.

"Now I think you'll have to find some baby books on economics."

"You can find one on tango for kids."

CHAPTER 27

1992 Spain

Before they left Spain, Archie wanted to shop for a ring for Layla. She wasn't so sure, but to avoid questions, she would wear it on her right hand as if it were a souvenir. Only they would know that it was a promise. They tried jewelry stores from the *Molero*, the *Joya Classica*, to the *Vera* before they circled back to *Molero*.

Layla returned to the display with the antique round emerald in a classic setting.

"It fits you," Archie said.

"This ring was a gift to the wife of an Andalusian olive grower for their 50th anniversary," the jeweler said.

"Fifty years!" Layla said. "Did you hear that?"

"How old is it?" Archie asked.

"The daughter inherited it many years ago. It lay forgotten in her jewelry box," the jeweler said. "She said her parents were devoted to one another. The ring has a good history, a sign of future happiness, no?" The jeweler showed Layla a note that came with the ring. The daughter had shown the anniversary card to the jeweler, but she couldn't part with the sentimental message and kept the card with her.

"You could have something nicer," Archie said. "You don't believe – "

Layla looked at him with a frown. "I had to warm up to the idea of a ring, but now, I'm on board. This is the one. Humor me." Layla kissed his cheek, and the jeweler looked away.

"Why didn't you tell me that you liked the one from *Molero* before?"

"I didn't know until I'd seen the others," Layla said.

"It's so small."

"That's the one I want. Besides, after you gave *Tia* Gabriella that block of Apple stock, you need to save your pennies."

"It doesn't look like much now, but Apple Computer Company will revolutionize computing. The feel of the computer, the look of the fonts – you wait and see. *Tia* Gabriella will have a fine in a few years."

"She won't touch it, you know."

"I told her that she can use it for her foster parents or single mothers," Archie said.

They stepped outside, and Layla held the emerald up to the sunlight. "The pineapple, the Apple stock, the ring – you love giving gifts, don't you?"

"More than you'll ever know," he said.

"I meant to tell *Tia* Gabriella that I'm meeting with Steve Jobs next week. He's talking about making a cell phone called a MacIntosh. That's a kind of apple in the States, I guess."

Before they slept that night, Layla told Archie about her parents tuning to Duke Ellington on the radio and dancing around the living room. She could still picture how her mother and father looked at each other, still see their bodies moving in symmetry, feeling the intensity between them, even though she was then too young to understand it. As she dozed off, he listened to her breathing and felt a penetrating loneliness at the thought of their parting tomorrow. He needed to ask her what it was like to come home, find her house destroyed, and then be forced to leave. Others didn't understand what it was like for children to flee their homes as he and Layla did – that it empties a part of you. Layla would. But he would not wake her.

CHAPTER 28

1992 Austria

Layla walked in from the Felderstraße and through the imposing, arched doors of the Vienna City Library to meet Archie. She followed his directions to the long, narrow reading room with its towering wooden bookshelves that reached the blue sky-painted ceiling and found him at a table with three short stacks of antediluvian tomes. The strange, bald, frowning man next to him must be the security official she was invited to meet. The two of them looked more like muscular rugby players than library patrons. Lost in his search, Archie appeared to have a handwritten list. His finger scrolled down the list, and the bald man would find the corresponding page. "This glyph to the left, Zoli – ah Layla!"

Archie's voice brought shushes from nearby patrons.

She scanned the oversized pages in front of them before she met his eyes.

"Layla, look at these fonts. Beautiful glyphs!" He lowered his voice. "Steve Jobs told me they inspired him. He took a calligraphy class and decided to make computer print beautiful, like letter art.

It's like a Shakespeare play, Layla. You have to *hear* Shakespeare, not just read it on a page. In the theater, you hear the beauty of the words bumping up against one another. You feel the passion, jealousy, inspiration, betrayal, strength, and sorrow."

Layla asked him if Havel had recently convinced him to read Shakespeare, and he admitted to *King Lear*. "But there's a connection," he said. "These fonts do the same thing for the written word."

He pulled out the chair next to him, and she sat.

"This is Black Letter from the 1100s." He slid the book so she could see. "It's like hand-drawn calligraphy." He turned the page. "Here's a kind of Helvetica Jobs will call San Francisco, and it will appear on Apple computers."

"He can get computers to use different fonts?" Layla asked.

"It's not just about the words, but the presentation. The font can convey the meaning, like the Canadian Marshal McLuhan's idea that the medium is the message. I wouldn't say the typography is more important than the message, but it isn't just a vehicle of delivery. It sets the best mood for the reader to accept the message. That's powerful."

"How do you know?"

"I see Job's curiosity and his change-the-world attitude. He and Wozniak's first computer design has been improving ever since. He believes in making things appear simple, but he's willing to work like a Trojan to make it as perfect as possible. He and I agree on something else – don't let money ruin your life."

"Where did you meet him?"

"I heard him speak at Lund University in Sweden in '85. He turned pages of fonts and pointed out the bold curves and pointy corners."

Layla marveled at Archie's ability to put the weighty issues on the back burner and indulge in childlike wonder. She caught his enthusiasm as he pointed out different fonts and their ability to enhance the reader's experience of mood and tone from whatever subject matter it captured.

He closed the book, and the old book smell wafted up. Layla breathed in. "Um – It's redolent of smokey wood."

"Or earthy, like coffee," Zolt said, peering over the other side of Archie.

"It's *bibliosmia*," Archie said. "The decay of books."

Once Archie paused, Layla looked at Zolt. "Are you going to introduce us?"

"Layla, I've known about you for quite some time. Archie's security officer." Zolt reached his hand across Archie.

Layla took it and gave him a firm business handshake. She could tell they wore their friendship easily. "So, tell me about yourself, Zolt," she said.

Zolt stood. "Archie can tell it better than I can. I'll be back," he said, and disappeared out the other door of the long reading room.

Archie said Zoli was an introvert and didn't like talking about himself. He was a half-sibling to many brothers and sisters. As a toddler in Israel, his mother would leave him all afternoon in the sun on the sandy vacant lot next door in his wet diaper. He was told he'd smile and wave to passersby. As he grew older, cousins chided him for the odd shapes and colors the sun had burned on his face. An aunt couldn't endure her sister's neglect of the child, and took Zoli to the Ministry of Welfare. Zoli was a loving child and tried to befriend the foster siblings, but his appearance was difficult to accept, and the families would return him.

Layla listened with her chin on her hand. She had heard similar stories from Syrian mothers, but this was different.

Archie told her that he spent his teenage years in and out of a variety of families and knew how to make friends quickly, gaining an understanding of people so that they might overlook his appearance. Despite this upheaval, he excelled in math and science. Archie first saw him during a guest lecture during Zoli's first college term. Like others, Archie was shocked by Zoli's face when he came up to ask questions after the lecture. Their talks continued, and Archie provided a scholarship for his remaining years and an internship in his financial firm.

Years later, Archie told Zoli that he was a turtle emerging from its shell. Once Zoli began to talk, Archie felt more of his warmth and humanity. When scholarship administrators told Archie of Zoli's background, he checked with plastic surgeons. Archie found specialists who provided relief from the Actinic Keratosis and rough, scaly patches on his face. Laser surgery, dermabrasion, and plastic surgery over Zoli's college years gave him a fine-looking face. His hair would not grow back, but the stares of pity and disgust diminished.

Even though he was a survivor, Zoli never got over the feeling of being an outcast. His need to outperform in academics and to search for kinship before others had a chance to reject him never left him. Along with gratitude for Archie's mentorship, he recognized Archie's need for protection against powerful media disinformation networks. He proposed a silent, secret network of agents in all the cities where Archie conducted business, using new technologies to track those out to harm him and help to give him a semblance of a normal life rather than one in hiding. Archie loved the idea, and the two had worked together ever since.

Archie told Zoli that he hoped to see him have a family, one his own childhood had denied him. Zoli refused. He had endured more than his share of rejection throughout his life and was satisfied to walk down the street without stares and pity. Archie and the security team were his family. He was honored to protect Archie as his life's work.

Zoli returned and sat next to Archie. "Are you finished?"

"Zoli has always protected us, sometimes when we didn't even know it."

Layla was moved by his story and told him so.

"Do you think I left anything out?" Archie turned to his friend.

"The indescribable humiliation of being the "other one." Zolt said. "I think the secondary level at school was the worst, but Archie didn't have parents either. He knew," He looked at Layla. "Not too many people know that story, but I knew I could trust Archie to tell it. I can see that he's not like these other financial titans. It's almost like a coincidence that he has money, a small wonder that happens to be there when he thinks of a reason to give it away. And he's always thinking of ways to give it away."

"Now I know your story, and it's my work to record women's stories," she told him. "So why is it usually so hard for men to tell these important stories? To open up?"

"You're comparing me as if we're all alike. It's socialization," Archie said.

"Men grow up not knowing that it's okay to be unguarded and appreciate things. They feel that it's a sign of weakness," Layla said.

"Not true. My life has revolved around protecting Rivka. She always comes first, and I've protected her. I always will."

"You're not hearing what I'm saying. I mean that you feel it's your responsibility to be the strong one, to take care. Rivka's a grown woman and a wife. She's a university professor. Of course, you love her, but she has her own family." Layla knew she hit a sore point when Archie averted her gaze. He was silent, so she gave an example.

"I didn't listen to the Grateful Dead but I liked Roger Whittaker. He sang that song, "Last Farewell." *Tia* Gabriella and I would listen to it over and over.

"Who is Roger Whittaker?"

"He's British, but he was born and grew up in Kenya. It's a song about a military officer in the 1800s who fell in love with a beautiful Polynesian woman and had to leave her to go off to war. His voice had a quality that kind of wrapped itself around me, and I thought it was terribly romantic. In the song, he wasn't afraid to die in the war – so brave – but his regret was the thought of never seeing his love again."

"You like nostalgia." Archie voiced his disagreement.

"It's the power of a love so strong that no war could stop it. I loved Mary Stewart's books. She's an English author who writes romantic thrillers that take place all over Europe just after World War II. When I was young, I'd read her books and fantasize about a big strong man who was also kind and tender, one who righted wrongs, who would sweep me off my feet and adore me."

"So that's why you're here with me." Archie winked.

Layla tried unsuccessfully to push down a giggle. A patron at the next table shushed her. "I dated a lot in college. In the back of my mind was always that Mary Stewart romantic, strong man and no one came close to that ideal until I met a man in the Spanish army. His name was Javier, and I would melt when he smiled at me. We'd go for walks and sit in cafes with cups of tea. Neither of us had much money, but we'd have Sunday dinner with his big family, all the brothers and sisters. All that warmth made me feel loved, and I loved them all."

"One big happy family." There was an edge to Archie's voice.

"One Sunday after dinner, in front of his whole family, he dropped to one knee and showed me an engagement ring. It was his grandmother's. It was so soon! I was speechless. He said, 'Now you will live here with my family. You won't go to school anymore. We will have a big family, and our world will be here.'"

Layla blinked as the memory returned. "I thought about stopping my classes, emptying myself. I looked at their smiling faces, waiting for me to say yes. This family I had grown to love began to feel like guards at a prison gate. I felt as if they were taking away my sense of self, and I don't want to feel like that again."

Archie wasn't sure what she meant. Maybe it was the feeling of being fenced in. But this wasn't the time to ask, so he said, "Hmm."

"I could feel my eyes turning red, and I told them I had to leave. I never saw him again." She looked at Zolt and then at Archie. "It took a long time to realize that those Roger Whittaker songs and the suspenseful books I loved were a fantasy. I wouldn't want to live that way. And here you are with your appalling wealth. I wouldn't want to live that way either."

"It is appalling," Archie agreed, "and besides you, Zoli is the only one brave enough to tell me. And the more I give away, the more tax I pay, it still keeps growing. I magpie here and there, and I don't finish things. But keep telling me what you think."

"I love that about you," Layla said.

Archie sighed. "Okay, Layla, while we're talking about

uncomfortable stories, I have one, and it's not pretty. Just so you know, it's not part of my spiritual inheritance. During welcome week in my first year of college, I met this girl in the stairwell of the dorm. Neither of us knew anyone. She was comfortable to be with and easy to talk to, and I hadn't dated much.

"For two days, we hung around, explored campus to get our bearings, swapped stories. I wanted to present myself in the best light, so I only mentioned that I'd moved from Israel to Vienna, not the hard stuff. We checked out the library and decided to visit the record collection on the fourth floor. We got in the elevator, and another student slipped in after us."

"We both hit the fourth-floor button. Our fingers touched, and we looked at each other. She was sweet with long, swingy hair, and she grinned at me. Something happened. Here was a girl I'd had a two-day friendship with, but this new girl was looking right at me and smiling. I didn't even think. I put my hand on the back of her neck and leaned in to kiss her. I knew she wanted it, but she slapped me and it stung, and I backed away, mostly embarrassed, and the elevator took forever. When the elevator door stopped, she stomped off, and I looked at my friend to figure out what had happened."

"Are you kidding? She wanted it? How many of my depositions have those words, and how many women were sent to hospitals or left in alleys because a man knew she wanted it, or she dressed that way, or he knew by looking at her that she was a whore?"

Nearby tables shushed her.

"You expected your new friend to go along with it?" Layla said. "That is the most asinine –"

"I'll never forget how she looked at me – like I'd hurt her. All she said was, "*Dummkopf.*"

"I would have said more than that!"

"She walked away, and I never saw her again."

"Why are you telling me this?" Layla asked.

"Because I never want to feel that way again – so guilty. Taking advantage can hurt people you care about. I was the cause of that look and no one else. I wanted you to know that's not me, but it was me once."

"I can think of half a dozen men who would have done the same thing as if they're entitled to, but I didn't think that you were like that," Layla said.

"Guilty as charged."

Zolt said. "I've seen far worse."

"Zoli, I'm not blaming you," Layla said. "He pays you to protect him."

"It's more than that," Zolt said. "Follow me."

Zolt led them to the bank of windows overlooking the parking lot. They looked down. "When we were at school here, this was all trees, remember?

Archie nodded.

"Was it this window?" Zolt asked.

"Maybe. Or this one," Archie stood before the one next to him.

"One day when Archie and I were studying here, he talked about Vienna or his impending financial career – maybe both – as constricting encasement." Zolt waited to make sure Layla knew what that was.

"Archie pointed to the windowsill and watched a ladybug shed its shell," Zolt said. "We watched because we'd never seen that happen before. He opened the window and –

"We had to wrench it back and forth until the window gave way, and the ladybug opened its wings and flew free," Archie added. Zolt looked at Layla. "Now, how many people do you know who would do that?

CHAPTER 29

1992 Czech Republic

Havel's invitation was welcome but a bit cryptic. Although Archie and Layla had visited Prague on business, they had never been to the Prague People's Theater or sat in the red-velvet-draped President's box.

Archie and Vaclav sat away from the eyes of the rest of the audience, surrounded by 19th-century splendor, and gold-leafed details. Layla stood at the velvet rail and looked up. Hanging from the center of the ceiling painted with Greek mythical figures was a grand chandelier sparkling in the nation's pride: hand-crafted Czech crystal. She had questions about the theater's history, but Havel wanted to talk. "When you see her, you will know. We have so much in common. No one can ever replace my Olga, but Dagmar is a good woman."

"Dagmar?"

"Yes yes. She's performing here tonight. We'll meet her after. She's been in dozens of movies, TV shows, and she's not only a comedienne, but a fine actress. You'll see. I've seen the show three times already."

"Vaclav, Olga's been gone only a year. I still miss her terribly." After Olga's painful death from cancer, the shock in Layla's voice was not lost on Havel. "Are you sure you're not moving too fast?"

"The people love her! Not only that, but she is a woman of substance. She speaks for social justice. She has a foundation to help those affected by floods and fires. But you are right. I think this is happening because I miss my Olga. Because our love was great, the pain without her is also great. I believe Olga would approve of her. Oh, the curtain is going up. Sit down, sit down!" Havel took Layla's hand and squeezed, leading her to her seat away from the railing. "This was Mozart's favorite theater. The sound – you'll hear every word."

"The raven himself is hoarse
That croaks the fatal entrance of Duncan
Under my battlements. Come, you spirits
That tend on mortal thoughts, unsex me here,
And fill me from the crown to the toe top-full
Of direst cruelty. Make thick my blood,
Stop up th'access and passage to remorse..."

Archie listened to Dagmar's portrayal of Lady Macbeth, and with suspended disbelief, Dagmar became the ruthless lady. He saw Havel in the darkened theater, his face lit by the stage lights and from within by the poet's heart.

Layla was one of the last to end her applause before the intermission. "Vaclav, she's formidable. I can't wait to meet her."

Havel knitted his eyebrows and observed the two of them. "Am I blinded by my feelings? Is this a bad idea?"

"What have you told her?" asked Archie.

"Nothing at all directly. But I have written her poetry."

Layla touched his shoulder. "Vaclav, she knows."

At the end of the play, the audience stood to applaud, and the Czech faces, usually serious, broke out in smiles.

They met in the back room of Flambée, a cellar restaurant around the corner from the Old Town Square. Archie and Havel led the way to the table, and drinks had been served by the time Dagmar arrived. While they were dressed for a theater evening, Dagmar wore simple black pants, a turtleneck, and a jacket. With her stage makeup removed, she was still attractive, her face framed in lustrous Lady Macbeth golden- curled waves. She leaned to kiss Havel's cheeks and nodded to Archie and Layla before sitting. In one swift movement, she slid herself closer to Havel in the restaurant's half-circle booth.

"Introductions aren't necessary," Dagmar said. "Havel has told me all about you." There was a hint of mischief in her voice.

Waitstaff arrived with a drink for Dagmar and appetizers for the table, although no menu was offered. "I've been here so often that they know what I want better than I do," she said.

Havel talked about the clocks he had added to the Palace, some of which Dagmar had helped to select. Archie described the sights on his most recent hike with Layla. Dagmar, not one to hike, asked Layla for a recommendation for walking shoes as walking was her favorite mode of traversing Prague.

Havel took a phone call. "It's boring everyday stuff," he explained as the staff removed the phone from the table. "But it's vital – roads and water supplies have been neglected for years and repair is slow, but the need is immediate."

"While you're here," Dagmar turned to Layla, "You must stop by the amphitheater on the banks of the Vltava at 2:00. Each day a barge stops by with a puppet show for kids, but there is much adult humor that goes over their heads to the parents. I know we seem to be quiet, serious people, but we love to laugh." Dagmar blinked at Havel. Archie assumed that they were sharing a private joke.

CHAPTER 30

1992 Syria

Days later, Layla returned to Syria. Trying to make up for the unhurried days with Archie, she took extra depositions from women caught in the fighting between rival factions. The line of women waiting patiently to testify seemed never to end. Soon after her return, Layla called Archie. She missed him more on the days after they'd spent time together.

She tapped the number on her new cell phone as she looked out over the city from the roof of her Damascus flat. It seemed safer to make a call from here, and the reception was better.

"Archie, your life reminds me of the Yeats poem, the one he wrote after World War I when the Russian Civil War was still raging. It's called 'The Second Coming.' I think of the line, *'Things fall apart; the center cannot hold.'* We argued those lines in a college poetry class about the best and worst of us. The best are not willing to sacrifice much, and the worst have such passion and intensity that they're willing to do anything – to poison or murder – to get what they want. They're so sure that the chaos that follows is justified." The book was in her room below, and she wished she'd brought it up with her.

"And his *spiritus mundi,*" Archie said, "the spirit of the world was our collective soul, our memories."

"The collective Russian souls, so many opposition groups that they couldn't find the center, the moral foundation, the core of their ideology. Here, you are trying to gather a majority in the center to help people find one another. The censorship is pushing against you."

"It comes in waves, doesn't it?" Archie said. "The States had it in the 1950s during their Cold War. They tried to eliminate "subversive" people from getting jobs. Their Supreme Court made a declaration for academic freedom that I've used in some of my guest lectures in Budapest. It goes something like. ' Scholarship cannot flourish with suspicion and distrust.' Students need freedom or civilization will stagnate and die. That's the censorship Eastern Europe is battling now. During the American Civil War, there was Frederick Douglass who was censored for his anti-slavery rhetoric. He said, 'Liberty is meaningless where the right to utter one's thoughts and opinions has ceased to exist.'"

Layla responded, "We had some testy discussions about European colonial slavery as if we'd banned it long before America, but it was only a handful of years before."

Archie continued, "In his poem, Yeats didn't consider the downward spiral of propaganda and its passionate supporters. When I first opened the school, I returned to my hotel room one day to find the door latch covered in fine powder. I took a cloth and soap from the washroom and scrubbed it down. It wasn't long after that I began to sweat and become dizzy. I fell to the floor and dragged myself to the phone to call the desk. I was unconscious when they took me to hospital."

"They tested me for every kind of poison they knew about but could find nothing. It was a warning: watch what professors you hire for your school. Watch what they teach their students. We're watching you. I know that if I were a political opponent, I'd have been assassinated by now. In Eastern Europe, I never spend more than one night in any lodging. Western Europe is better; a few nights are okay. They have better surveillance."

"Did they ever find – "

"Never," Archie said. "Since then, I've heard of others – independent, pro-democracy supporters, and people who want fair and free elections who suddenly become ill. It's always suspected. I have a toxicologist in Vienna working on it. After each incident, I gather and send everything I can find to him. The poison cannot be identified, but symptoms are the same."

Layla was quiet. Had he said too much? Why would any woman want to continue a relationship with a man who could be poisoned at any time?

"You never give up, and neither do I," she said. "We rarely discuss your financial burden, but I see how it trips you up. You aim at fairness and spend your wealth to make it happen, but your money has made your life poorer for it, a danger. You live from place to place, unable to call any place home. Instead of a yacht in Dubai, you support Marek's *Fortuna* barge. Instead of building a Mediterranean palace with walls and guards, you give microloans so that African women can send children to school."

"The alternative is too bleak to imagine," Archie said. "We'd have Europe run by Ministries of Propaganda, piling one scheme on top of another to confuse and conjure up fear, telling people *their* leadership is the true one, and that what they see with their own eyes is wrong. The threat of unleashed forces fuels me. That and my army of student journalists."

They had talked so long that only starlight revealed the sparkle of her ring. Even the birds were quiet.

The next day's depositions were lengthy, and Layla stared at the stacks of file folders on her desk before she put her pencil down and looked at Fatima, the woman who had just shared a harrowing story. "Your bravery in telling us what happened means more than you know. This violation is more than sex. Men have thought of sexual violence as a normal tool of war for hundreds of years, and change is slow. But now, in the Balkans and the Democratic Republic of Congo, and here in Syria change is happening and you stepped forward to help other women. Thank you for speaking out."

She waited for Bibi, her Syrian translator, to say the words. Fatima nodded to both of them before she left. Bibi dropped an additional stack of file folders on the desk. "Bibi, did you get the impression that Fatima and Amoud were about the same age?" Layla asked.

"That was my impression. You might suggest that in the notes," Bibi replied. "What do you say, two more for today?"

Layla looked at Bibi, who was not only a translator but a good friend. They had worked on these projects for three years. Bibi brushed her long hair back from her forehead, damp from the Syrian heat, and her eyes looked tired.

"Good work, Bibi. It's been a long one today." She looked out at the waiting women. "I think I see four left. How about if we tell the fourth one that she is the last? She can tell anyone else to come back in the morning."

Bibi nodded. "In that case, you must go out for a drink with me after," she said.

Layla nodded. From her Palestinian upbringing that forbade drinking, it still surprised her, no matter where she was that people could go out and find places to talk and drink.

Soma Cafe was in the middle of an area of Aleppo simmering with nightlife. The two women waited a bit longer for a table in a corner, making it easier to check the surroundings. Not only were they wary of Archie's Soviet observers, but of the husbands and partners of the women who gave depositions.

"Arak on ice," Bibi called to the waiter over the music of the band.

"Grapefruit juice and soda," Layla shouted.

Bibi looked at her. "I brought you here after the day we had, and that's all you're getting?"

Layla looked at her and smiled. She had confided her feelings about Archie except for this last surprise.

"Oh – I get it. Good for you if that's what you want!"

Layla changed the subject. "Did I tell you about coming to Spain from Palestine? You know how sometimes memories come back to you? It was after the Six-Day War, and I was alone and four years old. *Tia* Gabriella searched for favorite foods and painted my room aqua – my favorite color then. But still, I wanted home – the rubble-filled streets, the listening for mortar shells, the hiding with my parents in our home, the only place to go. All the things that made Gaza dangerous, I longed for my family and to be in it together."

Their drinks arrived, and Layla took a sip. "Maybe," she said, "thinking of that young mother today, this is the first time that I allowed myself to feel anything about it."

"A toast to us – all of us!" Layla said as they lifted their glasses.

"It's a different lens you look through when you think of the

little one," Bibi said. "The fourth deposition was the hardest one today. Did you notice how anxious the young mother was at first?"

Layla nodded. "Her shoulders were shaking."

"Your questions and the way you ordered them, I think that helped bring her some understanding of the chaos of the whole thing."

"We find ways to pull at the threads of evidence that will prove effective when Syrian law doesn't favor women. She'd waited as long as she could, but she needed to go to the market to feed her children." Layla said.

"To think that those men attacked her in the street in front of the children," Bibi said.

"And no one came to her aid. They were afraid they would be killed."

"And then what they did to her children right in front of her, one by one," Bibi grasped her glass until her fingertips were white.

"The government does nothing. Fear makes people easier to control." Layla took a sip of her drink to clear her throat. "The mercenaries, those secretly trained groups, are not bound by the laws of any country. From one spot to another, they leave chaos and broken lives in their wake. But enough." She tracked the moisture on her glass.

"Ritter is adventurous, but he's traditional too." She smiled. "He gave a pineapple to the barge captain in Prague as a good luck gift." Layla and Bibi referred to Archie by his secret name, Ritter, the name of a coffee *haus* in Vienna.

"It's a welcoming gift for a new homeowner. I've never known anyone to do such a thing. And he has this arresting look that he reserves only for me, that conceals nothing."

Layla turned to see a flak jacket in her face. A man grabbed her wrist and twisted it. She jumped from her seat and kicked, but he grabbed her leg. Two men with faces covered darted out from behind him to zip-tie her hands behind her. In seconds, the men had forced her to walk between the triangle they created with short knives pointed at her sides, warning her not to speak.

"Adhhab *'iilaa aljahim!* Help!" Bibi stood and shouted.

The music and voices were too loud. Already, she couldn't see the men or Layla. Finally, a waiter came, and Bibi told him to call an ambulance and the police.

Bibi grabbed their shoulder bags and pushed through the crowd, but people danced in aisles or stood unaware that anything had happened. At the door, she ran shouting Layla's name. People on the street stared, but there were no men in black. A police car pulled up, and Bibi explained in her distraught voice. The officers stood there, so she ran terrified behind the *Soma Cafe,* and the officers followed.

Layla's breathing was ragged, and knife wounds were hard to count. "We've got you, Layla. You're going to be okay," Bibi said, although she felt that those words were far from the truth.

CHAPTER 31

1992 Syria

At the hospital, Bibi used Layla's phone to call *Tia* Gabriella. She asked her in Spanish, "Notify Ritter, you know?"

"I know. I am afraid of what he might do," Tia said.

Bibi knew better than to say Archie's name in public.

Within hours, two guards were posted outside Layla's door. Bibi fluffed Layla's pillows as much as she could, afraid to touch her or disturb the tubes and monitors. A brusque woman rushed in with a clipboard. "Don't think of turning anything off." She glared at Bibi.

"Of course not," Bibi was exhausted.

"So we understand each other. The baby is alive. If she dies, we go to somatic support until the baby is born."

"But that could be… 28 weeks or maybe more." Bibi was sure the woman was mistaken.

"That's right. And if there is a choice and only one can live, it must be this child. If anything happens, prepare to be questioned."

"I didn't catch your name," Bibi said with her own abrasive voice, but the woman had already left.

The next morning, Archie appeared from the airport. His haggard appearance was not only due to Layla's attack but also a result of his red-eye flight from a D.C. meeting of the Aspen Institute. Spotting the guards, he passed by the nurses' station directly to Layla's room. A nurse blocked his way.

"Yes, I'm Ritter," he replied. The guards nodded as he opened the door. Layla's face was swollen, and her left eye, black. An oxygen tube was taped to one cheek. Gauze and bandages covered her torso and left arm.

In the chair, asleep, was Bibi. The nurse started to list Layla's injuries and Bibi awoke to the litany from the nurse and an attractive man standing over her. His eyes were tired and sad.

Bibi began to translate the knife wounds, abrasions, concussion, broken ribs, and an unknown substance that appeared to be a topical poison. The lab was working to identify it, but its characteristics didn't fit any poison currently known. Before a poison was identified, two hospital workers also became ill from contact with Layla.

Archie picked up the phone by Layla's bed and called EAPCCT in Vienna. " Dr. Schroeder," he said. When he reached a lab associate, Archie left a message that he would send a sample of a poison that needed identification as soon as possible, whatever the cost.

"Thank you, Bibi," he said. Gently holding Layla's hand in his, he whispered, "You will live. Our child will live." Archie leaned over Layla trying to ignore the tubes, and spoke to her with a reassurance that he didn't feel.

Bibi said softly, "Maybe she can't hear us, but let's keep talking." She saw his face change from sadness to anger.

"Let's find out who runs the hospital lab."

For four days, Archie and Bibi sat with Layla. Archie brought flowers. Bibi told Layla stories of her dog. Archie read to her the love poetry of Rumi – which he didn't care for, but he knew was her favorite. Fluids coursed into her through the tube in her arm. No nourishment seemed to stay in her body, and her glowing olive skin grew ashen.

Investigators around Aleppo reported that the three men, including one who had drugged the security guards assigned to Layla, left nothing behind. Each day the chance of finding them became less likely.

Then Dr. Schroeder called. They had exhausted every possibility for the type of poison used, except for one: an advanced Soviet nerve agent illegal in every country. It was a chemical weapon: Novichok. Dr. Schroeder expressed his sorrow that there was no antidote at this time. Atropine could counteract some effects, but only if it had been immediately administered.

The next day, Dr. Scholz made a cursory check and instructed nurses to change the equipment to life support for the fetus. He shook hands with Archie, his rough, scrubbed surgeon's hand in contrast to Archie's smooth one.

"What did Layla's aunt say?" Archie asked.

"I spoke with her at some length, explained the poison, brain trauma, the stab wounds to liver and kidneys, and lung punctures. I assured her she was not feeling pain. Her brain function is unknown," the doctor said. "Ms. Gabriella was sure that Layla would not want her body to be kept alive until the birth of the child."

"That's 28 weeks."

"Yes, possibly," Dr. Scholz said.

"*Tia* Gabriella didn't want that, and I'm sure Layla would not want that," Bibi said.

"The baby is all that we have left," Archie said.

"It's the law. We will keep her alive until the child can be safely delivered." Dr. Scholz stood back while the attendant checked the mechanical ventilator.

"The baby is healthy?" Archie asked.

"We can't be sure, but there is a heartbeat. As long as there is a heartbeat, we must follow the law. It is a tragedy, all this." Dr. Scholz left.

"Ritter, we can't let her live for months hooked up to monitors and tubes."

"It's not something we ever talked about." His forearm brushed his eyes. "She can't decide, but our child – "

"No, Ritter, it's not about what you want." Her look dared him to look away. "This is the last thing you will ever do for her. You heard what Dr. Scholz said about his talk with *Tia* Gabriella. Think of what Layla would want."

For a man who always depended on rational truth, a logical decision was not to be had. He'd spent his life protecting and helping. Now he would be selfish. "I'm going to keep the child," he said.

"You were good for her," Bibi said.

"I *am* good for her, and she is everything to me."

"I could hear it in the tone of her voice when she talked about you. The way she'd look into the distance as if she was imagining you. She was seeing a therapist you know. Many deposition lawyers do. It's about the secondary trauma."

"I didn't know."

"The stories are haunting. After many days and dozens of stories, with tragic details, we can't shrug it off."

Archie shifted uncomfortably. "Sometimes, she would begin to talk about it. When I'd ask her questions, she would change the subject."

Unaccustomed to this helpless feeling, he tried to think of something he could do. "Can you think of anything she might need from her apartment?" he asked.

Bibi said she'd think about it.

He told her about the time Layla had invited him to cook with her in her apartment shortly after he had met her aunt in Madrid.

He warned Layla that Elias had told him before how unhelpful he was in the kitchen, but she ignored his protestations. He showed up at her door with wine. "A Viennese *Grüner Veltliner* for madame, minerally in flavor, more exotic than sauvignon blanc, with notes of lime, lemon, and apricot."

She laughed at his elaborate description and escorted him to the counter that separated the dining area from the kitchen. On a small table she had set for two, he found glassware. With a towel placed over his arm, he poured two glasses, presenting her glass like a sommelier. He hoped he could get away with just pouring wine, but Layla had other ideas.

She wiped her hands on the kitchen towel tucked in her waist and hugged him. "You have onion duty," she said.

He looked at the selection of knives in the block and chose a chef's knife with a well-used handle. After the first cut, he sliced his thumb. "This is honed sharp enough to kill a horse," he said.

"That was *Tia's*. She gifted it to me when I got this apartment. Don't drip blood in the onion," she sang, looking for the bandage tin in the cupboard. She wrapped a large one around the cut on his thumb.

He looked at the bandage design. "Hello Kitty?"

"I bought boxes of them for the children who come with their mothers to give depositions. You'd be surprised how many need bandages."

Soon the fragrance of onions sizzling in butter permeated the galley kitchen. "Watch, Archie."

The onions he'd chopped and dumped into the bubbling butter were browning too fast, and he struggled mightily with the spatula. Camp cooking was so much easier than this.

Her judgment was swift. "Not too hot - caramelize them. Get them sweet."

He dialed down the flame and watched her open the *masala dabba,* dipping the scoop in the cardamom, turmeric, and garam masala from their tin compartments before tossing the seasonings on the chicken. "Where is your measuring spoon?" he asked. These were whole containers, not the small spice jars his mother used. "It's going to be too hot," he warned.

"Not at all. It will be rich with aroma and richer with flavor," she said. "Go back to your pine nuts." With a nudge of her hip, she pushed him back to his side of the stove. Archie inhaled the cloud of aromas, especially the pungent, earthy sumac.

This was a new side of Layla with her grin of concentration, a woman full of surprises. She took a sip of wine and gave him a nod, a sign that it would pair well with the *Musakhan*. On Marek's barge, she'd told him she didn't like cooking, but she seemed to be getting a kick out of sharing her stove with him, nudging him around her kitchen.

Now that the onions appeared less angry in their butter, he concentrated on the smaller pan. Unsure about how dark the tiny pine nuts should be, he noticed when their scent grew woody, and their color changed. He turned off the burner and tossed them in the air, catching them back in the pan, feeling like he'd found his rhythm.

Just as he thought that all the ingredients were ready, Layla ripped open a packet of shiny crystals and dissolved a spoonful of them in a small bowl of chicken broth.

"What's that?"

"It's tears from the Greek mastic tree. They score the older trees in mid-summer and harvest the sticky resin, so it looks like the tree is crying. Remember our trip to *Mercado de San Miguel* in Madrid?"

"It was huge. Tapas, nuts, fruits, pastries – there was no end."

" I found the mastic there." With a wooden spoon and measuring cup, she stirred the crystals into a syrup and poured it over the chicken. "Smell."

"Archie leaned over the pan and took in a woodsy scent that changed the balance of the dish. "I've never smelled anything like it that I could eat."

She dipped the wooden spoon into the velvety sauce and gave him a taste. "Let's take some on our next hut-to-hut hike."

Once the chicken was sauteed, she slipped naan under it to soak up the seasoned sauce. Next came the onion layer, lentils spooned warm from the oven, and the seasoned chicken on top.

Archie sprinkled his pine nuts.

She turned down the heat and swept a shock of his hair from his forehead. Her warm hand followed down his cheek. "Oh!" She ripped the kitchen towel free from her waist and carefully wiped the streak of sauce she'd left on his face. "The pine nuts are a perfect bronzey brown, Archie. Who says you aren't helpful?" She gave him a wink.

He grabbed her hand, whisking her around the kitchen, watching the playful glint in her eye.

"Come away with me," she sang.

"Anywhere you wish," he said. He couldn't look away from her.

Layla stopped. "The parsley," she called out. Pulling a handful from the counter, she told him to chop it while she poured water into the glasses. "Smaller bits," she told him, looking over his shoulder.

He laughed and tossed some parsley at her.

"Like this." She squeezed herself between Archie and the counter, took the knife from him, and minced the remaining bits of green at a fast clip, before tossing them like little jewels on top of the *Musakhan*. Together they leaned over their achievement, steam rising to their faces, a simple pleasure of their procreation.

Bibi nodded when Archie had finished telling the story. Layla had made *Musakhan* for her and her nephew, too.

"I'm flying to Vienna in two days, back to the EAPCCT and Dr. Schroeder. Where can I find you?" he asked Bibi.

"Layla could always find me wherever I was. You could find me at my disabled father's, or maybe fixing a flat bike tire in Aleppo outside the Justia office, or watching my nephew's soccer game. One place you won't find me is watching my dear friend die a slow death that some law has forced on her against her will."

He could see Bibi approaching to hug him goodbye, but he couldn't feel it. He held her hand and thanked her.

By Layla's bedside that evening, Archie was awakened by a nurse taking vital signs. Her routine exam of the baby took longer than usual. She left and returned with a doctor who checked again. Archie realized they could no longer hear the baby's heartbeat. Silently, the nurse closed the door behind her. Archie placed his hand over hers committing the feel of it to his memory, and after a time, drawing it back until only their fingertips touched.

He woke with a start to a touch of his hand. Layla's fingers felt his. "I'm here, Layla. It's me, Archie."

"Oh, Archie, I hurt," Layla said.

Through her bandaged face, he saw her eyes flutter open and close again. He knew she had seen him. "You're going to be alright, Layla. I promise you," he said, pushing the button for the nurse over and over again.

Archie sang one of his favorite songs to her. The song told of birds that had flown, willow trees by the rolling river.

"Rest and be free of hurt. No pain…"

He hummed the next lines, unable to say the words.

"Listen to the river sing sweet songs to rock my soul."

He blinked his reddened eyes.

"The river by the willow tree, rolling along."

Once the doctor confirmed that Layla would live, he called Tia Gabriella. His flicker of hope grew to a flame until Zolt called.

"Archie, get out of there. Get away from Layla. Your presence puts her in danger. For once and for all, you have to leave her if you want to save her." Archie did the only thing he could think of: visit his sister Rivka.

CHAPTER 32

1992 Austria

Zolt listened without speaking, taking notes as Archie explained what had happened. He checked off Archie's security arrangements for the flight to Vienna, transfer to the EAPCCT, and the hotel. Once he got off the phone, he could arrange for new investigators in Aleppo and a lead he had heard about from Havel in the Czech Republic. His sources found a connection between a woman identified only as Z, and an operative near Washington DC, but no name had surfaced yet. It was a man in his fifties, which was nothing to go on. Could it have been an attempt to capture Archie during his recent speech at the Aspen Institute? Finally, Archie paused.

"How long ago?" Zolt said the words and covered his eyes, feeling loss, but more than that, a guilty relief. He couldn't imagine Archie's life trying to keep an infant son alive and safe. He heard the hope in Archie's voice and hated to tell him never to see her again, but if his job was to keep the two of them alive, there were no other options. Now, with Layla's terrorist attack investigation alongside his regular work, his words were clipped, short, and efficient, not what Archie needed to hear.

After the call, Zolt focused on the next steps. He called his team, which, in turn, called specialists in law enforcement and investigation in Aleppo and New York. He thought about another emergency where time was crucial: the British pound debacle. "Somebody had to do it, Zoli. I saved the pound. But nobody sees it that way."

Looking back, he and Archie had taken an extraordinary number of chances. Archie would have found another way if the same opportunity had presented itself today. That's it. He would find another way, and the man in Maryland was the key. He heard the knock at his door. After his talk with the team, he would go to Madrid and find out what he could from his contacts.

CHAPTER 33

1992 New York

Weary from the flight, Archie anticipated a warm welcome from his sister. She would walk him through his sense of loss and into the world again on his timeline. He stood on the sidewalk before her Brooklyn brownstone and scrutinized the windows. The panes were decades old and should be replaced with something more energy-efficient. He'd look into it. Buying this brownstone was the least he could do for her. His slow steps stopped at the solid wooden door he'd replaced last year. He knocked.

"Archie, let me look at you!" Rivka leaned across the transom to hug him, but her pregnant belly got in the way. She laughed. "Come in!" She stood back, and he grabbed his suitcase again, taking his shoes off to walk sock-footed on the cool black and white foyer tile. "Good timing, you!" she said. "Wilson is on assignment in St. Louis, and Logan – we're naming him Logan – is due in ten days."

"How do you know it's a boy?"

"Ultrasound. Amazing, isn't it?"

She led the way upstairs to his room, painted in slate blue. A single, narrow window overlooked the busy street. He looked down through a leafy tree branch to see a boy on a skateboard buzz by.

"You're so quiet, Archie," she said. "You've had a loss, and we'll talk about that. Get settled and come down to the kitchen. I'll fix you a drink," she said.

Archie looked to Rivka more as a confidante than a sister. A brandy was waiting for him in the kitchen. He tried to tell Rivka about Layla, how the sight of her electrified him, how her purpose blended with his own, and how they loved hiking. "She taught me the tango," he said.

"You? Archie, you weren't much of a dancer." Rivka didn't believe it.

He knew Rivka didn't understand him. "I need to take a walk," he said.

"I never trusted lawyers. You can't trust any of 'em," Rivka called as he closed the door behind him.

He settled on a bench in Prospect Park where pigeons and families shared space. A breeze blew a newspaper from a bench across from him, and without the energy to pick it up and dispose of it, he felt the weathering of his own life. He watched the paper roll and drift out of sight. Rivka had told him that Americans took it for granted that their news was legitimate, but that she didn't. They tuned in to Peter Jennings at 6:00 or not. Archie wondered what that would be like. The familiar emptiness in the pit of his stomach returned, and he stopped at a news seller to pick up the daily New York paper before he walked back to the apartment.

"Archie!" he heard as he walked in the door. "It's time!"

Logan would not wait. All seven pounds of him rushed into the world within an hour of checking in at New York Presbyterian. Three days later, mother and baby were home.

Archie unlocked the door for her, and Rivka made her way to the kitchen to make a pot of tea. She handed the sleeping bundle to Archie.

"When is Wilson coming to see his son?" Archie looked at the calm, sleeping baby in his arms. One side of Logan's mouth hinted at a smile as if he were dreaming.

"The newspaper extended his assignment," Rivka said, an edge to her voice. "Another two weeks, maybe three."

Archie pitched in. No matter his loss, Rivka and his new nephew needed him. He folded diapers, put soiled ones on the porch for pickup by the diaper service, and spent hours rocking Logan, looking into his face from the light that filtered through the living room window. His hair was dark and wavy, a baby version of Archies' hair. His eyes and impish mouth were all Rivka. Archie didn't intend to listen in, but he could hear Rivka's irritated voice as she spoke to Wilson over the phone. Pans rattled in the kitchen, and Logan flinched his arms.

He found comfort in holding Logan and touched his face to the baby's blanket, breathing in his intoxicating, sweet, milky smell. When he lifted his head, he saw that Logan had been watching him. "I will always protect your mother," Archie told him. "And now, you too."

On the eighth day, the *mohel* came to Rivka's apartment. She made the introductions. *"Baruch Ha-Ba."* the *mohel* said over the newborn. "Blessed art Thou, O Lord our God, King of the universe, who hast sanctified us with Thy command-ments and given us the command con-cerning circumcision."

Archie told a story of their Hungarian grandfather, *Gyorgy*, who was something of a philosopher storyteller in his town of Visegrad. Logan turned his head so that his kippah skewed over his face, so Rivka tied the strings under his chin, and the *mohel* gently lifted him from Archie's arms. Now that his arm was free, Archie took a photo to send to Wilson in St. Louis.

The *mohel*, elderly and experienced, raised a glass of wine and placed a few drops in Logan's mouth. He spoke a Hebrew prayer. Rivka didn't often attend synagogue, but her friends spoke of the *mohel* as if he were a family member. He talked soothingly to Logan as he used his instruments and expertly performed his work.

Archie looked at Rivka when the baby turned the volume up beyond his usual wails of hunger. He expected her to react, but she only nodded and lit a candle.

After the bris, the *mohel* gave Logan his Jewish name, *Gyorgy*, after their grandfather. Archie lifted the same wine glass and drank first, then handed the glass to Rivka.

The *mohel* nodded, *"Mazel tov!"*

Rivka returned Logan to his crib for a nap, and Archie saw the *mohel* to the door. "I'm sorry to hear of your loss. I can see it in your face," he said. "You don't know if you feel like living or dying yourself, like Hamlet. What if dying is more of a nightmare of suffering? It's a gamble." He put his hand on Archie's shoulder and left it there. "Be gentle with your hope. Breathe, slow down, and know that not everyone has a love so great that they feel the depths of sorrow you feel. I know people who grieve and start scholarship funds or charities in memory of lost children, all well and good, but how do you get meaning back into life? You will find a way."

"Are you a therapist as well as a rabbi?" Archie asked.

He gave Archie's shoulder a fatherly pat before he left.

What the *mohel* said was true. Layla had become his meaning, and he knew what it was like to want to live and die at the same time.

Rivka turned to Archie. "I'm glad you were here for this, to usher Logan into his life."

For the boy's father, Archie took another photo of Rivka and Logan. "I'm honored, Rivka." If only Layla could have been here standing next to him.

After dinner, Archie watched Rivka shake her head out of a vacant stare. He could tell she felt Wilson's absence, not only for his son's birth but on this traditional eighth day after. "Remember the olive fights on those hot days working in the groves on the kibbutz?" he said.

The corner of her mouth turned up. "I got so sick of those olives. I never wanted to see another one. I won't eat them even to this day!" she sighed.

"Remember my pet rooster, Rusty?"

"Didn't one of the families give it to you as a chick?"

"I raised him. He'd sit in my lap and listen to music with me."

"Nobody could touch him but you. He clawed and scratched me," Rivka said.

"He never scratched me and he'd come when I called his name. We had some great conversations. He looked so focused as if he were listening to me. That last family got mad when he scratched their daughter – and he ended up on the dinner table."

"I remember you asked for a new family after that," Rivka said.

"And there was the cow barn. The three boys in that family were always fighting, and I could never get along with them." Archie chuckled. "I didn't mind when they told me to go to the barn to milk the cow and bring some back for dinner. One day, a worker pulled a lighter from his pocket and taught me how to light the cow's *gaz*. We lit the *gaz* once and started laughing uncontrollably. When I tried, the cow backed into a hay bale and set it on fire. We pumped buckets of water, and I couldn't believe we didn't get caught. But I wasn't allowed dinner when I returned to the house empty-handed."

Rivka's eyes brightened, and she laughed. "I played with the girls. We cut out paper dolls, strung beads, and drew pictures — you had all the fun."

CHAPTER 34

1992 New York

By the end of the second week, Archie had established a comfortable routine with his new kinsman. From the rocking chair, he told Logan the stories he remembered from the kibbutz. There was the fox and the goat who became fast friends, although they were different. Their parents objected, but their friendship prevailed. Archie sang him a tango with the rhythm of a lullaby. Over the chair was a shelf of books and Rivka's collection of antique animal traps she'd started in college. Fortunately, they were high enough that Logan couldn't toddle over in a few years and snap his tiny fingers in one.

"Logan, I'm going to tell you about Layla so there will be two of us who knew the funny things she said, how she taught me to cook and dance, and how she'd measure time in music. She always flipped her pillow to the cold side, slept on the floor when something was on her mind, and she feared peanut butter sticking to the roof of her mouth – but not breaking her leg on a hike, foreign adversaries, or even death."

"She was so full of spirit, I couldn't hide a thing. Hah. She said

I was handsome enough. She never tried too hard like other women, but she made me stand taller, Logan. Always she was herself." His voice caught. "I wanted her, and I'm the reason we're apart."

He kept reliving memories until he must've dozed off because he woke with a start. Logan was still asleep. "We've been here on Earth for six million years, Logan. Think of all those before us who didn't know us and all those who will come after. But you and I will have known Layla. Now she will live in us right here." He took Logan's tiny hand and rested it on his chest. The tiny fingers held his thumb. "When you're older, I'll take you hiking near Vienna and Switzerland. You'll meet Aunt Gabriella in Spain." He nuzzled Logan, allowing the feelings to well up inside. "Layla did important work, and when she's better, we'll help that work to continue."

He heard the hum of the trash truck on the street below and carried the baby to the window. Pointing through the trees, he explained to Logan what the truck was doing, having watched it the week before at about the same time of day. How ordinary it was, watching the truck, knowing that it would be back next week, but he would be in Vienna by then. He had emptied the baskets around the house and taken the trash out for Rivka, which was the least he could do. The truck made his life seem unreal. This truck was the reality with its punctual, predictable pick-ups from homes where people lived and watched children grow. He once told Layla he wanted an everyday life, whatever that was. A few days in a hotel with a change of clothes brought up from storage and travel to the next city seemed lifeless.

How did he get here? His mind was restless in the present as it obsessed with what-ifs. If it wasn't for the landmine incident, he wouldn't feel so responsible for Rivka. If he hadn't excelled in probabilities, he wouldn't have gotten the scholarship to Vienna. If Elias hadn't invited him to dinner, he would never have met Layla. That dinner was the beginning of the best years of his life. He looked down at Logan. If anything should happen to this boy because of him…

Rivka walked in with a steaming mug. He looked up through glazed eyes.

"Drink this," she said. "It's herbal tea. It tells your body to settle itself." She noiselessly placed it on the side table, patted his shoulder, and walked away.

Each day, he called the Spanish investigators who had connections with Syria, but there was no discovery, no new information. He arranged for specialists from around Europe to assure Layla received the best care. When he couldn't postpone company meetings any longer, he made excuses. In his absence, the Czech free press was losing momentum to government-backed propaganda newspapers that were springing up like weeds. His associates warned him that he needed to respond to accusations that his wealth was bending reality to his will, away from everyday people.

He told Rivka that it was time for him to return to Vienna. He arranged for a doula to help each day. "Keep her as long as you need," Archie said.

"That's very generous of you, dear brother."

They sat at the dining room table after Rivka had nursed Logan into a sound sleep. Archie had bought a bottle of Israeli wine from a merchant down the street, a red from the Judean hills, but not too sweet. He poured two glasses. Rivka downed hers and motioned for another.

"I only have three classes scheduled at the university next term. I figured I'd take it easy during the first term back after Logan," she said. "One class is new, Revolutionary World Movements 332." She stopped to drink and then picked up the bottle to check the label. "Good. Never had that one. So we're starting with the American Revolution, then on to the French and Spanish and German."

"I can send you some pieces from the Vienna library on the 1814 Holy Alliance," Archie said.

"Thanks, but I don't think so. I want to include our Israeli Six-Day War. These self-indulgent American students need to know that others have inalienable rights too." She downed the glass and set it before Archie for a refill.

"Are you sure? It's okay with nursing Logan? Look at this." He held up the nearly empty bottle. "Back in the day, Victorian women used belladonna. I'm looking at your eyes. They reminded me of black mirrors like the paintings of Victorian women."

"Oh Archie, stop it with your trivia."

"Not trivia, esoterica."

"I've got another two hours at least before Logan wakes up," she said. She talked about her fellow professors at NYU, sounding disparaging and dismissive of them. "The painfully American wool-gatherers look too far down the road instead of seeing what is right in front of them," she said.

"What about people from the Temple? You have friends you can call on when I'm gone?"

"I don't need anyone any more. I have my work." She changed the subject. "I was contacted by a friend of Elias, your old roommate, about some information that might be useful in my class."

"A friend of Elias?"

"Friedrich Heinz. He sent me boxes of primary sources, interviews, and charts that gave me a whole new take on political motives and whipping the masses into a mad frenzy," she laughed. "American students are small-minded and loyal like dogs, all guns, guts, and God."

"That's stunning." Archie was surprised. But he knew that if anyone checked and double-checked sources for teaching, it was Rivka. Her wild, sprawling contradictions, her irrepressible spirit – he loved it all, but this seemed so wrong.

"And another thing, the Protocols of the Elders of Zion was true. Henry Ford believed it. The desire of the Rothschild family to shape history and take over the world with their banking empire was undisputed. You know one of them, don't you?"

"That's antisemitic trash, Rivka. It's a bad joke."

They had been talking awhile. When she placed her glass before him for another refill, he saw that the second bottle was nearly empty.

"Oh, don't look so worried about me. I know what I'm doing. More than that little Palestinian whore of yours. She was only after your money." Her eyes narrowed, waiting for a reply. "I've had enough of your boring tales of happiness, anyway. Let's talk about how you used to fight."

"Layla and I shared everything. I told her the fighting was not me."

"The shrew. You're weak weak weak. You're an emotional shipwreck."

"When she shared what was on her mind, I could never feel closer to anyone. I was privileged to see into that beautiful mind now and then." He shook his head. "You know, the organization she worked for was up for a Nobel Peace Prize."

"I like people who aren't in rehab."

He recognized Rivka's talk as an alcoholic haze. "Rivka, ever since you were four years old and came to see me bandaged up in the medical tent, I look at your face and see that girl with no one to look out for her but me. I will carry that responsibility all my life." He couldn't keep the anger from his voice. "Layla talked about you too. She said you were the inspiration for my life's work. The Freedom and Open Society microloans and the University that helped so many young people get a leg up in the world might never have happened if it weren't for my sister." He stood and faced her. "Don't ever speak out against Layla again."

"I have to check on Logan." Rivka left the room without another word.

By morning, the empty bottle and glasses were still on the table.

It was a long two days' wait for his flight to Vienna. Archie spent as much time as possible with Logan, wondering how much he would change before they could be together again. Archie watched the little fingers stretch and grasp, thinking of the times he placed his hand on Layla's belly. With his energy, he didn't look forward to the tight schedule and consequential decision-making that faced him in Vienna. The Russian literati said it best. If they were right about anything, it was about suffering. Neither his financial success nor his effort to give money away, could prevent it. With Logan in his arms, he watched from the window while a woman on the sidewalk below walked her Scotty dog and a man, part of his security detail, tucked a newspaper under his arm.

Archie's last night in New York passed like a slow ache, and then with meteoric speed in a waking of emotional impulse. He reached for Layla, eyes open with tears too stubborn to break free. Layla had as little meaning to Rivka as a dust mote swept from under her chair. After a death of one child and the birth of another, he looked to the rest of his life as something to endure.

"Do come back soon and see Logan. He'll grow fast and you don't want to miss that." Rivka said.

Archie agreed and nodded. Rivka was independent to the point where he rarely thought of her prosthetic and her many steps to the third floor to retrieve Logan. Even so, they'd helped each other these past weeks. As his plane crossed to the continent, he worried about Wilson's commitment to his family. He'd never once spoken to his brother-in-law since he came to New York. But indeed, if something were wrong, Rivka would have told him.

CHAPTER 35

1992 Austria

Elias spooned out the last bite of his two soft-boiled eggs from their glass and picked up his coffee. Archie and Elias had chosen Cafe Central in Vienna's *Innere Stadt* that day. Once frequented by Sigmund Freud because of its dusty, frayed decor, it fit their moods. The prices were reasonable, and the latest newspapers rested in wooden holders by the door.

They had arrived just before the red-uniformed marching band turned the street corner on its way to the Summer Palace, a tourist favorite. They ordered lunch and waited for the snap of the snare drum, and the harmony of the march tune to fade down the street before they spoke. Archie looked up from his newspaper and ordered a *cafe mélange with* steamed milk, and foam, from a waiter whose mind was elsewhere.

"Archie, I'd never seen you happier than when you were with Layla."

It was the first time they had talked since Archie had returned to Vienna. Until now, his schedule had made for no allowances. He had eaten only a few bites of his food.

Archie turned a page of the newspaper spread on the table in front of him. "You know when we were hiking, I tested her, walking faster, taking more challenging trails, and she always kept up. And the surprise meeting with Havel. He shook his head. "She was testing me – "

"Archie, you need to see Mom and Dad. Go talk to them."

Archie looked at him. " I thought I could leave my grief in New York, but it followed me back here. Layla forced me to see things I didn't want to see. Did you know that Palestine has never had elections? Never known a peace process?" He cleared his throat. "You think something is solid, then it's gone. We were so different, but we both wanted the same thing."

Elias could see that Archie's thoughts were miles away when a friend approached and Elias invited him to sit down. "Archie, remember Alexandr?"

He didn't seem to notice. "After living my life with the switch off, she turned it on."

Elias changed the subject. "How's Rivka?"

Archie withdrew his wallet and motioned to the waiter. "Rivka invited me back in time for the birth of Logan. You should see him, Elias. He's strong. He kicked and grabbed my thumb with his fingers. A few years and I'll take him hiking."

Archie then became aware that someone was sitting next to Elias.

"Alexandr from our MBA program? He's Czech," Elias said.

Alexandr's face became animated. "I'm thinking of Scholz's Econ 402 class." He laughed. "Scholz tried to trip you up so many times."

The three men reminisced over university days and Archie noticed the easy camaraderie between Alexandr and Elias, the way their shoulders bumped and their expressions mirrored one another.

"You were on the swim team, weren't you?" Archie asked.

"I remember when I first started on my school team in Czechoslovakia," Alexandr said. "I was eleven. That was late, but my family had to raise money to pay bribes. There were bribes for everything. But it all fell away with swimming. I'd never felt so free. Then there were the demonstrations. We paid bribes to cross the bridge, to buy butter! I hadn't thought about it much before, about communism, I mean. It's a big country. I thought it was our protector, not our adversary."

"At university, I doubted why the Soviets wanted us, why it mattered if we felt a part of the USSR or not." Alexandr's voice grew stern. "We didn't know whether or not to believe the fearful rumors of people being poisoned, jailed, or simply disappearing. They said it was for our protection, but it didn't feel real. What I was taught to say became so different from what I was afraid to say." Alexandr looked from side to side, an old habit from years of caution over listening ears. "So yeah, I was on the team at college."

Archie mentioned Marek and the *Fortuna* on the Danube. "If you ever go back, look him up. He'll have some stories to tell you, too."

Before they left, Archie asked if Elias remembered his friend Friedrich Heinz, a man with a treasure-trove of historical documents.

"Common name," Elias said. "Can't say I remember him offhand. Alexandr?"

Alexandr shook his head.

"Was he supposed to be an old school chum?" Elias asked.

Archie was puzzled, but in her tipsy state, Rivka could have gotten the name wrong.

In the family dining room, where he used to listen to eager over-talking during his university days, Archie and the Bauers shared a comforting meal of *Mutter* Bauer knew Archie liked it. They spoke of a concert, a botanical flower show, and their pride in Elias's taking the reins of the family business. They listened to Archie unburden himself about Layla. *Mutter* Bauer cleared plates and brought coffee while Max shared news of Vienna.

"I just learned that back in the eighties, Vienna played a pivotal role as a go-between for Russian and American spycraft," Max said. "The FBI caught the Soviets stealing cutting-edge microchip technology that they needed for their air defense. Their space shuttles depended on it." He raised his eyebrow and waited for Archie's response.

Archie hadn't heard about it, but he wasn't surprised.

"The Soviets were hoovering up electronics and chips from Silicon Valley, and a Viennese man helped uncover the theft. The Austrian posed as a crook willing to sell secrets to the Soviets. It was called Operation Intering, and over the years, the Austrian funneled secret US technology to the Soviets. Although the FBI had sabotaged it to work only randomly while appearing as a voltage overload, Moscow celebrated him as a hero." Max laughed. "They spent millions on these faulty parts with plans to duplicate the entire US computer industry, but when they got too close to the Austrian, he vanished."

Archie told Max that he had studied the Cold War spycraft of Vienna, one of Europe's most important intelligence sources.

"But now we're moving to aid the United Nations," Max said. "The Vienna Declaration and Programme of Action has been finalized for the UN, Archie. I suggested you as a speaker," Max said. "One of the features is the protection of children."

"I have someone better, Max," Archie said. "Elida is a woman of the people in Kenya, a mother, a goat-herder, and an activist." He thought about a recent letter he had received from Elida and her work to improve lives in her community. "More people need to hear the stories she has to tell about human rights for children. Put me in touch with the Director."

"I think…" Max tapped his finger on the table. "*Herr* Director Eder likes to cycle. Rather than a stuffy office, you'd have better luck convincing him if you took a bike ride with him along the Danube, one that ended up at the Austria Center near his office. Just a thought."

"What will you do now, Archie?" *Mutter* Bauer asked.

He looked at these two kind people who had taken him into

their family and encouraged him on his way. He could go for a month without seeing them, yet he knew that they were here, and he could talk to them without any filter. Being with the Bauers made him feel stronger than he had in weeks. Yet, seeing the lines around *Mutter* Bauer's smile and *Herr* Bauer's thinning gray hair was unsettling. He couldn't think about what the world would be like without them.

"I have a meeting with my journalism students. I have a special job for them. Have you heard anything about Chertok, the communications magnate?"

"Only that he's someone you shouldn't get involved with, Archie. I hear he's close to publishing a book with Habsburg, some isolationist leech he is. You can give it up and stick to the financial world, get your mind off things, live a safer life without looking over your shoulder," *Herr* Bauer said.

"I have Zolt for that. And I still have financial clients."

"Yes, I deal in the safety of the bond market, and you talk about Apple. I've heard of your Steve Jobs," Max said.

"His personal computers will open up libraries around the world. When everyone has access to technology, it will be like a bike for our minds, he says."

He wasn't expecting *Mutter* Bauer to walk up behind him and squeeze his shoulders. "Don't wait so long to come back to us. You are a son to us, you know," she said.

CHAPTER 36

1992 Prague

So, what will you do now?" Vaclav asked.

Archie bristled at the words of caring. Why did everyone ask him that? The two walked in Stromovka Park where Archie sat under a willow tree beside the pond. He looked over the shivering surface to see what it might be thinking. This restful, calming spot, felt clouded so that even the stones seemed homely. Nattering irritation, a claw of guilt, and Vaclav's slapdash about moving on did little to cheer him.

"She told me once that one of the women she interviewed was not allowed to leave her house without a man. The only man in her life was her husband, whom the military had killed. After days inside, her daughters had no food, so she sneaked out of the house. The authorities caught her alone without a male chaperone. They jailed her, and she endured attacks over days. When she was finally released and accompanied to her home, her daughters had died."

Vaclav stirred uncomfortably and Archie looked at him. This wasn't easy for Vaclav either, but there were no words to tell his friend how much it meant that he was here.

"I must keep Layla's work alive until she's ready to return. If we let the opposition take over, the people lose whatever rights they have. Protesters are jailed, but the independent journalists make it harder to silence the power of the truth," he said.

Archie picked up a smooth stone and turned it in his hand. If only he had that photo of the two of them from Marek's boat. Over the pond was an outcropping of rocks under leaf-heavy trees. "I can see her glance over a dinner table, her arched eyebrow all provocative, her voice singing in Spanish – "

He recalled a time with her after he'd abandoned his usual caution. "Now that you've decided to let your guard down, there's no stopping you! So what's with the trivia?" she'd asked.

Vaclav told him he hadn't heard this story.

"It's esoterica!" Archie pretended offense. "I have only a few memories of my father from when I was small, but I feared his disapproval. I found factual esoterica was a way to gain his attention and keep him from thinking I was boring."

"Boring?"

"Trivia comes from *Trivialis*, language that belongs to public streets. It's everywhere, from gold yields to sugar production in the Caribbean islands to Ireland's potato famine. Esoterica is fact that is hard to understand. I've always collected it. I read *The Farmer's Almanac* in German. Did you know that almanac has been collecting facts since the 1400s?"

Layla smiled and shook her head. "What am I getting into?"

"Take television. The average person in the 90s watches 39 channels and seven hours of TV daily."

"Here's one," Layla said. "A novelist once said journalism is what maintains democracy."

"Exactly. That's esoterica. Bravo! If I said that champagne was used as shoe polish, that would be trivia."

"Archie, you are so lucky you found me," she said. "Any other woman would be running for the doors by now."

Vaclav saw the trace of a smile. "So when will you visit her aunt?"

Archie tossed the stone in the pond. He had spoken with *Tia* Gabriella and she insisted that he come to see her. He hoped they would have a wheelchair dance together in memory of better times.

CHAPTER 37

1992 Spain

Archie had only been in Prague for a few days when he was notified that *Tia* Gabriella had suffered a stroke. He contacted Zolt to check for evidence of substances left around her house and caught a plane to her healthcare facility in Spain. Getting permission to see her wasn't easy, but he was allowed a short, supervised visit. Surprisingly, the community women she worked with came and went without restriction, hugging, chatting, and interrupting as if he wasn't there.

Gabriella looked up at him from her wheelchair, her eyes narrowed, and her lips pursed. She was afraid and defensive, not the ageless, swaying flamenco dancer he remembered, her scarf floating around her.

He slowly reached out for her hand, but she drew hers back. "I'm doing everything I can to find the men who did this," he said. "I'm here to help you – anything you need."

"Bring Layla back. I need to see her. You could have killed her,"

Tia Gabriella said.

The aide told him to leave.

Tia was angry, and he needed an ally now, not someone who would magnify his loss. Archie hid his face in his hand and tried to steady his breathing. *Tia* Gabriella had spoken the words he dared only to think.

The next day, he came back. The aide allowed him to stay longer, but the parade of women interrupted any meaningful conversation. He shared one story of Layla when she hurt her knee on their first hike. How strong she was. *Tia* Gabriella's pursed lips softened as she listened.

On the third day, he stayed with her for hours. He talked about his visit to her home, the tango, and *Tia* Gabriella's long red scarf. She nodded and spoke about Layla's growing up years, her awkwardness around boys, and how she seemed to be near when weaker children needed someone to protect them. Archie's hunger to hear these stories was insatiable. There wasn't a dry eye between them when it was time to go.

"The nurses say you are good company for me," Gabriella said.

He asked if he could come back to see her. Her furrowed brow softened. At least she didn't say no. That was enough.

He spoke with the attendants. She had no living relatives, but the band of community women was her family. Her visibility and Zolt's guards lessened Archie's fears for her safety. She wasn't lonely, but Archie's nagging guilt over Layla and *Tia's* vulnerability gave him the impulse to ask the staff to notify him of any changes in her condition, wherever he was.

His flight to Vienna was scheduled for the following day, but he met with Zolt at *Tia's* home during his last day in Madrid. Zolt had talked to neighbors and checked outside doors. Nothing was found that might have caused her downturn. "Maybe it was the shock over Layla's attack," he said.

Together, they walked the perimeter of the house. Archie saw the weedy flower beds and laughed. "Here's what we'll do, Zoli," he said. "We'll weed her flowers and take pictures to send her." The physical exertion was good for both of them. After an hour, the man next door brought a water pitcher, and they drank heartily. By the end of the second hour, they were ready to take pictures. The colorful kalanchoe was now visible next to the English Ivy. Multiple Swiss cheese plants shaded smaller hydrangeas. A Madagascar dragon tree was untangled from lacy laurustinus. Archie imagined *Tia's* smile when she saw the photos.

As he packed for Vienna, he regretted the great distance between them. First Rivka's injury, then Layla's brush with death, and now *Tia's* stroke – all the money in the world couldn't fix what he had caused.

CHAPTER 38

1993 Vienna

Havel was finishing work on the Constitution Court document when Archie called from Vienna. He turned to glance at the newly installed President's coat of arms for the Czech Republic mounted behind his desk. The motto read, *Pravda vítězí*, Truth prevails. He held the phone with his shoulder as he made pencil checks on his copy. "I think of the Constitution as a living document meant to adapt over time, not set in the stone of its origins or twisted to fit the past," Havel told him. "We will stay a step ahead of authoritarians who interpret laws in a way that takes away human rights. Their sparkling lies disguise their manipulation. Our Constitution Court document is anchored to Western thought. Unity means equality, and equality means strength. Twelve of the fifteen justices are appointed and waiting in Brno. I have to finish this."

Archie could hear the rustling of papers. He asked about Dagmar, and the two discussed the latest news of the New York World Trade Center bombing.

"Have you called Rivka?"

"I can't get through to her," Archie said.

Havel could hear the pain in Archie's voice. "Lines are overloaded. You'll hear soon," he said.

"She may be calling now," Archie said as the two men exchanged hurried goodbyes for Archie's incoming call.

"Rivka, are you all right? Is Wilson there?"

"Relax, Archie, we're fine."

"The Twin Towers are only a few miles away from you. And that Yousef fellow, the ringleader, was there at the Mosque where they plotted their crime. That's right in Brooklyn. It's a new kind of terrorism, Rivka. Zolt said that he heard the FBI knew all about them and were close to capturing them."

"The FBI. What do they know? We can't trust them."

Archie waited. If he expected Rivka to say anything, it wasn't that.

"Logan's fine. Wilson is on assignment in California, but he called. I've been talking about the history of terrorist movements in class. This situation is one of those teaching moments."

Archie detected a tiredness in her voice. "I heard they caught five of them, but one is missing. Zolt said something about a rental van's VIN."

"He's probably fled the country by now. They're Palestinian, you know. It figures."

"It's terrorism, Rivka. They weren't going to end with the Trade Center. They were going for the Holland Tunnel, the Lincoln Tunnel, and the UN Building. Even a dozen planes."

"They had a ton of explosives. Have you seen the pictures? There's a crater the size of a football field under the parking garage," Rivka said.

"They meant to topple one building and have it fall into the other. And that Brooklyn Mosque where they got their crazy ideas, Rivka – do you and Logan go to Temple nearby?"

"Not to worry, Archie. Since my student's wedding last year, we haven't been to Temple."

"Rivka, I don't think I've ever been so relieved to hear you. One more thing and then I have to go. This Yousef's uncle, Khalid Sheikh Mohammed, is in a terrorist group called Al Qaeda. He is a powerful, evil man. I've asked Zolt to watch for intelligence about him from his Middle East contacts. If he tries again, we'll find someone in the FBI – "

"Archie, not the FBI. We have militia units, armed paramilitary groups. I've talked with some of them."

He was startled again. He must've misunderstood. Rivka must be talking about something else. "I have to go. If you need anything, just call me."

CHAPTER 39

1993 Spain

In haste, Archie tied up some careful negotiations for Havel in preparation for returning to *Tia* Gabriella. Zolt informed him that Gabriella was in hospital. He flew back and gathered neurologists for testing. He had to rule out that the vibrant woman, the fighter he knew, could have a more serious condition. In her wheelchair in the courtyard of the care facility was a frail, thin version of Gabriella. She brightened when she saw him.

"How's that Apple stock doing?" she asked.

"Up 24%."

"Time to sell?"

"Not yet." He grinned at the wiley look in her eyes. "Let's see what it will do."

"How about giving it to the women's shelter?" she asked.

Archie paused, trying to gauge her train of thought. "Maybe you'll want to use it to take a cruise when you get out of here," he said.

She made a light sound, a gossamer laugh. Archie talked of Bibi, Layla's translator, and of how he had hired two attorneys learning Syrian law to make things easier in preparation for Layla's return to her deposition work.

"So you're saying it took two lawyers to replace her," *Tia* said.

Archie shook his head. "Never replace, but carry on," he added. He told her that the last two men who attacked Layla were found guilty in the International Court and were serving life prison terms.

Tia Gabriella sat silently absorbing the news. "She's able to visit me now. She was proud to have graduated from a wheelchair to crutches.'

"How is she? I need to know," Archie said.

"Layla appreciates the specialists you contacted for her care."

There was a silence until staff brought *alfajores*, a shortbread sandwich cookie with caramel, and tea. She offered Archie the cookies and thanked him for cleaning up her garden and sending the photos. "Sell the house quickly before the weeds grow back," she said. "I can't go back there. Give the money – "

"I know. To the women's shelter." Archie finished her sentence. "I found Layla's ring in a box by the window. I sent it to Bibi if it's okay with you."

Gabriella nodded and he could see she was tiring. He held her hand before he rose and noticed her attempt to control the tremor.

On the first night of Archie's return to Vienna, Zolt brought up a carafe of *glühwein* from room service and placed it on a table between them before delivering his message. Gabriella had fallen again. The secure care facility they had found for her in Madrid confirmed Parkinson's-related dementia. The nurse said Gabriella would forget that she couldn't stand up as quickly as before. Archie drank a glass of wine, and then another.

CHAPTER 40

1997 Spain

Archie and Gabriella drank tea as Archie told stories about his first camping trip with Logan.

"Archie, this rehabilitation facility is too much." She looked around the solarium and through the tall windows, which offered pastoral views of green hills and cypress trees.

"I want you to be safe, *Tia*, and this is the safest."

"Regardless, I thank you." She looked up at him. "I was so furious with you after Layla's death. It took time to regain trust," *Tia* Gabriella gave Archie's arm a little push. "Relationships need building and maintaining to get attention and keep it. People are nostalgic for a time that never was, the old days that only existed in their minds."

"*Tia*, I know." Her words were a relief to him. "I hear you – that bump of nostalgia, the fuzzy lens that clouds the unsatisfied, that pacifying defense mechanism. Do things as they've always been done, or cut through the chaos with civic debate. We'll gain their trust and pull the curtain back."

"You need to meet this woman." *Tia* nodded to a slender woman reading alone in the corner, gray curls piled on her head. "She is a mysterious one. No one knows much about her, but she reached out to me because she knows about you."

"My new friend is recovering from a neurological illness, but she is protected also, like me. She is a writer from Moldova. Before her latest review of the state of Russian journalism was scheduled for release, she was poisoned. The State considered her views too Western and shut down the sale of her book. Her family flew her here and she is recovering. She was certain that once the book was distributed, the news would be too big to justify a personal attack. I remember her name. It's Zorica."

Archie thought of the woman in Madrid that Zoli had mentioned, whose only identifier was Z. "Had they threatened her before?"

"Many times. It made her write faster. Unfortunately, all materials and evidence she used in her manuscript have disappeared. Could you help to find them?"

"What did she have?"

"Names, dates, places, and incidents from informers. It was too dangerous to make copies. Now, what she had is gone. The State controls reviews. Even Indigenous communities are banned from writing or speaking in their native tongues – which was in part so that informants couldn't pass information."

"I'd like very much to meet her."

Gabriella's recall heartened Archie. Maybe the dementia diagnosis was wrong. He wheeled her chair to the corner and names were exchanged.

"Zorica, I told you about Archie," Gabriella said.

"Zorica *Abromovich*," Archie said. He recognized her from her photograph on the cover of a book he had read. "I'm in rarefied company. I read your *Treatise on Truth*. I'd like to help you – and your contacts may help us, too. I have journalism students who might contact you without arousing suspicion."

Zorica's dove-gray eyes looked at him. "I hear you have relations in Brooklyn," she said. "The terrorist attack must be a great worry for you."

Archie was furious with himself for saying too much to Gabriella: now this woman whom he knew only by reputation, knew of his family.

"I hold many secrets," Zorica said. "Yours are safe here." She tapped her heart. She told him that the missing evidence took years for her to gather. "Ruthless men in high places must've known the value of my information if they were willing to kill me for it." Her voice was edged with tension. Archie noticed her fragile hand as she closed the book. Gabriella placed her hand over that of her friend.

"Let me tell you what I remember."

CHAPTER 41

1997 - Archie Tours Kenya

For a year, Archie had put off his tour to meet microloan recipients in Africa.

On the night before the tour, Zolt brought up a carafe of *glühwein* from room service and placed it on a table between them before delivering his message. Gabriella had fallen again. The secure care facility they had found for her in Madrid confirmed Parkinson's-related dementia. The nurse said Gabriella would forget that she couldn't stand up as quickly as before. Archie drank a glass of wine, and then another.

He felt torn to cancel and fly to *Tia* Gabriella, but the organization would set up the tour, and a conflict in the Czech Republic or Hungary would come up, or the university would require lobbying in parliament to keep truth alive, or he would use all of the above as an excuse not to meet Juma, the child who was now a teenager. Archie kept Elida's letter that Layla had given him, one of the few artifacts that traveled with him wherever he went. He had to go to Africa.

Elida now watched over her nephew Mulilo after the death of

her brother and his wife. Mulilo was now a boisterous five-year-old, according to Elida's letter of invitation. Archie was saddened to discover in her letter that malaria had taken Juma's life, not uncommon in Kenya.

When Archie arrived in Kenjaja and met Elida for the first time, he was surprised that there was no welcoming group. He preferred it that way, but it was unlike the other communities he'd visited. Elida had brought running water to her village as well as limited electricity. Yet the people they passed didn't return her nod when she greeted them by name. They peered suspiciously when she took Archie's small group to the village square where people lined up with jerry cans for clean water. Thanks to her work, the walking time for fresh water had been cut in half.

Threading their way through busy streets to her home, Elida pointed to her five goats in a pen behind the house. She took Archie and his group inside and motioned for them to sit while she made tea. The house was simple and clean, free of the noise and dust from chasing dogs, shouts, cars honking, and handcarts with hawkers selling figs and citrus outside – free of the hiss of mutton barbecue, or samosas.

"Everyone in Kenjaja does not appreciate my improvements," she said. Change is hard, but I overlook the frowns and turned backs. I remember Juma and look to what is best for Mulilo's future."

On the table in front of Archie and his assistant, she placed cups of *rooibos* tea with milk and spices. Her village group had decided that the next improvement would be farm market umbrellas for the searing heat, and she explained that the umbrellas would protect not only the customers on market days but also the produce and farmers.

Mulilo burst through the door. "Where have you been?" His aunt said. "I told you Mr. Archie would be here. He wanted to meet you."

Mulilo's exuberance left him. His shoulders dropped, and he placed his school bag in a corner. He walked to Archie and stopped.

"I'm sorry, Mr. Archie. I was playing soccer with my friends."

Archie tried to take in fully the situation's gravity. "I see. So, how are your school subjects?"

"I like geography and lunch. Numbers are okay, but reading not so much."

Archie nodded. "Suppose you show me how you kick a soccer ball."

Mulilo's grin returned, and they stepped outside into the sun.

By the time Archie and Mulilo returned, their shirts clung to their bodies from the heat of the street game. Archie hadn't kicked a soccer ball since his days on the kibbutz. 'You're raising one fine soccer player," he told Elida. Then, he mentioned his nephew, Logan. "Maybe he could teach Logan to play the game."

Archie's assistant looked at him. Archie was not one to play games or talk about his family. Yet he and Elida were chatting like old friends. When Archie's group gathered their belongings to leave, Archie asked his assistant if he could give a toy or something else to Mulilo. The assistant checked his bag of papers, and a laptop. He drew out a pencil, and Archie frowned. He stood in front of Mulilo and bent to one knee. "I'd like to give you something," he said. "It was given to me by a wise old man when I was about your age." He took the battered compass from his pocket and explained how it worked. Mulilo put out his hand, and Archie placed the precious gift in it.

"Ohhh…" Mulilo examined the treasure.

"Remember, True North," Archie said. "The compass will help you find your way."

Mulilo showed his aunt and grasped the compass, pushing it down to the bottom of his school uniform pocket, much like Archie had years ago.

Archie and his assistant stepped into the busy street. He turned back and watched Mulilo's lively wave goodbye.

CHAPTER 42

1997 Switzerland

Moments before their address to the Club of Rome in Winterthur, Switzerland, Archie questioned Havel. He seemed scattered after a late flight and wanted to know if anything had changed since they had last met.

Havel brought up Archie's encounters with Habsburg and Chertok years ago, wondering if there had been any move of the needle since then.

Archie snorted. "Like pouring sand through a sifter." He peered at the seats on the stage, the bright lights, and around the curtain, a packed audience. He changed course to the task at hand. "You're the man they came to see," Archie said. "I'll go first to warm them up." Havel nodded, and Archie walked onstage dressed in a sweater and corduroys. It was a casual but meaningful gathering.

"My esteemed colleagues of journalists, historians, academics, presidents, diplomats, scientists, and members of parliament, you have been dismissed by Moscow as "cosmopolitans and interlopers." He paused. "You know that's because only Moscow wasn't invited." A hint of nervous laughter expanded through the audience.

Archie spoke of the bedrock of freedom and truth in journalism, his eyes tracking the audience, searching for faces of like minds in the crowd, and pushing to convince the listeners of the crucial nature of solid news. "The problems of humanity are connected to poverty and inequality. We gather not to point fingers at enemies but to discuss pressing global issues. When countries brand neighbors as enemies and use them as scapegoats – blaming them for problems of their own making – they are covering up their shortcomings, distracting their people from their treachery. If an enemy doesn't exist, one has to be identified."

"The authoritarian leader commands them not to believe the proof they see. Proof is unnecessary for these false leaders who hammer belief by constant repetition. Doubt and fear about a neighbor is enough. When NATO was forged, peace left a hole, and a new enemy had to be created. The us-and-them strategy required new propaganda and new motives for violence. It could be founded on a religious belief or a skin color, but the blame is as old as humanity itself."

"Today, we have the human power to mitigate the heavy use of the world's resources and prevent the catastrophe of world famine by 2050." Archie continued. "Water shortages will drive migration when over 100 million people will lose their homes from land that is uninhabitable. This is bigger than the Kremlin's creation of fear and distraction by shutting down the free press in its country and beyond. The only way everyone will know is if journalists around the world expose the smears, poisonings, and jail sentences. Disinformation is the enemy we can fight – not each other."

The group applauded politely.

Archie sat in the white upholstered chair next to Havel, who covered his mouth and said to Archie, "So much for not pointing fingers."

Havel took his notes with him and spoke about growth statistics. He told stories of walks among townspeople, asking them about their lives and capturing the attention of the men and women with his poetic descriptions. He ended with observations about new colorful paint on buildings after years of Russian gray. He felt less fear and more optimism among Czech citizens.

Effusive, warm applause filled the museum lecture hall, and before it could die down, the Danish mathematician Jerg raised his hand for discussion. "Archie, about your school." He looked around to see which of his friends was listening. "How do we know your brilliant journalists weren't hand-picked to support your ideas?

"Jerg, these ideas are more than mine. They're from arid areas of Africa, polluted areas of India, and deforested Brazil. Do we view the Greek philosophers as being biased to the left or right? How about Renaissance thinkers? University Europe Central has a committee of seven board members of whom I am one. Three of those board members are in this audience today." The group looked around and one hand went up. Archie nodded to his Viennese counterpart, brave enough to identify herself.

"Each of my journalism students received a majority vote before being allowed to investigate their stories. I'll tell you, Jerg, the competition is fierce. If one misses a date, an attribution, or a confirmation, the rest will tear the work apart!"

After the lengthy discussions that followed, Havel and Archie took a walk to the Winterthur Museum garden. "I thought that went well," Havel said. "Should we head to Zurich for dinner?"

"Let's walk around first. We'll be moving targets, not stationary ones."

At the garden entrance, he and Havel remarked about the unusually early Chaenomeles.

"We call that flowering quince."

"Or Japonica –the same."

"*Today we have naming of parts. Japonica.*" Havel recited from memory.

"*Glistens like coral in all of the neighbouring gardens, And today we have naming of parts.*"

"Anti-war poem, is it?"

"From America, yes. Henry Reed. By the way, I spoke with Layla. She's seeing a Spanish politician she met during her rehabilitation.

"Is he legitimate?" Archie bristled. "I'll have Zolt investigate."

"Calm down. No need. I've already done so," Vaclav said. "He's a good man, but he's not the man for her."

They circled the rearing horse statue in the center of the pond. "The response from the Club was good.

I was hoping for more. Could have been worse." Archie motioned toward the rookery for the cover of birdsong. "Jerg annoyed the hell out of me."

In the rookery, Archie felt more confident talking about the university. "Vaclav, I need strings pulled. You know the Chechen leaders. I have a student, Erika. You may remember that I told you about the story she was working on, a fugitive from a supposed Orthodox bible-burning dissident who ended up in Kosovo. She was working on assignment for her newspaper when extremist authorities took her passport, so she's stranded there. They reported her to Interpol, claiming that the document was stolen so she that would be taken into custody. Now that she's trapped, they're harassing her, claiming her journalism to be obsolete. Zolt's been working on it, but he tells me Interpol needs confirmation to release her. Can you arrange it?"

"Ah, that would mean they're using Interpol to help fight their enemies. If Interpol has instated a Blue Notice, it's tough to retract it. Maskhadov owes me a favor. How about – " he scratched his chin. "Let's offer some international pressure in support of the Chechens at the same time. After all, they are defending themselves, fighting for justice. The cowards in the Kremlin claim that they are wearing the skins of warriors destroying terrorists when they are in fact attacking civilians. Their delusions can't will themselves into reality."

"Hmph," Archie looked at him. "You sound less like a poet and more like a President every day. I'm meeting with Rothschild tomorrow morning before our flight. Do you have an idea what this is about?" Archie said.

Havel was silent.

"How much do you know about this *Bratva* outfit that Zolt talks about?" Archie asked.

"The mafiya group? We investigated the murder of a co-owner of a company used for money laundering. We found a room full of weapons – anti-tank grenades, explosives, ammunition of all kinds. Now that our courts are functioning, our businesses don't need *Bratva* to collect debts, so they're expanding to other areas. Their roots are deep. It's hard to get rid of them. Find out all you can from Rothschild."

CHAPTER 43

1997 Switzerland

Becuase you strike out on your own, you and your cadre of student journalists, you think you're independent of the Soviet bloc." Alex Rothschild didn't waste time on pleasantries. "Your so-called independence only isolates you. You are fearful of every hotel room and every corner. What kind of freedom do you have if you live like this?" His thin-lipped smile was forced. "You can keep your freedom, Archie, and I'll keep mine."

Rothschild sat with Archie in a small private room with only a table and two chairs. The two Austrians had vastly different worldviews. A buffet on the narrow side wall held hot *kafé crème* and a plate of local *butschella* with raisins and citrus.

Archie looked at the sweets and rose from his chair to pour a cup of kafé. "Your freedom is forced conformity and double-speak." He chose a pastry carrying it back to the table. "The Czechs can profit from their own business, free of manipulation and bribes. Your freedom is from government persecution, as long as you come to heel." He knew only a part of the vast invisible network that

Rothschild condoned. "Those who don't come to heel face violence-fueled fear and anger. That retreat deeper into doubt and isolation from the world makes an ever-widening gulf. Your imagination is jailed, Rothschild, imprisoned, and punished by rules. Your thoughts are out of line. You tweak words, pushing them to sound like half realities."

"I am free to disagree with Havel. I'm not isolated and powerless or driven by those like me dictating what I do," Archie continued. "We are not distrustful and suspicious of our people. We are not limited in what we read or listen to. This freedom of thought is something we share, and it strengthens us – not weakens us.

"We get credit for ideas we create," Archie sipped his *kafé crème*. "Families have hope for better lives than their parents. Your people invent something and the government takes it over, taking both the credit and the profit."

"It's called power and influence," Rothschild said.

"My students know who they are and would be ashamed to be anyone else." Archie's hands grasped the sides of the table. "We have no illusions like the Americans who say they are born equal. That idea worries your leaders, who bully with anger and fear. Your people submit to the strong man who stifles critical thought, even if it takes an army to do it."

Rothschild laughed. "That equality idea may be in the Declaration, but after the U.S. Civil War, it's just a proposition, nothing more."

Archie knew that he had to bring *Bratva* into the conversation but couldn't stop. "Has there ever been a time when words were corrupted to hide the truth as much as today? We have a spirit in us, in our culture." Archie looked at his hands, trying to keep from clenching them in fists. "It cannot be corrupted or buried or slammed beneath a shoe. Our initiative will overtake your suspicions and your readiness to risk it all – you'll see. Watch us and learn what true strength is."

Archie's utterance of risk turned his thoughts to Logan. Thank God Logan was safe living in the States, even if they hadn't figured out the matter of equality yet. Americans had no worries about the rule of law being corrupted. No matter what came along, the law would be there to protect him, not to be twisted at the whim of some despot like it had been in the Czechoslovakia before Havel became President. Free speech was *not* in retreat. "I'm thinking," he told Rothschild. "If you have to defy your laws to please your authoritarian regime, what kind of world is that?"

"It's a dream world, Archie. You see yourself as the superhero from the West, out to conquer the evil East. But superheroes are a fantasy. Our truth is in power, and we have *Bratva*, more powerful than the law. The people desire the powerful, like a god. Keep them fearful, and they're afraid not to believe in the power. We don't have to like the Stalins and Lenins to ride the coattails of power."

Archie stood to go. "Truth in power? We've sat at the same tables, Rothschild, where everyone's in a balancing act, keeping all the plates in the air, no matter what it takes, to keep from losing position and power, looking for a new loophole, paranoid about being found out, willing to do anything to stay at the table. With more power than ever, even your *Bratva* is never enough."

With Rothschild's intractable stance, Archie felt an even stronger wobble in the world, and a heated fury. "Here we are arguing – without plotting to obliterate each other at least. Peace is cheaper, you know. Yes, I help Havel. I'll keep spending to help him and his people if I'm down to my last shilling." Archie wanted to stomp off, but that was the last thing Havel needed him to do now. "The best way to reach the truth is to communicate. Isn't that what we're doing?"

"You're wrong. Truth can be created, formed from something else. Once more people start to believe it, and it takes hold, it becomes truth. It's the belief in it, not the veracity," Rothschild said.

"Those creations you talk about reproduce like viruses infecting people before they are aware of the sickness. You can't run a country with a virus," Archie argued.

"So you want to censor the truth you don't believe in? Once a new truth takes hold, you will be the one the crowds will rail against – a virus to quarantine. Your ideas will be so foreign that they will be unthinkable. They'll claim you're destroying their culture, and they'll turn their backs on you," Rothschild said.

"What about the Sophists? Cicero? Isaac Newton? Bertrand Russel? Sartre? The reasoning of our own Elizabeth of Austria?"

"Reasoning?" Rothschild looked at Archie as if he had said the most preposterous thing. "There's no fire in reason. No bread and circuses. Think of Orwell's feelies. Entertain them, distract them, and light a fire under their feelings against those who disagree. That's how to create truth."

"Havel and my journalists use reason to restore human rights, not Russia's violence-forced peace and accord," Archie said. "Justice can move people more than any desire and people refuse to be determined by the world as it is. Reason is just a part of Havel's toolbox for liberation."

"Pfft! You sound like that German Kant – those colonizing Europeans and their slavery. Russia didn't colonize. Imperial Russia only colonized itself."

"Another created reality! My journalists would eat you for dinner in that debate. Your short-sighted, hopeless beliefs can only end in tragedy. Truth has no place for hate and greed. Truth seeks out stability for all humans."

"Your ideas are reversed. You see what's good as bad," Rothschild said.

"Good means we work like hell to survive," said Archie. "Bad means we do nothing and let the Kremlin rattle its sabers so the Americans will nuke them, and guess who's in the crossfire?"

"You're catastrophizing. An American president would never be hotheaded enough to – "

"*Veritas*, Rothschild. Truth hasn't changed at all. Never will."

"Archie, you sound like my cousins. I'll tell you what I tell them: lighten up. Your life is a doorstop."

"And history is one argument after another," Archie said.

"You and I know this. The papal bull, the Doctrine of Discovery from the 15th century, tells us what we already know – that

European civilization and Christianity dominate all other cultures. How else will America come to terms with its Indian problem? Its Negro problem? Through religion. Archie, we Jews have been seen as wealthy world dominators for centuries. That trope has morphed a million ways, and the blame is endless. If we're responsible for every world problem, why not embrace it? That invisible oppressor makes us the scapegoat anyway, so let's run with it," Rothschild said.

"Keep up your reckless spending, running in circles." Rothschild stood and pushed his *kafé* aside, forming a resolute angle with his hands flat on the desk. "We have our candidates who claim to be tough on crime. They will agree to build a few city parks, repair a hospital or two, and get the votes. The people won't care what else they do. Archie, you can go along with me or over me to put up with the next man. But I tell you, he will be a helluva lot worse."

CHAPTER 44

1997 Spain

Archie got the call after midnight. *Tia* Gabriella had broken ribs and vertebrae. When the hospital warned him that it looked like abuse in her elder care facility, he took the first flight to Madrid.

When he walked into her hospital room, she called him by name. "Where am I?"

He was relieved that she knew him, but Gabriella was confused. She patiently answered his many questions, although some answers were jumbled.

"I want to go home and see my friends," she said.

"*Tia*, is anyone hurting you or making you afraid?" he asked.

"No, no, no," she said, as if he'd asked a crazy question.

At last, Archie released the tension in his shoulders and called the care facility. *Tia* had fallen in the night when she got out of bed. On the phone, her caretaker at the facility seemed distraught. When she learned that Archie was nearby, she provided a list of *Tia's* needs outside the care facility. "We need someone to take her to outside appointments," she told him.

Archie assured her he would arrange for a dentist for some necessary work and an ophthalmologist for her blurry vision.

"*Tia*, when the hospital lets you go, we have some appointments to make," he said.

"Archie, what am I doing here?" was her common refrain. Her distress broke his heart.

"You'll be able to leave soon," he said. "What do you say we go shopping for dresses to visit your friends?"

Her face brightened and he saw a glimpse of Layla in her smile.

"Layla is naughty," she said.

"What do you mean?" Archie's ears perked up.

"I thought she was in her room doing homework, and she sneaked out of her bedroom window."

Archie smiled. "What did you do?"

"She went to the square to be with her friends after I told her no. She went to eat churros and drink hot chocolate. I could see the remnant on her upper lip here. *Tia* motioned to her own lip. I told her homework first, and she defied me! She found me in her room when she tried to climb back in through the window!"

Archie stifled a laugh. Clearly, Gabriella had not forgiven her for this long-ago indiscretion. He gently placed his hand over hers before he left and told her that his people had caught one of Layla's attackers, and Austria had agreed to hold him. Archie was preparing to take the attacker to the International Court. They had information on the others, with connections pointing to the Syrian government.

Tia Gabriella began to smile and patted his hand.

Zolt asked if he could talk to Layla about end-of-life care for Gabriella, but Archie refused. "Would you want to live this way?" Zolt asked. "I wouldn't."

Archie wondered what Layla and Gabriella would want. Gabriella seemed content, even if she was confused. He refused to think of losing her. "I don't know."

"I will look into palliative care." Zolt turned to leave before Archie could get angry with him.

CHAPTER 45

1998 New York

Are we there yet?"

"Take small steps down these rocks. See that last one? Take one more small step," Archie said.

"Look at all that water!" Logan plopped himself onto the trail to watch the waterfall tumbling down. They sat in silence, listening to the rushing sound.

Archie didn't want any more time to pass before he took his nephew for a hike. After his soccer game with Mulilo, he realized that he had overestimated how far a six-year-old could walk with his pack. On the first morning, Logan spent half of the hike riding on *Dod* Archie's shoulders.

Logan picked a cornflower and showed it to Archie. "Mama would like this."

"Sure she would. How about a swim?" Archie said. He stood and pulled off his pack, boots, and layers of camp clothes down to his shorts. "Can you swim, Logan?"

Logan frowned.

"You want to try?" Archie asked.

Logan took off his layers of gear as he had seen Archie do. Archie swam to the middle of Elka Park's Kaaterskill Falls and back in time to help Logan into the water. "Watch the rocks. They're slippery."

Logan's balance was sure. He stepped over the rocks into the deeper water.

"We'll start with a float. Are you ready?" Archie told him how to hold his arms and legs and tip his head back before he let go. Logan collapsed and disappeared under the water.

Archie changed his plan. As long as Logan was still interested, he'd teach him to float at least. Logan's arm was flailing with his head up and one foot down.

After several attempts, Logan exclaimed, "Look: I'm floating."

"You can feel it, can't you?" Unexpectedly, Archie's pride in his nephew overcame him. He imagined Logan hiking in Switzerland with him, touring Africa and bringing water to a village in need, or a grown-up Logan lecturing at his university in Hungary in front of a packed lecture hall. He turned to smile at Logan and told himself he would never let anyone hurt the boy. They floated together in the calm waters, looking up at the falls through the leafy canopy.

After noon, Archie regretted staying so long at the falls. It took him some time to light a fire and prepare their lunch, Hungarian venison goulash.

Logan complained, "I'm hungry. When will it be ready?"

"Gather some sticks for the fire while you're waiting," Archie told him. "But stay where I can see you."

When the goulash bubbled, and the aroma made Archie hungry too, he poured a fruit drink for Logan and a coffee for himself. "Logan, it's ready." Archie looked all around, but Logan was gone. He dashed around the camp in widening circles calling his name. A pounding grew in his chest as he thought of his role in Rivka's loss, how he wasn't there for Layla, and now this.

"Uncle Archie, I found a bird in a tree."

"Logan, you left me. You scared the shit out of me."

"Mama says I can't say shit."

"Your mother's right. Let's have lunch."

"Look at the bird."

Archie looked up and saw a scarlet tanager, its shiny red wing feather groomed by the bird's beak. Logan liked birds.

When they returned to their lunch, they came across a raccoon with a paw in the hot pan. Undeterred by the fire and humans, the panhandler continued to scoop up their lunch, the fur on his back raised in defiance.

Logan laughed. "He's wearing a mask on his eyes!"

Now, Archie was feeling hungry and out of sorts. "Yeah. Let's see if I can find some granola for lunch."

The last day's main meal of canned stew filled them up. They sat around the fire afterwards. "In school, we got to talk to astronauts on the space station, and they described the earth from up there – how fragile it was like a blue marble with just a shallow atmosphere around it and the right amount of oxygen for us to live," Logan said. "Without enough oxygen, we would die. It's like you, protecting people – when dangerous people want to hurt us." Logan took a few bites. "Don't tell Mom, but I wonder about God."

"Logan, what do you wonder?"

"God is supposed to be good. He's not an excuse to do stuff."

"Like what?"

Logan looked at the ground. "Like hurting people who are different." He picked up a stick in his hand and made lines in the soil.

"The astronauts come from different countries, and they get along," Archie said. "I was talking to someone the other day about your Declaration of Independence and equality. The man, Alex, said equality used to be an inalienable right. It means that it can't be taken away, but it's unimportant. What do you think?"

"I know a right can't be taken away," Logan said. "I think we'd be mad if somebody took equality away." Logan thought about it. "But when I heard the astronauts, I thought that maybe God can't keep bad things from happening to the people you know, but something's keeping that atmosphere around us. The astronaut we talked to said no other planets we know of have that kind of atmosphere, just us. Do you think we really went to the moon? Mom says it was a hoax."

Archie blew out a long breath. "Logan, she's your mother and you respect her, but yes, I know we went to the moon."

By the following evening, when the two tired hikers had returned to Brooklyn, Archie was sure Rivka would never let Logan go on another hike with him. He watched Logan run to his mother and hug her leg.

"Tell me about your hike," she said.

"I saw a scarlet tanager, Mama. I want to go back tomorrow."

Archie was relieved. Losing Logan in the woods would be their secret.

Rivka hugged her boy and thanked her brother.

CHAPTER 46

1998 New York

It was late, and Rivka was turning off the lights before heading to bed. She jumped at a knock at the door. "Archie," she called.

"It's okay. Zolt called and said he was on his way. I'll talk to him." Archie was tired after the hike, but he knew this must be important as soon as he opened the door.

"We need to go for a walk," Zolt said.

Archie looked up the stairs. Rivka was watching, but he waved to her. The house key was in his pocket, and he locked the door behind him.

The sky was dark and starless, the sidewalk empty. They passed a streetlight and a corner traffic signal before Zolt said a word. "I was looking for intel for Havel and found something else."

"Don't tell me about palliative care for Gabriella. I know you mean well but now is not the time. She and Zorica – "

"It's about an arm of the Federal Security Service."

"The FSB is stepping up its provocation of people's worst impulses, and confusion? They plunge their victims into a life where even an existential silence isn't possible. I look at them as the antithesis of you. Your loyalty, Zolt, your fidelity is to the truth, not to me or Havel. Anything less is a betrayal. Any FSB operative with half a conscience would be squirming in guilt right now," Archie said.

"Havel's position is precarious, subject to change at any moment. The FSB *kompromat* takes hold, and his people lose faith and trust in him. But I'm talking about something else," Zolt continued.

"Sounds like Sazan, that Mediterranean island from the Cold War with bunkers and a ramshackle resort. Chertok has started construction to bolster it as a "retreat" now that Hungary and the Czech Republic are almost NATO nations. The FSB is preparing for retribution in case of a Kremlin nuclear attack. Chertok's already stockpiling defensive weapons, establishing communications equipment, and modernizing bunkers.

Zolt dropped his head. "That shell company Dominion Directive has problematic connections to Moldova."

"That's not Moldova's choice, Zolt. They've had 1,500 Russian troops stationed there since their agreement with the leader to remove them. Russia is walking a fine line in Moldova, trying to establish an army base, squeeze its economy, and pressure Russian-speaking locals in Transnistria, to strengthen its influence and undermine the government. The troops are not moving. They claim to provide security but they're developing a very lucrative arms and drug-smuggling operation."

"My contacts confirm that the FSB is trying to wrest control from the military," Zolt said. His contacts included Zorica, they mysterious Moldovan friend of *Tia* Gabriella, whose contacts had been helpful to them both. "The military claims that this is protection, a practice run for the Czech Republic, but it appears to be preparation for annexation. They force detentions and crack down on anyone brave enough to speak out. With only a few million people, Moldova lacks the wealth to fight all the meddling and disinformation."

"I'd like to get a journalist into a safe space in Moldova – on the right bank of Dniester, of course. We need to get counter-evidence into print that Moldovans are not fascists who are out to kill the Transnistrians on the other side."

"When Moldova reaches out to the EU, and things look promising, Russia shuts down gas pipelines and bans imports," Archie continued. "Just when life in Moldova starts to improve over life in Transnistria, sanctions take them back to square one."

"The violations of free speech and evidence manipulation are all on the rise with no group strong enough to shoulder the costs to fight it."

"Take the SARS outbreak – they claimed the Moldovan government caused it," Archie said. "One more grim fairy tale to sew instability and division. We need a safe path for student journalists."

"You're not thinking of Nicoletta and Kristof. That's incredibly risky."

"Let's make the path, Zolt."

Breathing slowly through pursed lips, Zolt's impatience grew. "It's something else – but I know a photojournalist who records stories of the people. He's constantly moving, so he won't be easy to track. If he gets evidence of the propaganda, potential rigging of voting precincts, money laundering, and poisoning of the pro-Moldova presidential candidate and publishes it around the world, he should be safe. He would agree that we need to halt this move now to stop a more significant move on Havel and the Czech Republic.

"We can start with their security zone." Archie said. "Your photojournalist hikes incognito with Kristof and Nicoletta through small Moldova towns, talking to townspeople and mayors, finding out where their loyalties lie. There have been threats against those who speak out against the propaganda before the election. Word of mouth is trusted. I believe the new candidate for Moldova's president has the support of the workers, so Russia will try to prevent a fair election. Online propaganda supports their opposition leader, so he has a following. The photojournalist spreads the truth and might save the courts as well as the election."

"Archie, I've been trying to tell you. It's something else, not Moldova. It's closer to home. It's like they kicked down the door and walked right in. I wanted to tell you that the FSB is in the States too."

"What?" Archie stopped walking and looked at Zolt. "I know there has been some money laundering in real estate but – "

"It's more. Not just interfering in free elections in Europe, but here it's the US Army and the Navy. They call it the Moonlight Maze, and it's about influencing the troops. Here's the New York News headline." Zolt pushed buttons on his Nokia phone in front of Archie.

1996 Turla Revelation: FSB's Advanced Computer Hacking Yields Towering Stack of US Military Intel, Monumental in Scope.

Archie reread the headline. "The Russian *mafiya*. Where are they?"

"Their American headquarters is in Brooklyn," Zolt said. "Their motto is 'we always collect.'"

CHAPTER 47

1998 Estonia

Russian computer hackers here in Logan's New York borough added pressure to Archie's days in New York. Zolt's message bent time, and he felt forced to act. Zolt had already found more protection for the journalists. He had scoured the records to find military members recently released from tours of duty. Archie's pay scale was a welcome surprise to them and their families, and they were already familiar with the villages they would be watching. He suggested that Zolt do the same in Brooklyn with American military members who had finished their tours of duty.

Archie accepted an invitation to visit the Estonian University of Tartu, despite his concerns for Rivka's and Logan's safety. The provost offered contingency plans and invited Archie to the campus. Tartu, long recognized as one of the best universities in Europe, welcomed him warmly. Archie met with administrators and explained his desire to keep his university in Hungary but recognized that government pressure made it difficult for them to stay. He explained that as they talked, Hungarian authorities were forcing their own government-approved curriculum. They claimed that Archie's independent ideas were polarizing and creating chaos. Pamphlets distributed around campus claimed Archie was a baby killer, a former Nazi, and the leader of an international group of traffickers and pedophiles. One of his worst offenses, they claimed, was helping refugees. At least they got the help for refugees right, he thought.

Would Tartu consider a branch campus? The provost, Mr. Kask, assured him that local newspapers would be willing to work with his independent journalism students, and Archie was warming to the idea of an expansion. Not one book or website needed the required approval of the government of Estonia. The men agreed on the goals of rigorous, open independence and truth, making little mention of Chertok's Reynard News kompromat and attempts to influence his beloved Estonia, the country of his birth.

Tartu was Estonia's intellectual center and oldest university. Just north of the city center, Provost Kask walked the cobblestone streets with Archie along the banks of the Emajõgi River to Supilinn or Soup Town. Walking into the historic neighborhood felt like stepping back into a well-loved medieval village. The provost directed Archie to *Olde Hansa* for folk music and a flavorful bowl of lentil stew served with Olderman's hearty brew. Together, they worked out some preliminary details.

"What you're doing reminds me of Vilnius University," Kask said. Like us, they have banned state-controlled media. They have a university and village journalists network, and the word spreads with connections to the BBC. Once propaganda is proposed, it is exposed before it has a chance to take hold. They're too late when the government tries to fire old professors and bring in ones that promote only the Vilnius government line. I've thought about creating our own link." Kask paused to motion a friend to the table. "Imagine what we could do for all of it with your Hungarian journalists, the Vilnius journalists, and connections to the BBC."

Archie finished off the last spoonful of stew. Kask introduced his friend, the dean of the Department of Media Studies, and the men shook hands. "A free press is fragile," the dean said. "Russia's goals are to take bigger bites out of the republics. Attacks on education are paramount because they know it's one of the best ways to expose propaganda. When voices are extreme, truth goes from being a lifeblood to a casualty." The dean nodded and left.

Archie was reminded of Havel's words in *Power to the Powerless.* "Havel said that banning independent thought becomes the most scientific of world views; because the regime is captive to its lies, it must falsify everything. It pretends to respect human rights. It pretends to persecute no one. It pretends to fear nothing. It pretends to pretend nothing. Here you are banning state-controlled media when you share a border with Russia." A plate clattered in the kitchen and startled them both. "My journalism students dig deep into stories and tell village people what they need to make sense of things. They write about the villains who want to change the balance of power, those who widen the gap between what people believe and what is happening to them."

As Archie gathered his papers to leave, the waiter returned, asking if he'd like some oxen meat. "I assure you, the meat is from well-kept cattle," he said.

Archie turned to the Provost with a bewildered expression. "Thank you. We'll have our check now," Provost Kask said. The waiter bowed and left.

CHAPTER 48

1998 Austria

Archie had exchanged letters with Elida since his visit to Africa and the soccer game in the street with her nephew Mulilo. When he arrived at his Vienna office, the staff placed Elida's correspondence at the top of the stack on his desk, and it was always the first envelope he opened. Elida declined additional loans he had offered, telling him that she was more than able to take care of herself. So Archie sent books. He smiled at the thank you notes in Mulilo's handwriting that arrived in her letters. Archie still traveled with Elida's letter that Layla had given him, but since he had met Mulilo, now a six-year-old, he tried to think of something more that he could do and decided to make Elida a future offer. Two weeks later at his Vienna office, her reply was waiting for him at the top of the stack.

Archie,

I value our correspondence since you came to visit us. I was astonished at your generous offer of secondary education for

Mulilo in New York when he is older. I explained to Mulilo that it was a scholarship similar to yours for your education in Vienna, and he agreed. I accept your offer, as long as you know we will not stay. After Mulilo's education is completed, we will return to Kanjanja. There is so much to be done, and we love the growth and change in our village too much not to take part in it.

Since Mulilo and your nephew, Logan, are of similar age, perhaps they could strike up a brotherly friendship. Mulilo will miss his friends but we have discussed this as an opportunity. Mulilo knows the old stories of our village and wants to share them with Logan, but he studies hard, too. The American children's literature and history books you have sent will help ease the adjustment to a new culture. We look forward to this future adventure.

With God's blessings

Yours sincerely,
Elida

CHAPTER 49

1998 Czech Republic

A Czech teen can buy a pair of Nikes designed in Oregon, made in China, and shipped to Hamburg, now all affordable." Havel marveled at the array of products available in the Czech Republic from container ships arriving at Germany's biggest port. "The shipping from China is cheaper than the trucking from Hamburg." He and Archie waited in their theater seats for the end of intermission. They had been watching Dagmar in the lead role of *Departing (Odcházení)* at the *Vinohrady* Theater.

"I've been cautiously recommending the shipping companies," Archie said. "We can learn from what happened in the States, where auto companies outsourced whole factories to Mexico and China. It left workers in factory towns with no jobs to feed their families, and inequality skyrocketed."

"True enough. We must find a balance. Look at our Škoda cars. The company nearly collapsed in the Cold War, but today, with access to designers and engineers worldwide, we ship over 400,000 cars to 70 countries. There is no end to good factory jobs here. More trade means interdependence. International trade benefits the people more than the strongman dictator. Now Dubai has skyscrapers, Bollywood has movies, and men have Viagra!"

Archie laughed. "People are slow to accept change, but fast to react against it, Havel. Be careful. They may love the shoes, but blame you for bringing them from China."

"Speech teach, Archie. I give the people lessons in globalization, a bite at a time, so their busy lives can take it in. We don't have the oligarchs who take it all for themselves. I remind them that we're saving our profits to fix our bridges, maintain the electric grids, and get out this great new broadband."

"So many *greats*. Constantine the Great, the Great Society, Alexander the Great, Catherine the Great – your Czech Technical University in Prague is a model." Archie had to admit that he would like to develop a technology degree at his university,

"The Great Depression, the Great War, Make Germany Great Again, yes, yes, we started with our *bíbieskas* like computer bulletin boards, and now we have small newspapers online. The States have the search engine Netscape Navigator, and we have *Seznam* — such change. Nearly two percent of the world is connected to the internet, and it will light a fire under us. You will see."

"Yes, but nothing will replace a real newspaper delivered to your porch or picked up at a stand, Havel. Technology moving too fast creates a backlash of resentment against globalization from the rising middle class. They feel that their cultural power is being attacked, disrupted, and it's up to them to defend it. They feel caught in an undertow of progressive change, and must claw back. Remember what Tocqueville said a hundred years ago. It's still true. It's *relative* deprivation, not *absolute* deprivation, that sparks revolt," Archie said. "Not everyone is ready for the future."

"How can you be so sure? Maybe *you* are not ready." Havel smiled with his lighthearted teasing and turned to the stage where the lights flashed, and the curtain opened, revealing Dagmar in a brilliant red gown. "I wrote the lead part in the play for her," he said. "I think she carries it well."

CHAPTER 50

1999 New York

The yearly hikes in Elka Park became highlights of the year for both Logan and Archie. Now that Logan was seven, Archie added an extra day to the hike. Logan played on a soccer team that year, and Archie figured he could handle more time and a few extra pounds in his pack. As much as Archie enjoyed time with his nephew, every look into his face made him wonder what it would have been like to be here with Layla and their son.

Logan wandered into Archie's room the night before their hike. He found *Dod* Archie laying out his hiking gear from the guest room closet. His uncle often brought a few pieces of new, foreign gear, and Logan was curious. Once more, Archie pulled something from his flight carry-on bag that Logan hadn't seen.

"This is *Amadou*." He showed the child-sized hat to Logan before plopping it on his head.

Logan grabbed it off to take a look.

"*Amadou* is a fungus that grows on the sides of trees like mushrooms. The word translates to 'lure' or to 'grasp' or 'spark'. Fly fishermen use it to dry flies. It looks like a horse's hoof when it grows on the tree."

Logan ran his hand over the material. "It's soft."

"Hikers like these hats. They're made in Transylvania."

"That's the vampire place with ghosts and Dracula."

"*Amadou* starts life as a parasite that kills the tree. Then, it dies and becomes its most important self, nourishing the soil. It feeds the forest with its death."

"That's weird. Can I wear it to school?"

"You can wear it on our hike. That's what it's for."

"What language is *Amadou*?"

"It's French," Archie said.

"How do you speak so many languages?"

"Most everyone does in Europe. The US is a big country. You can travel from state to state and speak the same language. It's not that way in Europe. Instead of the next state, it's a new country with different customs and language. To be comfortable there, you learn the language, that's all."

The hikers left after daybreak and passed an abandoned house and barn from the last century. They started with the Codfish Point Trail, which was busy in the morning. "Look out for stones and tree roots," Archie said.

Logan had to stop and talk to the dogs and their owners on their way to Platte Cove Falls. Huckleberry Point Trail in the afternoon offered beautiful views of the Catskills and Hudson River. They weren't in any hurry and stopped to pick huckleberries, ripe in mid-July. Logan took off his *Amadou* hat and before long, had it filled it with berries. Archie kept watch for bears. His nephew wasn't the only one who loved the tart, juicy fruit.

They dropped their gear for lunch. Logan arranged stones for the fire, and they sat there waiting for their stew to warm.

"So, did you call your dad last week?" Wilson rarely called Logan, so Archie encouraged him to call once a week.

"He couldn't talk long. He's on a story about a UFO sighting. Last month, it was about some guy who claimed to know who was in on Kennedy getting shot." He looked at Archie. "I don't believe that shit."

"Don't let your mother hear you talk that way."

"Dad doesn't care about anything I do."

"Logan," he wanted to say something and changed his mind. "I look at the man you're growing up to be. I couldn't love you any more if you were anyone other than who you are, and you are half your dad."

"He wants people to think that stuff is real."

"That's not going to happen here. America isn't just one place, one way of thinking. You have journalists you can trust to tell the truth." He wanted to tell Logan about the struggles of his student journalists in Hungary but decided to wait. "Fortunately, not too many people believe the stories about UFOs and Kennedy. Those fanciful stories aren't going to hurt anyone."

"I don't tell Mom. She gets angrier and more afraid when I tell her I don't believe stuff. She said the walls have ears and she makes us hide in the closet. She says we're invisible in there."

Archie was unsure if this was the product of a seven-year-old mind, or something else.

"I look through the closet keyhole when I see light under the door. It makes my stomach hurt to see her mumbling and turning pages, sitting on the floor. One time, she kept talking about a shadow government. What does that mean, *Dod* Archie?"

"If it's what I think she means, it's a term that started in Turkey. It means double government, a way of demonizing an opposing political enemy, exploiting everyday citizens with organized crime outfits."

"But it's crap."

"Some people feel powerless. Maybe they were hurt when they were children, maybe there was a fire or storm that wiped out their village, and they felt that no one cared. They feel helpless like they don't matter. So they look for something to hang on to, some person or idea bigger or stronger than they feel."

"Like the idea that Elvis is still alive?"

"Yes, like Elvis, or if they believe in a different leader who will fix all of their problems if they just believe and show loyalty to him without question. They feel good about this unshakable power, the glitter of it, the pride they have in it. They're willing to give up their own ideas to pledge loyalty, to let this idea be their master."

"Is that what happened to the German people with Hitler?"

"Something like that. And now Russia is demanding that type of loyalty too."

"I don't get it."

"Sometimes people are tired. They don't want to think. They want things to be easy, to be told what to think."

"So that's why my teacher always says 'why'. It's hard when he says 'why'. There isn't just one answer."

Archie stirred the fire and waited to answer. "It's hard. It takes lots of studying. These believers don't realize what they're giving up to be part of the group. They're overwhelmed by anxiety and doubt. Some think that if they're loyal, they won't feel so powerless. They'll feel secure. Instead, they are taught to be fearful. When they're afraid, they can't make sound decisions. They get stuck in their fearful loyalty. They believe if they can just own the opposition, make them feel helpless, rule over them, humiliate them, make them suffer, then they will win."

"Do they think they could rule a bunch of people who don't want what they want?"

"They're so fearful, they don't think how impossible it would be to force powerful beliefs on people who know otherwise. Beliefs don't always work to help people, but they are powerful anyway."

"Aren't strong people powerful too?"

"If I have power over someone, more muscles than someone else, you could say I'm stronger. But that's different from longing, hungering, aching for power. That's a weakness when we reach for someone else's strength instead of making our own."

"I don't have to believe you, ya know."

"No, you don't."

"Mom says you're full of *schmegegge*."

Archie stirred the stew. "No one has it figured out, Logan." Maybe Havel was right. He didn't feel ready for the future. "It looks like our supper is ready," he said, picking up a bowl by its handle. "And I brought *stroopwafels* for dessert." Logan's hands reached out for the thick, steaming stew. "What are you looking at?" Archie asked.

"I'm looking hard," Logan said. "At everything. I want to look so hard so I don't forget. So this place doesn't leave me. Then, when Mom says that stuff, I can remember this, and I'll be okay." He ate a spoonful of stew. "When Dad leaves it's like the hole your tongue finds when you lose a tooth. You're the tooth that grows in the hole. You still love her, don't you," Logan said.

"What do you mean?" Archie was surprised.

"Layla. You still talk about her. I feel like she's with you even though she's off in Europe somewhere. You still love her."

"I can't stop myself." Archie's breath caught. "Love tears and pulls and she's the reason."

"What reason?" Logan said.

"Why I keep taking risks. Layla would want me to, and so I go on. And for you, because revolutionary acts – "

"I know. Like George Orwell," Logan said. "In a time of deceit, telling the truth is a revolutionary act. But I'm never gonna love a girl."

"Why would you say that?"

"It would hurt too much if she found someone else or if she – I'd never go through that. It's not worth it."

"Logan, you will love someday, and then you will know. The good is too good not to try." Archie smiled to himself. "If love wasn't so powerful, it wouldn't hurt so much, but you can't stop it. A rabbi once said to me, '...Not everyone has a love so great that they feel the depths of sorrow.'"

CHAPTER 51

1999 New York

A freed slave 2,000 years ago, the playwright Terence, said, 'Nothing human is foreign to me.'" Archie scooped the remainder of his stew from the bowl. "We are all heirs to other humans. One person's heedless reaction shouldn't dictate a thousand arrows piercing the rest of us. Our ideas are just part of who we are. Think of what we have in us that existed before we evolved into humans. Over the past 400 years, you have had over 4,000 ancestors who loved and struggled before you were here. All of those relatives are a part of what we feel and think. Explore that, Logan."

Logan didn't finish his stew. "I'm not that hungry. I'm tired."

Usually, Logan ate quickly, but Archie wasn't concerned.

"Nothing the afternoon hike won't fix. This time, we're going to – "

"My belly button hurts."

Archie didn't want to say it, but he told Logan they could stop if he needed to.

"No, I want to keep going."

The longer Platekill Mountain Summit wasn't difficult, but Archie thought Logan could learn some bushwacking, or hiking off-trail. Further on, other hikers thinned, and he noticed a distant bear walking up the side of a hill. Before the hill, they came upon an abandoned clapboard farmhouse with two broken windows like black eyes. The jagged tooth of a front door hung on one hinge. Logan was fascinated and walked to the front porch before Archie could stop him. A board clattered and Archie watched Logan disappear beneath it.

"Logan!" He ran to the step and saw a hand reaching the porch top. He could see nothing else in the darkness below. Archie threw his pack off and crouched down. Reaching his arm down as far as he could, he felt a hand. With a hefty pull, he raised Logan and his pack out of the muck under the porch. "So, what'd you find?"

"My stomach hurts. It really hurts." Logan grimaced and slapped his hands on the sides of his jeans, covering the fear in his voice. "I felt rusty gears and old bottles," he said. "I think I heard a rat too."

When Archie asked where it hurt, Logan looked up, his face crumpled in pain. "We're going back," Archie said, picking up his nephew and heading back to the SUV, over a mile away.

Slowly, he retraced their steps. With Logan's added weight, the lurking bear, and uneven ground that could catch him off balance, the hike seemed interminable. Each time the trail turned uphill, he thought about ditching their backpacks. As the afternoon sun dipped low, Archie spied the trailhead. With great relief, he unlocked the door and buckled pale, sleepy Logan into the SUV. After the engine hummed to life, Archie's heart thumped, and his hands gripped the wheel on their tense drive to the hospital.

After a few tries, he contacted Rivka, and she left her class in time to see Logan after his surgery. Logan looked at them both and lifted his hospital gown to show off the small scar on his lower right side.

"You want to hurry up and get better so we can go home," Rivka patted his hand. "This is a long way from the city and it's too hard to get a sub for my classes when I stay here with you."

"I can stay," Archie said. He thought he saw relief in Logan's snaggle-toothed smile. In the past, Archie had thought of ways he might offer to help his dad, Wilson, to have his own bad teeth fixed, but Wilson already resented his help. Rivka wasn't bothered, so he let it go. For Logan, he would arrange for braces.

The doctor came to check Logan's incision and chart. He told Archie that the outcome would have been critical if Logan had arrived much later. Archie thanked the doctor for operating in time, feeling like the medical team had moved heaven and earth to help the boy.

Logan put his hospital gown down over the stitches and pulled up the blanket again. "I heard the doctor say something and write it on the chart." His eyebrows knitted together. "He said my appendix was grossly unremarkable. My appendix got me this far, and now I don't have it anymore, but he shouldn't make fun of it like that."

Archie explained. "That's a medical determination, Logan. It doesn't make sense to us, but to other doctors – "

"Enough of this. Archie, you probably saved Logan's life. Logan, don't you ever go camping again if your belly button hurts."

Logan saluted his mother, settled his head back into the pillow, and closed his eyes.

CHAPTER 52

1999 New York

Archie had put on weight, and the decade-old hiking gear left in Rivka's closet was unforgiving. On their camping trip, he'd bent over to tend the fire and popped a button on his hiking vest. After a search of the ground that Archie told Logan was like solving a detective story, they had to admit that it was gone. After Logan had been home from the hospital for a few days, Archie took him to East 62nd Street off Lexington Avenue, where they found Tender Buttons. Archie had been there before. Their claim to fame was that Gertrude Stein famously frequented the shop. Next to the shoe repair shop, the slender, brick storefront of Tender Buttons stood with its big gold button sign.

Archie and Logan passed under the arched windows and black wrought iron balcony as if they were walking into a Dickens novel. Logan passed by the everyday humble buttons and paused at a rare and wonderful case with a George Washington button. Archie pointed out another case with a brightly-lit Civil War button, pleased that these little momentos captured Logan's interest. "There was an artist, a friend of Michaelangelo named Vasari," he said to Logan. "He believed that history was the mirror to human life and the plans we make are the spirit of history."

A surly salesman approached, and Archie asked if they had a horn button to match the ones on his hiking vest. The salesman turned without a word and returned with two buffalo horn buttons that were a reasonable match. Archie bought them both.

"If I lose a button, Mom just throws the shirt out," Logan said.

Archie snorted and changed the subject. They bought hot pretzels from a street vendor and ate them while they walked the rows in the parking garage. "Have you read biographies about your country's leaders? George Washington or Abraham Lincoln?"

Logan said he hadn't, but he was curious about history, and his mom agreed with most of it, except she told him his teachers were wrong about the Civil War.

"Mark Twain said, 'Biographies are but the clothes and buttons of the man. The biography of the man himself cannot be written.'"

My teacher taught us about Mark Twain, "Loyalty to petrified opinion never broke a chain or freed a human soul."

Archie watched Logan scramble into his seat, securing the seatbelt. He wanted to meet this teacher. "So, what do you think that means?"

"We see petrified wood on hikes," he said. "It doesn't change, like ideas. Some people know there are new ideas but won't change their minds."

Archie wished Layla could hear. "It's like the ideas that forced your grandparents to flee from Germany. Some of the Nazis' ideas came from American slavery in the 1800s – owning people and destroying them if they disobeyed, justifying their violence by believing that the enslaved people were not human. They thought what was best for them was best for the world."

The SUV turned from the parking garage into the sunlight. "We need to think about our actions and the ripple effects on the rest of the world. Your country knows this, and they're working to fix the mistakes of the past. You can be part of what makes your country better. But some European countries doubt that justice should be the same for everyone. I'm trying to get more stories of justice published. People need to recognize that justice is for everyone."

"You can do that, *Dod* Archie. You have more money than my parents have. You don't have to be careful about what you buy. You even own a university."

"You wouldn't want all of this money, Logan. It's trapped me in a life I wouldn't choose. Too much money goes to protect the few who have it." He tried to think of words Logan might understand. "Have you heard of *tikkun olam*?"

Logan frowned.

"It's a Jewish concept, meaning that the path we take to help repair or heal the world is a constant journey. If an unleashed force of money favored most people in this world, we'd be building up, but too many people only want to tear down."

Before supper, Archie sat at the kitchen table, sewing on his button. Rivka poured them a glass of wine while waiting for the brisket to bake.

"Look at you. Let me take you to Patagonia tomorrow. That vest is ancient."

"It's all I need."

"You need all the help you can get."

She chopped, sauteed, and seasoned companion dishes in a constant restless motion, celebrating the hikers' return. Logan slouched through the kitchen and sniffed the aroma of the brisket, one of his favorites. "It won't taste as good as *Dod* Archie's hunter's stew," he said, leaving the room.

"You're spoiling him," Rivka told her brother.

CHAPTER 53

1999 New York

Archie, I know this man who could use a loan. He's a sweetheart. He'd never hurt people."

She put the leftover brisket in the fridge, and the two sat at the kitchen table. Rivka told her brother about a New York real estate tycoon who was smart enough to claim his hotels and resorts were worth less than their appraisals to save taxes. However, he was short on cash, and the banks weren't lending. "Could you lend him a few million?"

"He's got to be private equity, Rivka. Legislators retire with all their connections and get jobs with these companies to schmooze little companies, buy them up, and sell them off for parts. Employees lose, the little company's former owner and investors lose. The only winner is the private equity company. And these sweet people you like go out and hurt people repeatedly. There's no law against it."

"And I'm not trying to get one. We're talking about savvy business people who have a right to the money they work for. If the little companies don't want to sell to them, that's their business. My student came in one day, excited because he had gotten a great part-time job with private equity. He came in the following week in tears. There he is sniveling to me after class about how his job was to evict people from the cheap trailers they'd lived in their whole lives because his company bought the land and raised the price, so they couldn't afford the rent anymore."

"Rivka, listen to what you're saying."

She gave him a stricken expression. "It's business! Ray, that's my student, should have known that. The kid needed to buck up. If his company is smart enough to make money by cutting corners, it's his job to make it happen. Where was his loyalty? Instead, he's crying to me."

"Rivka, he was evicting people who were losing the homes they'd lived in for years."

"So all they had to do was get a better job. They're lazy. It's their fault."

Archie wanted to ask his sister if she and Wilson were willing to get better jobs to take over the payments he made for their home.

CHAPTER 54

1999 New York

Where are we going again? Logan moved closer as a woman in a bulky coat sat beside him on the crosstown subway.

Archie told him they were going to the Friday Temple service. "I wanted to watch TV," Logan said.

The synagogue in Brooklyn had experienced some problems. "Out of 600 synagogues in the city, there is no shortage of threats," he said. "Zolt will secure the premises for the service, and we'll help the congregation to be safe."

"Is this the one with tunnels under it?" Logan said.

Archie looked at him. "Stay close. Remember before we left your mom said no futzing around."

"Mom said people built secret tunnels under one of the synagogues."

Archie changed the subject as they walked up the subway steps toward the synagogue. Line 2 had arrived late, but they could still make it in time. "Layla was in Berlin in November, the day after the wall fell," Archie said. Logan's curiosity wasn't deep yet, but very wide. He asked a few questions, and that was a start.

Archie explained the weight of November 9, 1989 – a headline-making event worldwide.

"Did the East Germans feel like the Jews who left for Israel?" Logan asked.

"If Layla was here, we could ask her how it felt. She interviewed East German people. I was shaving in Vienna when I heard the news that morning, and I almost cut my face."

Layla was in Berlin for interviews and had no idea that this would happen. She increasingly heard people say, "The wall is coming down." Then, there were shouts and cheers in the streets. She was carried along by a crush of people. She would try to make her way to a location to meet an interviewee and end up somewhere else entirely. The look on the East German people's faces was a lot to take in.

They might arrive on time, but it would be close, Archie said as they stepped up on the curb and crossed the sidewalk. The synagogue door was open. He described Checkpoint Charlie as Layla had described it. Families who were forbidden to see one another for 28 years were rushing through to the West at this security point, reuniting in hugs, screams, and tears, daring to feel hope with all the commotion. Others were spray-painting the wall or chipping off pieces for souvenirs. Layla had a faraway look, just trying to find words. There were some interviews she just couldn't get with all the confusion, but one reverberated with her."

"What was that?" Logan said.

"These newlyweds were separated from the wife's parents who were left in East Berlin. The parents met their grandson, who had graduated from Free University in West Berlin. For weeks, he had protested with others to allow safe passage. And that night, she took a photo of the Brandenburg Gate at night. The famous landmark had been obscured by the wall for decades, and was now lit up for everyone to see from all angles. There were people everywhere drinking and celebrating, standing on top of the parts of the wall that were still there, chanting, 'No East, No West.'"

"Layla sounds brave."

Popping sounds fired in front of the synagogue, and Archie grabbed Logan. He forced his nephew down onto the sidewalk, positioning his body over him. "Stay down – you're brave – might be fireworks, but stay down," Archie said.

A shot cracked over their heads, and Logan tensed up. The popping continued in an agonizing staccato rhythm, but Archie's body remained motionless over him. "Legs still – don't move," he said.

"Don't you get tired of waiting for things to get better?" Logan's voice wavered. "Sometimes, do you just want to give up?"

"Shh – see these people next to us?" His voice was barely audible as men and women nearby were stretched out and still. "In too many places, hope is beaten out of them." Archie kept his voice quiet through another round of shots. "They have only their fear to live with every day."

"I won't give up," Logan whispered. After plenty of tension and time, the shooting sounds stopped, and from ground level, he saw people slowly picking themselves up. *Dod* Archie's weight lifted from him.

Boots appeared: the toes of one of *Dod* Archie's security guards. "Are you okay?"

He felt a hand lift him, and Logan stood looking into his uncle's wild eyes, inspecting every inch of him for harm. That look in his eyes spoke so loud that his uncle's calm words didn't make sense. "Take a few breaths, Logan."

"I'm okay." He brushed the dirt from his pants and touched the scuff on his jaw where it had scraped the sidewalk. Logan was going to tell his uncle that he felt dizzy and not brave, but Archie turned to talk to the security guard. It was better if he kept that to himself. Maybe it was the noise and all the people running. He watched a muscular man and a NYC police officer handcuff two men dressed in black, their faces covered. One yelled as a medic wrapped his arm and leg in bandages that turned red. He looked away. Another police car pulled up, lights flashing.

"Not one congregant was injured," Archie told him. "Zolt knows what he's doing." The two walked up the synagogue steps where the rabbi stood at the tall wooden door. Bullet holes marred the carvings, and splinters littered the entranceway. With animated hands, the uneasy rabbi motioned that he had canceled services but offered counseling and comfort to anyone who needed it. Logan listened to his uncle's calm voice, telling the rabbi he would take care of the repair work on the door. He'd call tomorrow.

They walked slowly down the steps. "Should we tell Mom?" Logan said.

"If she reads about it in the news, we can tell her that Line 2 was late and we didn't arrive until after."

"That's sort of true. What about my face?" Logan pointed to the scraped red lines along his jaw. He looked at his finger and found traces of blood.

Archie frowned and lifted Logan's chin for a better look. "We'll sort it out," he said.

With little to say, Logan reached for Archie's hand as they maneuvered past the gathering crowd and returned to the subway. The sky was darkening, colors draining into evening grays. "I know this is tough," he told Logan. "If you want to talk about it later, you let me know."

Logan nodded. What would he say? He couldn't think about the possibility of what might have happened minutes ago. What if one of those shots had found its target in *Dod* Archie? His mind wasn't working right. He tried to talk himself into feeling normal again.

The repetitive clicks of the subway rails offered a restive calm. Logan nudged close to his uncle, moving with the motion of the car. "When will things get better?"

"People are tired of waiting for things to get better." Archie kept his voice low. "Let me tell you a story about another time when people couldn't wait, when I carried secret messages for Israel," Archie said. Maybe this was the worst time ever to tell Logan about the scar on his chest. Or perhaps it was the best. "When I was twelve..."

CHAPTER 55

1999 Hungary

Six students sat around a table, each with a paper name tag tented in front of them. Archie scrutinized their humorless faces with pride, the best journalists of the upper classes with mind muscles itching for the full-out distance run. They were gathered in a basement room of the university library, its damp stone walls and flickering fluorescent lighting reminding Archie to provide more of a stipend to the head librarian and maintenance staff. Even the air seemed stale and musty. The room was secure, but it felt more like a prison cell. Archie set a box of pastries in the middle of the table.

This wasn't their first meeting, and he reminded them that they had a right to inquiry and evaluation free of threats or punishment from the Hungarian government or him. "The farther your evidence and truth spread, the more likely you will be able to counteract ideas of *kompromat*," he said.

"Some of you know that in the Cold War, our Psychological Defense Agency shielded us from war with Russia. We ended up being the target they threatened about."

Archie explained that when fear of the Kremlin grew, countries wanted to protect themselves and tried to join NATO. That's when the Kremlin sent out more disinformation about their Cold Peace.

"Some in our country fiercely oppose the Psychological Defense Agency because they fear it will stifle ideas. They feel that Russian FSB fear-mongering is in our best interests. It confuses others about who to believe, so our reporting is even more important. Now, Tamas, what did you find out about the poisoned water issue you were working on?" He turned to the student on his left, who had a pastry stuffed in his mouth.

Tamas swallowed. "There were protests on campus last week. Police used batons, and students were hurt. The polluted river water the factories refused to use was approved for neighborhood drinking water."

"What did the water authority say?"

"They confirmed it was lead-tainted, but I couldn't get them to admit it on record or use their names. There is a cover-up. Area leaders were paid to look the other way. I want the headline to be *A Firehose of Fake News*."

"What about the protesters?"

"They say you put them up to it, that you are to blame, but the people are getting sick from the water. I have the false statements from authorities, and I'm gathering evidence individually."

"Will they agree to fix it?"

"They don't seem to be in a hurry to fix it – just blame others. I have my work, but there are many government sources, much kompromat, ready to deny the facts."

"Let's see if the university in Vilnius can publish your article without interference," Archie said. He admired Tamas' chosen research. Safe water was often taken for granted and overlooked until a catastrophe hit. His article needed traction. "From there, Latvia and Sweden. When the news comes from outside, Hungarians will wonder why Lithuanians knew first."

Erika was next. She bit her nail, and her fingers flipped through pages before she spoke. "I got arrested for taking notes," she said.

Archie hadn't spoken with her since Havel had arranged for the return of her passport and secured her release from Kosovo. "Are you all right?" he asked.

She nodded. "The FSB is spreading a story that Swedish people were kidnapping Russian children, prohibiting them from speaking Russian, and sending them to work. There were no Russian children and no working children under 13. Then they claimed that one of the alleged kidnappers burned the Russian Orthodox Elizabeth Bible. There is no proof that the man had the Bible, but his colleagues are afraid of jail if they support him," she said. Erika admitted that there was confusion over Swedish neutrality and lies about Bibles that the Psych Defense Agency could clear up, but disinformation made them distrust their source of truth. "I'm writing about what happened and what didn't happen."

"Good work on a complex issue. Get quotes from those who distrust evidence and see if you can find a friend of the Swedish dissident to quote off the record. Find out where he was at the so-called burning." Archie stood and paced before he spoke again.

"Remember, these panics are not new. People think conspiracies have never been like this, but they go back to the 1400s and witch hunts in Roman times. Now it's not witches. It's librarians or teachers."

"They're just trying to scare you, keep you from exposing them," said Albert, a thin young man with dark circles under his eyes.

"Professors teach us to be objective, but the other side is so extreme," Silka said. "How can we present both sides when the other side makes up their facts? We can't write about a lie as if it's a valid point of debate."

"I feel like a spy in my own country." Erika picked up her pen and wrote a note to herself.

Archie listened to the edge in her voice. He had spoken to their professors who were at the same time supportive of the radical commitment of these young journalists and worried for their safety.

"I interviewed the teachers at my old Gimnázium," Albert said. "Local officials warned parents to report teachers who taught history that was unsupportive of Moscow. History must not make children feel like they are not Soviet brothers and sisters. They want to change our history, to admire the leader, and hate the enemy, as if loyalty is one's reason for living." He spoke directly to Archie. "This was my school. I'm proud of our history. It can't be rewritten to please some Kremlin ally."

Endre put his pastry down. "Hungarian and Soviet cultures are one, they tell us. "You are nothing without the Motherland." But we have our Hungarian spirit. The leaders on our monuments are not Czars but poets," said Endre, wiping crumbs from his *Ecole Polytechnique* sweatshirt.

"Like Attila József," Archie said. He had seen the statue. He looked from one face to the next and listened to the crackle of competitive spirit.

"Exactly. Then there is the music of Germany, the philosophers of France. Moscow is more foreign to us than these," said Endre. "I covered a campus protest in support of the poets. I watched pro-Soviet demonstrators drag the poet away and order him to kiss their Communist flag. When he refused, they beat him. No one can erase this from my memory."

Endre tapped his pencil, deciding what to say.

"But the adults speak Russian at home and feel more a part of Russia than we do. We feel a *froideur*, a coolness about it when we look at the corruption, the weak legal systems. We want laws to stick, but our parents' generation expect to pay bribes."

"Parents don't understand," Erika said, her eyes peering out from behind long bangs. "Look," she leafed through her notes. "Thirty-five percent of Hungarian adults look to Moscow with respect."

Endre leaned over to see her evidence, a footnote next to the statistic.

Archie marveled at the determination of these young people and the stark evidence they discovered. Having their work published one day, and forgotten the next, would be a crime. He had to sort it out and think of something.

"How about you, Kristof? What are you working on?" Archie

asked, as he turned to the quietest member of the group.

Kristof mumbled his answer under his sparse mustache. "Poisonings and disappearances."

Everyone turned to Kristof. Although his voice was not commanding, he seemed to command influence among them.

"Pardon?" Archie said.

"This past year, we've lost two Hungarian citizens to poisonings, and one simply disappeared."

Kristof bowed his head as he read from his notes. "Idena Broneslava and Kelman Helinka, both outspoken critics of the Russian Federation, both poisoned by an unknown substance. Dr. Ilona Denuse reported that the same unidentified substance was the cause of death for both Idena and Kelman. Two days later, Dr. Denuse disappeared. The underlying causes of both deaths were listed as natural disease."

Kristof looked up, but no one questioned his research.

"I'm trying to find out what Idena and Kelman knew that could have made them targets."

Archie's mind dredged up his poisoning and Layla's, but he would never speak of them. He said that if Kristof ran into people who feared an interview, he could assure protection for their cooperation. "When I was a child living in Israel, my mother told me there was nothing worse than a lie. If I ate the last dollop of hummus or drank the last of the pomegranate juice, she caught me when I tried to blame my sister. Back then, we fought Palestinian guerillas, and you are fighting for the truth." Archie sat back in his chair.

"Who has heard of David Halberstam?" A few hands went up. "In 1962, he wrote about Vietnam for the *New York Times* before Americans knew that they had been misled about the progress that U.S. government officials claimed. In '63, President Kennedy asked the newspaper's president to transfer Halberstam out of Vietnam because his reporting was upsetting. *The Times* refused to remove Halberstam, and he won prizes for his work. *The* Times' mission of news without fear or favor has held for a century.

"For many people in our country, truth is hard to find, even scarce. You're not telling your readers what to think with every word you write. They will decide for themselves based on your facts. I'm impressed by your independent investigations, but be careful, all of you. If you feel you are in danger, I have people who will work behind the scenes to ensure your safety. No one should put their life in danger to discover the truth."

The students gathered their notes and reached for the last pastries from the box.

Kristof was last to leave. "I need to ask a favor," he said.

Archie pushed in his chair over the cement floor.

"I want to talk to Vaclav Havel."

"Havel," Archie repeated. Of all these investigations that needed protection, perhaps Kristof's was the most complex – just the kind his university needed to encourage. "I don't think that would be impossible…"

Archie walked Buda streets, wanting to do more for his journalism students. Would university publications be enough to change minds? There had to be more that he could do, but it was a gamble. He smelled fresh baked pretzels and stopped at a vendor. The paper crinkled, and the pretzel was warm to the bite with just enough salt. When he tipped the man, the vendor's smile told Archie that he owned the wagon. Everywhere around him, he saw the energy of new businesses, signs with proud family names, fruit markets, tobacconists, lace for tourists, and hardware for repairing old Soviet-era plumbing systems. He passed an old theater where workers were installing sign letters for the name of a new production. The area was pulsing with ideas once thought "not possible."

He wished his sister could see this. When he spoke to Rivka on the phone, she chided him, asking why he would support that struggling university in Hungary, the country of their birth. 'It is a little country the size of Michigan. Its output is like our Kansas. It's nothing. More people live in New York City than in Hungary. Give it up."

But he could not.

CHAPTER 56

1999 Czech Republic

Kristof was hoping to see the inside of the Palace, but Archie led him to an upstairs office in the opposite direction, a block past the ancient Orloj clock tower.

On the one hand, Kristof was disappointed with this simple ancient, wooden staircase with its old-fashioned grillwork leading to a secret office of the Czech Republic's first President. Then again, he felt heartened that the country's first President wasn't impressed by opulence and the showy power that a palace provided.

"*Ahoj.*" He watched as Vaclav slapped Archie's back in greeting. "Please sit down." He motioned to the two wooden chairs at a folding table that served as a desk. Vaclav's pre-war swivel chair stood on the other side. Behind the chair was a small window gritty with dirt and a broken window blind half raised over it. Vaclav lit a small kerosene lamp that caused the leader's face to glow. "I just had the room swept for bugs before you arrived," he said. "Moscow knows about this room and the sparser I keep it, the easier it is to find their bugs."

Kristof couldn't resist. "Have you found many?"

"Ah – the journalist begins with his questions! I'll say this, Kristof. We've found enough to know that we're a thorn in Moscow's side, and they're not giving up easily. Enough to know they feel the need to step up their chaos and division. They haven't the power to make themselves stronger with their stories."

"Most other journalists at my university agree that the repetition of propaganda ingrains itself in people's minds. The longer they repeat these lies, the harder it is for journalists. Our truth sounds like lies to them."

Vaclav nodded. "On this, we agree. Archie tells me you are promising – a brave journalist, at a time when we sorely need them."

"We appreciate your time," Archie said. "Kristof impressed me with his investigation, so when he asked to speak with you, I knew it must be important."

The two arguably most powerful men in Hungary looked at Kristof. He told them, "Years ago, my friend moved from Czechoslovakia to Russia with her family. She was at university like me and studying to be a journalist. She was investigating the suspected poisoning of a well-known local barber in Norilsk. They have put her in jail, and now Moscow is threatening to kill her family if she doesn't retract her story. We need to help her. She is a good journalist, and we need her back."

"Did your journalist friend discover what the local official was doing before the poisoning?"

"She met with the barber's wife for tea a few times to ask about his customers. The wife mentioned a series of conflicts with one of them, a former official who grew quietly wealthy over the past few years. But the wife died – a mysterious fall down the stairs."

"Did she discover what this former official was doing before the poisoning?" Havel asked.

"She said it was very difficult. No one would talk to my friend. When she asked, they said it was not possible to get answers. She has notes that she keeps hidden, but she fears that they may fall into the wrong hands. Things are dangerous." Kristof looked back and forth between the two men. "She is my best friend."

"You need to know what you're getting into." Archie said. "Twenty-two journalists are now jailed in Russia. One is a Radio Free Europe reporter who failed to register as a foreign agent. She was visiting her mother. Many are held without trial in Lefortovo, an old, crumbling fortress built to interrogate criminals. This is how Russia sends signals that journalists aren't safe from their reach."

"So tell us about this young woman, Kristof," Havel said.

"Like Kafka, she is the harshest critic of her work." Kristof hoped his Kafka reference would interest Havel. "Kafka's alienation and disconnection is her own, and she says I am her Kafka." His face reddened. Had he meant to say that? "I mean, when we write together, we can finish one another's sentences."

"I am a fan," Havel said. True enough, he thought of how much that first day in his office reminded him of the castle that Kafka made famous. "I think more often of the Frenchman Alfred Jarry's influence, but there is no Czech like Kafka. Tell me more."

"There is the bug, the insect. On June 3rd, the anniversary of Kafka's death, she walked through Old Town and left insects she'd made by the places he frequented. She used twisted pipe cleaners and felt to make bugs that she left near his coffee shop, a book store, a park bench. She's in danger, and I can't hold enough of her in my hands," Kristof said. Kafka's words were not lost on Archie and Havel.

"Russian prisons are a nightmare. She's renounced her parents' Russia. She wants freedom without the influence of the Russian *kompromat*. She told me Kafka lived during a time of technological upheaval, and here we are again in a new one. She struggles, Ser Havel, to live her life without compromise." Kristof blinked his eyes. "I have to help her."

"Archie?" Havel wondered about connections.

"I'm not sure that my network extends to Norilsk, but let me ask my friends in intelligence if they have connections that might help us," Archie said. "We have to think several steps ahead of our adversaries' capabilities."

"Kristof, it sounds like your good friend has found some damning evidence that Moscow is eager to make disappear. They are more than able to do it. Men will talk to their barbers." Havel leaned toward the young man. "But remember, we won't underestimate what Archie Hoffman is capable of."

Kristof told them as much as he knew. Now that they had spoken together, he knew this would be a story he would tell his children someday. When he listened to Archie and Vaclav speak of counterintelligence and infiltration, it sounded like ideas that came from a spy movie.

"You have the heart of a poet, the patience of a fisherman, and now you'll need the stealth of a wolf. Let's go to work," Havel told Kristof.

"Once we get her parents out of Russia and into a safe country, we'll look at what we have," Archie said. "There are ways we can get your news out beyond the Czech Republic to Western European countries. Once they see what's happening, the pressure builds. The Kremlin will have the challenge of defending the poisoning of its own people. And her name?" He turned to Kristof.

"Nicoletta."

CHAPTER 57

2000 Austria

It started in America. But hundreds of European dot-com startups suddenly sank on March 10th when the bubble burst. Clickboo, a sporting goods company start-up, was spending spectacularly, struggling to stay above water while sales were in fractions. Traders looked to the news that described the stock market as a force with human abilities and demands. Initial Public Offerings dropped dramatically. Hundreds of companies scrambled to consolidate and ran into other companies, anxious to sell with no one to buy.

In his Vienna office days before, Archie had suspected the rout and had sold much of his tech investment beforehand, transferring to boring defensive stocks. Even his prized Apple stock plummeted to 22 American cents a share. As an advisor, he made multiple calls to warn his investors. Tech companies were growing too fast with little capital to back them up. Money wasn't cheap anymore. Greedy stock speculation, formerly as effortless as dart throwing, was now a dangerous game. When the day came, Archie took a steady stream of calls, smoothing the ruffled feathers of those who hadn't heeded his advice. If they stayed the course, these solid companies would reward them. Fortunately, Europe was not as severely injured as shareholders in the States were.

Archie was looking through his diminished portfolio when he took a call from Rivka. "They'll kick us out of our brownstone," she wailed. "It's ours! You have to find a way to keep paying for it. It's our home. We can't leave. Archie, do something."

"Rivka, I'm not a billionaire now. So I got dinged by the headwinds, but I'm alive, and you're alive. I'll trim the sails and stay the course. Logan and Wilson are with you. Think of what's important." His voice sounded relieved, a burden lifted.

"Dinged? Archie, you got *shellacked*. We're not on the kibbutz anymore. Life in New York is expensive. My salary at the university isn't enough. If you can't pay, we'll be out in the street. You don't know how crazy things are here."

"Archie sighed. "I can still pay your mortgage."

"But what about the SUV?"

"That too."

Her voice calmed. "Don't worry me like that."

"I keep telling investors at meetings every day that the investment isn't gone until it's sold. If you're invested in good companies, they will go up. All we do now is wait."

"That's easy for you to say. What if you're wrong? Then where will we be?"

Archie's heart sank. Did Rivka have any feelings for him anymore, or was it all about paying bills? "I can take care of you, Rivka. I'll always take care of you."

"Okay, but more importantly, I need your help. This is bigger."

"Of course. What is it?"

"These liberals, have you heard? They're connected with the FBI and the CIA. They're part of the Deep State, the secret fourth branch of government. Now, they're forcing young people into the sex trade. They hold them in an underground base in Mammoth Cave in Kentucky."

"What?"

"I know. Isn't it terrible? I shudder to think of something like that happening to Logan. Anyway, this man was accused of kidnapping these children on flights to his private island along with important men from all over the world, high-ranking men in politics and corporate life, so that they could have sex with the kids. Of course, it didn't happen. It was just a story to take attention away from Mammoth Cave. So this man is in jail now, and he's going to spread lies about taking celebrities to his island for sex with minors. The only thing we can do is kill him before he lies. You have contacts, don't you? Someone who could get into the jail and make it look like an accident?"

"No, Rivka. You're confused. This Deep State thing is a myth. It's disinformation. Think it through. If it's so secret, how can you know about it?" Archie didn't believe what he was hearing. "Rivka, these – stories – are coming from foreign state-controlled news outlets, not the US. They're masters of manipulation and are weaponizing information to confuse people. There are thousands of their *mafiya* groups around the world. They bribe people in government and operate mostly in frauds and scams, but they're now changing to money laundering in the US, including credit card fraud. They are so deep in the legal sector that it's difficult to catch them."

"Archie, you're making this up. You think you can hold the world like Atlas, and it spins at your will? You're so naive. The people I know have proof. I can't talk about this anymore. It's just too frightening."

"I'm just saying be careful. These people are dangerous. They assassinate political adversaries and interfere in elections."

"You're wrong. It's the sex traffickers. We have to stop them. I thought I could trust my brother to understand. All right, then. I'll go somewhere else."

Archie tried to talk, but she had already hung up. He rolled his eyes and whistled. It's just her concern about finances, he thought. She can't be serious.

CHAPTER 58

2000 Czech Republic

When Archie arrived at Prague's Natural History Museum after more than a few misdirections and dodges, his feet were already wet from walking along mud-covered streets. From the outside, the museum looked as if it hadn't sustained any more damage than a high water line around the exterior. Water from the flood that had disrupted half of Hungary had receded. Still, the mold and mildew left behind threatened the priceless cultural artifacts in the city's most family-friendly museum.

Floods from heavy rainfall damaged half of the country in the days after the banks of the Vltava overflowed to flood much of Prague. People's homes were ruined, but the old town and castle were protected by mobile walls, which held back the water. The National History Museum saved many precious items that were removed in time.

Inside, a heaviness filled the galleries and alcoves, echoing with the sounds of volunteers pushing mud into the hallways, and then into the street. Archie's requests to locate Havel were followed by finger-pointing directions. People saved their energy for the brooms. In the midst of a handful of volunteers, he found Havel and Dagmar in the African/Asian gallery, pushing garage brooms to move the mud toward the doorway.

"Archie!" Vaclav called. "Someone get him a broom now!" He swept like a madman.

Archie knew better than to talk to him during this Herculean task. Rivka had called and Logan had run away from home. The first person Archie wanted to tell was Havel, who knew so much more about the human condition than he did—the man who might tell him how to help Logan. But now was not the time, so he took the offered broom and swept, folding the sludge in accordion-like breaks. After hours of work, taking special care around the soaked wooden display supports that were too big to move, the volunteers inched the mud closer to the doorway until the worst of it had cleared the threshold and the floor could dry.

When the room was free of mud, volunteers found spots in other galleries and continued their work. Seating had been removed, so Vaclav, Dagmar, and Archie leaned against a marble wall to rest. "We can't get this mud out soon enough," Havel explained. "It's the mold - dangerous to the artifacts."

Archie expressed sorrow over the flood that had overwhelmed half of the Czech Republic, the worst flood in a hundred years.

"It's beyond belief," Vaclav said. "Every able person has been hired to clean up homes, then businesses. The museums are our pride, our lifeblood, but I can't ask people to help when homes are still filled with mud and silt. So we have volunteers. Every day we clean another museum. Did you see the Vltava today? Calm, placid serene again." His head sank to his chest. "All this mud goes back to the river."

"I've never seen anything like it," Archie said. "And I've never seen you so tired."

"You should see the subway tunnels. Filled with mud." Vaclav said. "We are at a standstill."

Dagmar leaned back, pushing back a wave of hair that had escaped the bun secured with military efficiency. Her face was glowing, and her makeup melted. "He works like a maniac," she frowned at him. "I tell him to rest, but no."

"Two years they say," Vaclav closed his eyes with his head against the wall. "It will take us two years, at this rate, to repair the damage."

"I have two days," Archie said. "I can push one more broom for you."

"Yes, yes, I know you came here to discuss other matters. We'll get to that, but first, the mud and sludge."

The three walked to the next gallery, with its dinosaurs and ancient sharks, and started again.

"I can't wait any more. We've broomed two galleries, and you need to stop, Havel."

Vaclav tried to walk around Archie's outstretched arm, but Dagmar also added her arm.

"Vaclav, enough. Just listen to what Archie came for."

Archie waited until he knew Havel wasn't going to bolt. "I have a piece from Kristof to show you, and we're getting closer to releasing the friend we've been talking about." Archie didn't want to mention Nicoletta by name. "But what I need is an idea. With all the noise, my journalism students' words are buried. My students are doing great work, uncovering necessary information. But with the *kompromat* escalating, no one listens to the truth. Your people trust you. Help me here."

"I don't know what to say, Archie. It's a battle every day." Havel's exhaustion was bone-deep as he hunched his back against the wall. "I was planning a trip to the US with Dagmar, strengthening relations with NATO and promoting our entrance into it. We wanted to see the New York Public Library and Dagmar wanted to visit the Metropolitan Museum of Art's Costume Institute. Then, on to Miami to talk to Cuban Americans about human rights and the power of democracy at Florida State University. And instead, I have the flood.

"But I know about trust." He leaned on the broom in his hand. "Yes, all of the Czech Republic is furious with the flood, but I have built up their trust over these years with safe neighborhoods and new businesses. There is hope, and the people have stayed with me so far. I don't want to betray that trust. Every day, I must prove to them that their confidence was not misplaced.

"I see what you mean," Archie said. "I have to find a way."

CHAPTER 59

2000 Hungary

The basement secure room at the university smelled less musty. A good cleaning, a new coat of paint, and better lighting all helped. Archie opened the box of sweet rolls and looked at the gathering from his end of the table, the students' faces serious as they ordered the papers in front of them. Since their last meeting, Archie had ruminated over their big question: how would truth overcome the sparkle and flash of disinformation? Other university papers had agreed to publish their stories to get the word out, but it wasn't enough. Thanks to his conversation with Havel after the disastrous Czech flood, he had another idea – a moonshot challenge he had to try.

Archie reached into his pockets and brought out fistfuls of local currency. "As part of your journalism study, I want you to visit your local newspapers."

Tomas looked at the money. "No one reads them," he said.

Archie ignored him. "So we have these local papers from the areas where you grew up. They don't have much money, but you can help by uncovering evidence. It will take time, but you can do it. Show them your work. Make your fact-checking beyond reproach – and not one name misspelled."

At that, the eyes around the table turned to Tamas. He looked back and stuffed a bite of cruller into his mouth.

"Space in local papers is expensive, and you may not get much, so you must make every line count like that American journalist Russel Baker. He said writing a column was like doing ballet in a telephone booth. But we can help them expand readership, and they can help us."

"People have slippery memories," Archie said. "They forget what things were like for their families in World War II with Hitler. You can change that. Here's why. First of all, the autocrats watch the big news sources. They don't have the resources to watch all the small ones that need money and writers. When you graduate, you'll need a place to start. What better place to start than in your hometowns with people you know who will trust you to tell the truth? Take money for your transportation, food, and lodging, if you need it. Spend a night. Tell the newspaper editor you want three of their biggest weekly ads for three weeks. Some ads can go to local businesses, and some can announce your meeting."

"What meeting?" Erika said.

"Arrange for a town hall meeting for you and the editor at the local fire station. At the end of the third week, arrange for security. Firefighters will probably do it. With so many town halls on the same day, it will be difficult for the opposition to check them all."

"What will the town halls be about?" Kristof said.

"You decide. Talk about what you've told me – your research – the truth. Expose local corruption. You are establishing a conduit for more news and a relationship with the community. Teach the villagers about the difference between a government that works with them and a government that only wants a single all-powerful man who works like a demonizing machine to suppress them."

"What is this for?" Kristof asked.

Archie paused. "I was young after the Second World War. That sounds like a long time ago to you, but after the West rebuilt

Germany and Japan into free-voting, rules-based powerhouses, we thought that authoritarian strongmen wouldn't stand a chance."

"Now we know that for Europe to be safe, we need a free press with more access to evidence, not more power to shut it down or create *kompromat* from it. Words are cheaper than weapons. Your words can fix what is broken, and your evidence is more substantial than the strongmen. Do you want to give the world away to a country that sparks enough anger to destroy itself and Europe?"

Kristof blinked and swallowed hard.

"We think of power as an absolute, an understood moral value," Archie said. "But how powerful is one despot's nation against an alliance of nations with the will of the people behind them? Even in the new century, the shadow of the Russian Federation embraces those who feel they were left behind, that outlawing reality will give them rights that everyone else owes them. How powerful is one nation riddled with double-speak against a nation with a free press?"

Their time was up, but the students didn't move. "There was a famous broadcast journalist in the States, Edward R. Morrow. He said, 'Truth is the best propaganda.' You are too young to be on a Russian watch list – you have the strength of anonymity. If you ever doubt the importance of what you are doing, remember the future of free societies, and your free will – are powered by your words."

"We can beat lies by getting out in front of them, exposing them first," Archie said. "Millions of pages of disinformation are produced every day. The more of it we can denounce, the more we can refute with real evidence, the weaker their propaganda machine will be." Archie shrugged. "I'm not sure how this will work yet, but I know it will be important to each of you. Here is a way to get an honest reputation as a journalist. Think of it as imagining a better world for the next generation. Start small and work up. I'll see you in three weeks after your town halls. We'll see how it's going."

The students looked at one another. With their other classes, this was more work than they'd signed up for, but they divided the folded bills, traded time schedules for trains, and ideas for newspaper ads.

Archie turned to Kristof. "Have you heard from our friend?"

Kristof pulled a folded paper from his pocket. "Tell me what you know. Is there anything?" He handed the letter over, and his eyes begged Archie to do something.

My Dear Friend,

You can't write me. It is too dangerous. I have learned the system here in prison, and I bribed a woman who is also here on false charges. I won't say how this note got out, but a little extra food goes a long way.

Prison life is enlightening. I am writing articles in my head for when I am free and can get them on paper, which is scarce. You will find a way, a source to get these printed, yes? Everything the guards tell us is so far removed from the truth, that it is laughable. They try to wear us down but strengthen our resolve by the day.

I could tell you things, inhumane work, mistreatment, little food, but I will survive this. I worry for my family. I will get out in a year, I hope,

Your dear friend,
N

Archie put his hand on Kristof's shoulder. "Havel and I are working on this, Kristof. It would be dangerous to tell you how. Nicoletta's parents' safety has taken longer than we had hoped, but we can work faster on Nicoletta's release once they are secured." He folded the letter and gave it back to Kristof. "I know you will be a brave information navigator whom your community will trust. Don't give up."

CHAPTER 60

2000 Russia

Now that Nicoletta's family was safe, there was a small window of possibility for Zolt to plan a scheme for her escape. His team had collected intel on the Leforitsa - 9 prison guard change schedule, but its accuracy was uncertain. The high-risk plan left few options. Zolt adjusted the thick straps on his Kevlar backpack and counted the guards he could see in the prison tower and patrolling the catwalks over the top of the dark walls. It was a moonless night in early spring, but in the Russian north, bitter gusts of wind swept up his back as he sat in the shadows of a ditch. The water-resistant fabric of his clothing was designed for quiet movement, but thin. On his haunches outside of the prison, his knees scraped the still-frozen ground. It had to be now. In a few hours, predicted snowfall would make their tracks too easy to follow.

So much of his work was intelligence gathering, waiting, and watching. But when these life-or-death efforts presented themselves, Zolt remembered why he was willing to risk everything. Despite the unforgiving cold, he felt an electric impulse at the prospect of freeing Nicoletta. In his mind, he studied the route to her corridor and cell. He knew how many locked doors there were between the stairway door and her chamber. But how many guards would they face after the alarm sounded?

With a zip of his pocket, his cold fingers fumbled with the signal laser. Taking careful aim, he signaled the team in the woods that he was ready. They could not signal back. Their Russian vehicle waited with clothes and forged papers that should get them through any unforeseen checkpoint en route to a fishing boat in Turkey. From there, her train ticket to Budapest would deliver her to one of Archie's safe spaces near the university and Kristof. Together, they would write the article that might save her life.

Zolt crept along the extended wall of the prison yard. Capturing the terrorists in front of the Temple B'nai Shalom in New York had been quick—nothing like this interminable crawl. Another menacing searchlight approached with its sweeping expanse. Zolt leaned tight against the wall until it passed. Thankful for the absence of snow and bootprints, he made his way to the door.

From another pocket, he removed an electronic device with stiff fingers, only to watch it tumble to the ground. Scrambling to retrieve it, he tapped buttons and applied the device in a pushing movement to the outside coded entry keypad of the reinforced steel door. He checked above for movement of the emergency lockdown gate but detected no motion. Reconfiguring for the second steel door, he placed the device and pushed it once more. Nothing happened, but that was nothing to panic about. Malware had been installed on the motion sensors a few days earlier during a staged fight in the cafeteria. In a few minutes, he reset the code and applied it to the entry keypad, hearing the lock release.

The hallway inside was dimly lit, and the air carried the heavy scent of metal. Looming overhead were security cameras located atop the stairwell doorways. He waited to see the silver crescent of the camera and trod noiselessly up three flights when each camera was scanning the opposite side. As he opened the door, he heard curses and gruff voices. A shot of anxiety coursed through him, making him regret all the coffee he had drunk earlier. Sweat trickled down his back as he forced his thoughts to ignore the image in his mind of Nicoletta, motionless, from a guard's bullet.

The Russian voices faded down the hallway, and he opened the third stairwell door, entering Nicoletta's corridor. He waited for the camera's silver crescent and heard a cough. Counting the doors to her cell as he passed, he tried to make his footsteps as quiet as the sleeping inmate in each cell.

He squinted to see into the dark cell, with only minimal light filtering from the hallway. What if he had miscounted the cells? Adjusting his device, he released her lock and regretted the soft clicking sound. She gasped and sat up in bed. In the faint light, her short, nearly white hair and thin face may have been the one in the photos he had seen. Zolt raised his hands and slowly walked toward her. Would she be able to move soon enough? Slowly, he leaned over and whispered *Kristof* in her ear. Instantly, she gathered her journal, and Zolt backed into the corridor. Barefoot, she bolted out of the cell after him, leaving her prison shoes behind.

Zolt was surprised by the speed with which Nicoletta moved. As they raced down the corridor, his frequent looks behind him revealed that she was all skin and bones, clutching her journal in a tight grip.

A guard appeared from around the corner as they approached the last stairwell. Zolt lunged toward him, his hand shooting out, clamping the guard's neck and pushing against the wall with a squeezing grip. Zolt's hand shook as he watched the guard's eyes wide with panic. A wheezing sound from his throat – one arm swinging at Zolt's face – Zolt's grip, now shaky, was unremitting, and the weakened guard, who had ceased his wheezing, crumpled unconscious to the floor. In the uncomfortable quiet, Nicoletta looked at Zolt and gingerly stepped over the guard. Now they raced down the stairwell, careless of the noise they made or what the cameras saw.

Once outside the prison gates, sirens blaring in their ears – Zolt yelled, "Faster – ." His random zigzag pattern slowed Nicoletta, but the woods were within reach. "Can't run – " she gasped. He cut the razor wire in front of them and slipped through. Shots fired, and Zolt looked back to see her falling dangerously behind. Afraid she had been wounded, he turned and stumbled. They had come so far, and she was so close to the perimeter when snow began to fall. Nicoletta cleared the wire and caught up just as shots rang perilously close, and they disappeared into the forest line together.

Behind the safety of the trees, he told her what they would do. "A black car – clothes and papers –" Zolt tried to catch his breath. "Then a boat – we'll get you out of here."

Nicoletta gulped for air. "My feet – " she said, looking back at the prison lights and shuddering from the speed of the escape. "Need to wrap them – " She shifted her weight from one frigid foot to the other.

Zolt removed his backpack and took out a tactical flashlight, pointing it down at her bare feet, scratched and jagged with blood. He hadn't noticed that she had no shoes, but then again, her bare feet made for a quieter exit. The wooded area did little to shield them from wind gusts, and he watched her wrap her scarecrow arms around her thin Russian-issue prison garment and her journal. Sirens blared on, and in the scanning searchlights, he saw beads of perspiration on her face.

From the direction of the prison, they heard something new: dogs barking. Zolt had not prepared for dogs. From his jacket, he pulled an extra pair of socks. She pulled them on while he unzipped his weapons-laden jacket and gave her the insulated long-sleeved shirt he wore under it.

The shirt was still warm from his body, but the right sleeve was ripped and bloody. "Look – " she said. "Your arm – "

"Let's go. The boat won't wait," he said.

Their circuitous route through the pine and larch woods meant that stones, twigs, and needles pierced the socks, making them nearly useless. The barking grew louder, and Zolt could hear voices shouting directions. At the bottom of a steep slope, they spied vehicle parking lights on a gravel road. Zolt took her hand, and they climbed down together.

The driver's well-armed partner opened the back door. Zolt and Nicoletta were barely seated when the tires spun on the gravel, and they were off. Zolt reached into a sack and handed her a pair of jeans, a bulky knit sweater, and worn shoes, which she painfully slipped on before cuffing up the jeans to a walkable length.

In Russian, she asked the partner in front for a first aid kit and searched for a roll of gauze to wrap Zolt's wounded arm.

Zolt took the kit from her, ignoring her protests. "Feet first," he said, motioning to her and gently holding an ankle to inspect the cuts.

For Nicoletta, the pain of the cleaning swabs and iodine was worse than that of the scrapes from their escape, but in admiration, she refused to make a sound. For her safety, she couldn't ask his name. "You did all of this and now I am free," she said.

By the time they reached the pier, warmth was returning to their bodies. The driver parked the black *Samara* near the dock across from an old fishing scow; engines were rumbling in the darkness, and there was a bluish light shining through the foggy windows in the captain's wheelhouse. Nicoletta hobbled up the gangway in the shoes that were one size too small, grateful for warm clothing. As crew members cast off the lines, the engine sputtered and turned over; they were underway. Alone on the deck, she crouched low as she was told to do. With no written directions, she had only Zolt's instructions for finding Kristof in Budapest.

CHAPTER 61

2000 Hungary

Mr. Hoffman called in some favors so you and your family could be safe." Kristof looked at his Russian classmate and shuddered. Here she was, complicated, keen-eyed, and unbroken. Thinner than ever, she sat beside him in a Budapest coffee shop near the university where they'd had so many undergraduate conversations. He'd never shared so much of himself with anyone. Now, she would have been his classmate in graduate school if she hadn't been imprisoned. Until a few hours ago, he wasn't sure that he would ever see her alive again.

Nicoletta blew aside a quick puff of cigarette smoke. Her nervous fingers tapped the counter and then gripped the cup handle. "Archie got me out, but are we safe?" she asked. Her dark eyes were riveted on his. "My family had to change their identities because of me. To protect them, I can never see them again, and it's my fault." She shook her head as if the spoken words punished her. "I must work harder to expose the lies that forced my parents to flee for their lives. I have information to add to the article. The prison guards got bored. We got to know each other, and they started leaking. Let's find a place where no one will hear us." With her sore feet, she carefully eased herself off the stool and grabbed his belt, pulling him upright.

From a bench in a leafy park, he sneaked glances at his friend to make sure she was really there – the stubby, strong fingers that wrote bullet points with lightning speed, the angular shoulders that still shrugged with regularity, one dangling earring with tiny bells, its match lost since before he'd known her. "You call him Archie and you've never met him. He's Mr. Hoffman."

Nicoletta looked out at the trees and breathed in the air.

Kristof took a folded paper from his pocket. "These are the types of stories the paper is working on, so you can get an idea of how different ours will be. The village news isn't used to scandals."

Flood in Helmut farm barley field

County supervisor paid double, board to vote yes on oil company provision

320-year-old Orthodox Bible found in attic

She raised an eyebrow. "How exciting, that one."

Sewage backed up in Novo Selo, workers disappeared

Neighbors help AIDs survivor abandoned by family

Escaped pig still on the loose after 3 days.

"That fucking pig in the jail." Nicoletta stood up. "What he did to my friend – "

Kristof reached for her hand and held it until she sat back down.

"My friend, Tonya, was sentenced to prison in the Arctic, the Polar Wolf prison, for her article on the abuse of Chechens. The little food they gave her was rancid. Cells were cold. At night, she could hear the screams from beatings. She worked long hours outdoors in frigid weather, and then they sent her to solitary for having part of her shirt untucked. All of this was meant to break her spirit, but when they released her, she researched the leader's palace and the money he stole to pay for it. She showed me pictures, and they are grotesque." Nicoletta sucked in the smoke from her cigarette.

"They told me that next time, they'll send me to the Arctic. Tonya almost died for writing the truth. Their warnings won't stop us." She looked at him. "Now Tonya has disappeared. I have to find her."

"No one will blame you if you start taking stories of lost cows and downed trees," Kristof said.

"*I* will blame me." She pointed to her heart. "I am the Russia of Solzhenitsyn, Chekov, Pushkin, and Tolstoy, not the rogue Russia that imprisons us for truth-telling, not the slithering-bag-of-vipers Russia." She shrugged, "The buggy food, the taunts of guards, all bad, but the worst was the aquarium."

"What's that?"

"It's a glass cage they put you in when you are on trial, and they make a big deal out of padlocking you into it. They say it's for your protection, but that is not true. It is psychological abuse to terrorize the innocent. It's stuffy and hot, and all you can smell is your own sweat. It's about repression, caging their accusers and putting them on display as an example for all to see."

"I don't understand."

"What's not to understand? It's there to make you look and feel like a dangerous criminal. But I had a trick of my own. When it was my turn to speak, I spouted off one of our favorite philosophers, the Russian Isaiah Berlin, in Russian court. I told them that to deny us leads to destruction. Eggs are broken, but the omelet is not in sight. There is only the infinite number of eggs, human lives, ready for the breaking. And in the end, the passionate idealists forget the omelet and just go on breaking eggs."

"Isaiah Berlin – good choice. What did they say?"

"They didn't say anything for a while, and the silence told me that they had heard me. Maybe they realized that what I said was true – though they wouldn't admit it. Then the judge said I was too loud and convicted me."

"But now that Archie got me out, I'm thinking about a detention house that the guards were bragging about," Nicoletta said. "It has to be where they moved my friend."

"It's too dangerous."

"This is not a hotel. Here, they wear down their prisoners with hard labor and deplorable conditions. Then, they claim that the prisoner died of natural causes. There is no time to wait. They say is not possible to get into the detention house, but I will chew over it."

By the following afternoon, they had run their article by one of Kristof's professors, and their draft was complete. They took the train to Kristof's village, Visolloosollo, outside of Budapest and waited to see the village news editor. Kristof had been here many times: a one-story building needing paint, a red handprint painted on the door as a threat. A metal sign on the editor's room wall displayed his humor: *Paris Street.* The office was lived-in with folders stacked, bookshelves packed, and papers strewn across his desk. The editor listened to Nicoletta, but he wasn't sure about her. She was not Hungarian. Her language was fluent but coarse, and her heavy kohl eye makeup, multiple piercings, and spiky hair did not appear like that of a hard-working journalist searching for truth.

After Kristof gave their sources, the editor gave him an update on his article about the Hungarians Idena Broneslava and Kelman Helinka, both outspoken critics of the Kremlin, poisoned by an unknown substance. "Your sources check out so far. Do you have sources for discovering what information they possessed that made them targets?"

Kristof told him about a possible source in Spain, but his time was limited with his classes in graduate school. The editor interrupted him and fired multiple questions at Nicoletta.

"Look, you," Nicoletta fired back. "I just spent months in prison with murderers, thieves, and even a rat. I believe in exposing these bastards who want to destroy our countries and our people for fun and profit. I don't need – "

"What she means is," Kristof broke in, "I couldn't have found the evidence we have without her – tenacious – spirit. I've known Nicoletta for two years, and I believe in her. I have evidence and trust that what she has found is the truth."

The editor narrowed his eyes at them both. His local reputation was on the line with each issue.

Kristof reviewed their sources again and listened to the editor.

"We're not the *Budapest Chronica* or the *Prague Noviny Blesk*," he told them. "But we need journalism that breaks the spell of *kompromat*. Maybe you can ask your benefactor for money for research and fact-checking for deep-dive reporting. Our checkbook balance rises and falls, and right now, the fact-checker I can afford is me. Maintaining trust is my job. I serve the community." The editor poked his chest.

Kristof looked at the award on the wall over the editor's chair. The editor had talked with Kristof about his process of writing the award-winning article on the cleanup of a polluted lake, a lake filled with industrial chemicals and silt.

"Most of our readers want comment sections, sports, and features, not what they need to know," the editor said. "This is not babies or weddings. There is a cost for our paper, the cost of a cup of coffee. Many people will go for the coffee. I think your article will make them reach for the paper over the coffee, help them feel involved in the tempo of our country, and encourage them to keep their ears close to the ground." He looked at the copy and made his decision. "It goes above the fold."

Nicoletta and Kristof were stunned. *Above the fold* was the most prominent spot on any newspaper. Once the article was on the editor's desk, Kristof felt a new relief that was soon overcome by his worry over Nicoletta's next move. Once the article was out, Russia would have to let her go rather than lose face trying to reimprison her. On their walk to the train station, he reached for a side hug, unsure how his moody friend would take it. She hugged back even harder.

"Mr. Hoffman has to see what you found out. He has to see it first. He's not going to like it."

"This is too fucking big to hold back, Kristof. Didn't you say Archie wanted your university journalists to get out shit like this? We'll finish this second article together and tell your people that you have something. They should be ready to publish as soon as we get the word. We'll hold it back a day until you get the okay from Archie, but no longer. We are plank walking, but we will expose these bastards one funeral at a time."

"I have Zolt's number."

"Who is Zolt?"

Kristof explained that Zolt operated like a hospital triage supervisor. "He sorts through all the messages to Mr. Hoffman and only gives him what is most important. If anyone can convince Archie to okay releasing this catastrophic issue," Kristof added, "it's Zolt. He's the one who got you out of prison."

"This Zolt is a brave man." Nicoletta stopped walking and looked at Kristof. She hadn't known the name of the man who had given his shirt when he was wounded, who'd helped her escape. "Kristof, you called him Archie instead of Mr. Hoffman." She grabbed the lapels of his jacket. " And back there, you told the editor that you believed in me."

He returned her look and felt his face blush, the impact of her stare etching itself in his mind.

CHAPTER 62

2000 Hungary

By the time that Archie was in the air, the university students had been protesting for over 24 hours. He looked down at the monogram on his cuff and regretted cutting short his visit with his nephew. If the protest was over when he arrived, he hoped to gather his journalists to find out the details. Students and professors were embroiled in the university's forced closing, and a handful of his journalists had embedded themselves with the protesters. Before the flight, Archie had asked what they needed. Zolt told him that the students' toes were blistered from walking. Hiking had taught Archie what to do. "Take them ointment and socks," he said as he packed a few belongings to catch the plane from New York. "And Zolt, get ten boxes of those layered fruit pastries from the Ruszwurm Bakery."

Kristof and Nicoletta heard about the university protest and hitchhiked back to Budapest to join in. Students marched over the Chain Bridge, through Clark Adams Square, and onto the steps of Buda Castle. Kristof gauged the mood of the crowd while Nicoletta interviewed marchers and asked Kristof to get her interviews to his village editor. Scribbling notes, she imagined the story flying out of her notebook and into the world. Besides Save Our School signs, messages about freedom seemed to multiply, signs demanding to make the films they wanted, and having books chosen by professors, not the government. The journalists told her that the protest march had started with a few hundred marchers, but by the time Nicoletta and Kristof had arrived, locals had joined the students in a countless throng.

Torches appeared as the second night fell. Kristof saw Erika from his journalism class standing on the Buda Castle steps, speaking to the marchers. Mr. Hoffman must have released her from incarceration. "We want free access to our history and culture with nothing left out. If this is a test of strength, we will win!"

It chilled him to see soldiers on rooftops, guns at the ready. But there were so many protesters that the will of the students prevailed. Like the protests in 1848 and the 1956 uprising, they had the support of the people. Like Genevieve Marx's poem, they would not tolerate this to be "woven into forgetting."

We will not let the monsters overtake us," Nicoletta told Kristof before she ran up the castle steps. She stood on the steps and shouted to the crowd. Erika turned and handed her the megaphone. "Instead of being ripped apart, we are united in our independence. Our stories and our people will not vanish. In our radical enlightenment, we know our true friends from the false ones." She gripped the megaphone tighter while the crowd cheered. "We will not let the monsters take over the school!" she yelled. "We are the monster killers!"

Erika took the megaphone back and led the chant, picked up by the crowd. "Monster killers, monster killers!"

Nicoletta looked out over the sea of chanting people. She read the banners held high in the torchlight. *No red terror. No police state takeover.* She grabbed the megaphone and told them her story of going to prison for her work, and how much a free press meant to her. "Let us learn freely," she said amidst cheers from the crowd.

Nicoletta ran down to join Kristof and an older woman handed her a torch. The Buda Castle shone before them in its evening illumination.

Kristof looked at her. "You were magnificent."

"This unity, Kristof," Her eyes were shining. "Everything here right now is worth everything." She looked around. "Some of these older people must remember the 1956 uprising. I spoke with one *babushka* who lived through the times of famine – so strong. I need to interview more of them and record their history."

Kristof kept an eye on the water cannons positioned beside them. "I'm watching for a path of escape if we need one."

Nicoletta was invigorated. "We can break them."

"We'll take your story to my editor together. Everybody in the village knows my family. People will feel comfortable talking to me. I can introduce you, and they'll be comfortable with you." Kristof didn't remind her of the red hand painted on the editor's door, a warning about news that disparaged the Party.

Archie arrived late and stood behind the crowd with Zolt and the fruit pastries. Zolt and an associate held the boxes while hungry students devoured the treats. The sea of students and local Hungarian people dumbfounded Archie. Then he spotted Erica on the steps of the castle. Once Nicoletta began to speak, he knew what Kristof saw in her. She captivated the crowd and spoke to the power of truth. What a team she and Kristof made.

This was Kristof's last term of graduate school – if the university didn't close before the end of the term. Archie would miss his dives into evidence. Vienna had a lively collage of news sources, and Archie thought of Vienna's *Der Standard.* The editor would snap up these two young reporters, these information navigators. Next year, when Erica graduated, he would help her, too. He would remember this moment if he ever doubted his decision to create the university.

CHAPTER 63

2000 Austria

Zoli, we have to get this story out now. Havel's presidency is at risk unless the newspapers get the story out before the fiction spreads."

Chertok had blitzed the government-run news sources with a story that would eclipse the university protest and harm Archie. Chertok's sources told fabrications of embezzlement and the murder of an elderly Hungarian judge who had in reality died in his sleep of a heart attack. Paid actors called for protests to enrage citizens and for Havel to step down. Havel's security was sound, but only the news media could keep the minds of the people from being swayed. Archie had sent an encrypted warning message to Havel before they took the car to the airport.

"It's working. The journalism students' stories establish trust, and the local newspapers are working with them. We have to make sure that Kristof's and Nicoletta's story and their byline reach more small papers. The truth will make its way through before the protests take hold. By then, Kristof and Nicoletta will be too well known to target for revenge."

"You didn't tell Rivka that you were coming?"

"Absolutely not." Archie noticed relief on Zolt's face. "We can't risk an intercepted call."

In the car, Zolt handed him a sheet of bullet points about an American conspiracy group. Outside of Havel's story, Dominion Directive was working with Moldova's charismatic leader, Alexei Vacuna to undermine the people's will and strengthen authoritarian sensitivities in neighboring countries. Rivka was listed as the newest member of the eight directors in three American states planning to use Vacuna's tactics at home. At the bottom of the bullet-pointed page, Archie read that Nicoletta's informant had been poisoned and was in serious condition in hospital. And now Archie was flying to New York to protect his sister.

"That's our warning. Does Kristof need additional protection?" Archie said. "Has he been warned to check anything he touches and eat only packaged foods that he buys himself?"

Zolt nodded. "We have extra protection for Zorica now. She was instrumental in gathering this information from informants in her home country." The car pulled up to the terminal and Zolt gave him the last manilla envelope. "Read this on the plane. It's Kristof's and Nicoletta's second article. You won't like it. It will explain what I haven't had time to explain – a clear picture."

Once the plane was off the ground, Archie had a scotch and then another. The look on Zolt's face was a worry. That and the fact that he looked like he could have used another ten hours of sleep. What had Rivka gotten herself into?

Zolt told him that Nicoletta and Kristof were waiting for Archie's consent to publish. It was time-sensitive and he advised Archie to approve it before he read it. Archie was skeptical, but after those bullet points, he consented before boarding.

When he was in cruising altitude on his way to New York, he finished his scotch and drew the long-form article from the manilla envelope. The headline read, *American Woman Unmasked in Covert Plot to Destabilize Central European Democracy: Secret Authoritarian Group Exposed.*

Archie ruffled through multiple pages, unable to focus past the headline. Once he had started reading the initial paragraphs, he could tell that the evidence was extensive. Apparently, Nicoletta's informant had been in the audience during a keynote address Rivka gave in New York. He spoke with Rivka afterward about her points, flaws in democracy, its chaotic nature, and the need for stability through central authoritarian leadership.

The far-right group, The Dominion Directive, were completely absorbed in her speech about Thomas Jefferson and hidden documents that she had discovered in the archives of an unnamed university. In private letters and diaries hidden for centuries, she cast doubt on the Founding Fathers' support of democracy. In times of crisis, like the Whiskey Rebellion of 1794, Washington and Jefferson supported authoritarian regulations to keep the nation secure. Her speech ended with a rousing call to authoritarians. "The military is a tool that works for us. They are loyal to us. Only the most loyal deserve to play a part in solving the chaos of democracy. What are we willing to do to show our loyalty?"

The informant claimed that a "swell of applause" spread across the auditorium. The Dominion Directive's leadership told her that the speech was groundbreaking and invited her to join their cause – to promote shadow authoritarian military leadership in democratic countries.

Archie skimmed pages looking for the informant's name, but his index finger stopped on a sentence. When asked about her brother Archie's dangerous financial support of fledgling democratic leaders, she scoffed and said that her brother was the victim of a conspiracy. She said to Orlov, the informant, "Leave him to me. I'll set him right."

Koslov's phone call on The Sea Eagle – How long had Orlov been manipulating his vulnerable sister? In a rush of clarity, Archie dropped the article in his lap. He worked his jaw and stared at the call buttons and air conditioning vents over his head, the same as those above every passenger seat. That article sentence read like the crash of an ocean wave before the clawing undertow dragged it back to the sea.

He thought of Logan growing up in the US, the world's policeman, the tentpole of the West, with power enough to protect itself and help its friends with their shared values. It was clear to him that the US tentpole could crack at any moment, depending on who believed the evidence. He'd do everything possible to keep his journalists from hoisting the white flag. He'd provide more ad revenue to the village papers, ads for local bakers, mechanics, grocers, money for newspapers to hire his graduated students as full-time reporters – whatever it took to keep the newspapers afloat.

The nine-hour flight meant he would arrive in New York City shortly after noon. He connected the student's evidence to the evidence he and Zolt had gathered before he left. The European branch of the group planned to remove Havel from office by force and make it look like a heroic act by the people. Rivka would write a speech manipulating the American historical perspective and casting doubt on any authoritarian responsibility for the coup. Her manipulated facts would frame the angry locals in Prague as the culprits.

The week before, a handful of locals had been paid to storm the Palace in Prague against a false report that Havel had embezzled tax money and hidden it in a private account in an unknown bank. On television, Havel showed viewers the evidence of legitimate state accounts of the funds, but opposition protesters shouted that they didn't believe him. They condemned Havel's handling of the destructive flood's cleanup, which was too expensive and had taken too long.

Now Archie could see why Zolt had dropped everything to get him on a plane to New York. Rivka's speeches and activity surely aroused the suspicions of CIA officials in the States and her group grew fearful of discovery. Zolt told him what he already knew: that this group would stop at nothing to keep the CIA from picking up Rivka. Archie turned to the next page and found a note from Zolt.

Archie,

This is hard to write, especially now. With the Havel assassination threat in addition to our usual protectees, security is exhausted. Our men and women love their work. This is not about pay but about long hours that wear us down, make us less effective, and make us more prone to mistakes. We have limited flexibility with the Hungarian and Czech laws, unlike in Vienna. Our single-minded workaholics risk burning out. When issues arise with little warning, the time limitations make us scramble. Our people get worn out, trying to fight exhaustion and keep their focus.

Havel's security has been compromised and we can't be sure who to trust. Hungarian security is in the process of firing those who are loyal to the Constitution instead of to their alternate views. I have a CIA contact in the States with diplomatic contacts. With our help, she can lower the temperature and slow things down. We are here for you, but with this chain of events, we need more time to do our best work.

No legacy is so rich as honesty,
Zolt

Below the note, Archie saw the signatures of each member of his European security detail. With the speed of these issues, he had taken for granted the mounting dangers of their work. Rereading the names, he pictured their faces. His finger traced the signatures, and he vowed to meet with his New York security detail to arrange a meeting with the CIA operative if he could find her.

CHAPTER 64

2000 New York

When Archie arrived, government officials were there to drive him first to the impounding area to verify that the SUV was in his name. Archie saw the entire front end smashed beyond repair, windshield splattered with blood. This was the vehicle with custom accommodations so Rivka's foot wouldn't get in the way of her independence. The same vehicle he drove like hell to take Logan to the hospital.

Rivka's accident stopped her from revealing the Dominion Directive members and their connection to anti-government groups in Moldova. Because of him, the shadowy Moldovan group, in their attempt to end Havel's leadership, instructed its US branch, Dominion Directive, to eliminate his sister, staging her death in an elaborate betrayal. The US group obeyed, ending her life to protect the group.

"Have you checked for a cut brake line? An accelerator malfunction?" Archie asked.

"Everything checked out initially. The interior had a burnt smell like the power steering fluid hadn't been changed." The black-suited government official leafed through a clipboard of check sheets completed by the mechanic who had done the work.

"Archie had to admit that Rivka was not one to remember maintenance work. "Could the fluid have been drained? Can you check fingerprints?"

"It's hard to do with the heat from the engine. We've only done a preliminary check. It'll take a few days, maybe a week. She hit a white rental van that ran a stop sign. The driver escaped, and we haven't found them. No fingerprints, no registration or insurance, rented to Ainsley Smith, paid in cash."

Various government groups questioned Archie, including the NTSB, the accident investigation team, and the New York City police.

Last of all was a CIA operative. Archie was heartened by her thorough questions and the steps she would take to push the investigation ahead. He felt validated that Logan was growing up in a country that followed the rule of law instead of locking up or killing political adversaries. "My nephew is getting home from school," Archie said. Explaining this to Logan was unthinkable. "Someone has to tell him about his mother. Can this wait until tomorrow?"

The agent lowered her head, scribbled something, and gave Archie her card. On the back, she had written, *Talk to Zolt.* She assured him she had some sand to throw into the gears and slow the pace. "We have diplomats can take care of slowing things down. We work closely with them." Their investigation depended on it as well.

Logan returned from school, and Archie opened the door before the boy reached the steps to the house. "Something's happened to Mom. My teacher was acting all weird and huggy when I left. She told me you'd be home when I got there. I want to see Mom. Where is she?"

Archie tensed and took his hand, guiding Logan to the living room. "An accident happened. Your mother was a – remarkable woman. I can tell you more about her someday when you're older."

He looked into Logan's reddening eyes. Now, there was a hole in his world. "All her life, it was my job to protect her, and I failed." He waited for his voice to steady itself. "No matter what it takes, I will protect you."

Through the afternoon, Archie answered as many of Logan's questions as he could. When he accepted the blame for her death, Logan was strangely calm. Together, they searched his mother's desk and bedside table for a phone number to call his dad. He used burner phones out of fear of being tracked, and the numbers often changed. Tomorrow, Archie would search her desk in the CUNY Humanities Department office.

It grew dark. Archie knew they had to eat something, but neither was hungry. In the freezer, he found some soup Rivka had made. He warmed it on the stove and placed a bowl before Logan. In the middle of the table were a few pieces of unopened mail. Archie watched Logan wipe his sleeve across his cheeks as he ate.

In a few days, Zolt arrived from the airport. From the window, Logan was surprised to see Zolt with two women and a boy he'd never met. "Dod Archie, Zolt is here, but I don't know who these people are."

"It's okay, Logan. Answer the door." Archie moved to the table to take hold of the flowers he'd bought for Elida. When he looked up, he couldn't move. Layla stood before Archie, taking his hand. "I'm so sorry, Archie." She looked at him with eyes that said so much and embraced him burying her face in his chest.

Archie believed never again would he feel the electric intensity of her arms around him – the flowers fell from his hand. "Layla." It was all he could say as he reached for her.

"You're Layla?" Logan said. "*Dod* Archie talks about you all the time. He tugged at her arm. "And he says you tell good stories."

Layla pulled away. "Nice to finally meet you, Logan." She looked at the boy who had hair and eyes that were all Archie. "Your uncle and I have a mutual friend, Vaclav Havel, and he tells me you two hike together. If it's okay with Archie, maybe we can go hiking together someday." She turned back to Archie and waited for his agreement.

He looked into her searching expression and tried to answer, but words wouldn't come. Archie took her hand with the emerald ring and kissed it.

Zolt waited in the silence and cleared his throat which brought Archie out of his fog.

"Logan, I'd like you to meet Elida. She's the woman I told you about who raised goats with her nephew Mulilo. He's about your age. I'll stay here with you as often as I can, but Elida will be here with you when I can't be. You and Mulilo can go to school together." Archie said that Mulilo came from Kenya, and he hoped Logan would help the boy adjust to school in a new country. Logan awkwardly shook his hand. Mulilo was nearly a head taller than Logan. Neither boy reached past Archie's shoulders, but it wouldn't be long before they did. Logan took Mulilo to his room.

"I'm only here until the boys are educated," Elida reminded Archie. "I want to return to my village." She expressed sorrow for Archie's and Logan's loss and told him about changes since their last letters. "This move took place years before we had planned to arrive, so preparations were far from organized."

Archie watched Zolt show Layla to the kitchen and turned back to Elida. He told Elida how thankful he was that she'd agreed to move to a new country on short notice. They could hear the boys talking in Logan's room. "It will take time for Logan to understand what has happened. I'm not sure I understand it."

"They're kids. They have both had upheavals in their lives. Maybe they can sort things out together."

Archie watched her uneasily sink into the living room chair. He thought of Rivka in that chair, absently nursing newborn Logan and talking through a college outline. Logan's eyes would focus on her face and voice as if he understood her words.

"Zolt has told you about security for you and the boys," Archie said. "I know it's inconvenient and disrupts your privacy. Mine too. I get used to it; I hope you will. The team is experienced and will stay out of your way as much as possible."

Zolt and Layla joined them with glasses and a pitcher of water. "Elida, did Zolt tell you that he is from the Czech Republic?" Archie tried to lighten their conversation.

"On the plane, I told her how I would help her and Mulilo adjust," Zolt said.

Archie couldn't bring himself to mention that the security detail meant to protect Rivka was identified and killed along with her. He assured Zolt that there was no way the security detail could have prepared for the speed of the decision to end Rivka's life, and told himself he would be more careful now with tighter security. "It's important that you tell him if you're going someplace other than the grocery or shopping," Archie warned her. "Logan is a Boy Scout, and there is soccer practice. Mulilo could go if he wanted to."

Elida's face lit up at the mention of soccer, Mulilo's favorite sport. "I have an aunt in Greenwich Village. I'm also involved with the OSAA, a lobbying group that informs the United Nations of Africa's concerns. I hoped I could bring more awareness from here."

Archie felt disjointed with so many people in the house at once. If Rivka were here, she'd know just what to do to make everyone content and make it seem effortless. Not Archie. For him, it felt like tending a series of fires. "They're still talking about your speech in Vienna," Archie said. "Zolt will check and make sure you're safe going where you need to go."

Elida's shoulders fell. Mulilo's opportunity for education put their lives at significant risk.

Zolt took out his cell phone and stepped out of the room.

"Logan seems like a fine boy," Elida said. "What about his father?"

Archie shook his head. "We're trying to locate him. He's a journalist."

Elida nodded. "You know, I don't cook like Logan probably eats - hamburgers and such. Yams, millet, lentils, Joilof rice – that's what we eat."

Archie thought of Rivka's soup that he had warmed from the freezer and ate with Logan that first night. "Food will bring you together." Archie laughed. "You should see some of the camp meals I made for us. If he could eat those, he'll love your cooking."

Elida was insulted but figured that Archie meant no harm by it. Layla sat next to her and asked about Elida's work with the UN.

Logan leaned his head around the corner.

"You know, journalists are heroes, like doctors," Archie told him. He wanted to prepare Logan for the news before his return to school when classmates started asking questions about his mother.

"Mom hated journalists except for the kind like Dad."

"They are a way to check and balance the government. They're brave and sometimes pay a price for their dangerous work."

"They get good people in trouble, Mom said."

"Leaders who do the right thing can be ruined by lies, not the truth. Good reporters don't judge; they just report what happened. It takes time for people to trust the truth when they've relied on lies for a long time. But that trust can be built one small village newspaper at a time. That's what I'm doing."

"Does Zolt protect the journalists too?"

"He does, along with his team."

"That's a lot of work," Logan said, tight-lipped.

"I couldn't do my work without him." Archie noticed Logan tried to cover the braces on his teeth when he talked in front of Mulilo.

"Like that day at the Temple," Logan said.

"He saved some lives that day, ours too."

"*Dod* Archie, I want to show you something," Logan said.

He and Mulilo led the way back upstairs and into his mother's room. Opening the closet door, they saw laundry baskets full of folders and documents, a shambolic war room against the marginalized.

Then Archie noticed the closet walls covered in tin foil. "What is this?"

"She had been working on it since school started. If I chewed gum, she'd use the silver wrapper on the wall. It's kitchen foil, sometimes two layers thick. She got afraid, and she made me afraid, too."

"What made her afraid?"

"She said that the bad people were watching her. We weren't safe. The people who wanted to mix the races weren't loyal. Sorry, Mulilo, but she said that only the loyal people could live and we had to hide here sometimes to keep ourselves safe. She said it was microwaves. They couldn't get through the foil and into our brains."

"She hid here?" Archie said.

Logan nodded. "I told you sometimes that I'd come home from school, and she'd pull me in here too. For a long time. It was worse lately." He kicked the toe of his sneaker on the wood floor. "She hardly looked at me or talked to me. When she said it was okay to get out, it would be dark outside."

All the worries Logan had tried to express, he had brushed off as youthful exaggeration. "Did the security people know about this?" Archie asked.

"I don't think so. They only came upstairs if we heard noises, but that was before the foil."

Layla and Elida had joined them at the closet doorway, peering at the foil. Elida caught Archie's look. "The most courageous act is to think for yourself," Elida spoke from the closet doorway and Logan moved to stand beside her. Archie knelt inside the cramped closet to look into some of the laundry baskets. He picked up a collection of paper copies with one staple in the left corner.

You desperate pedophile molester kidnapper using your lies on young journalists to spread your denial that you bring dirty, dangerous immigrants here to steal jobs from hard-working, God-fearing European Americans —

Archie recognized this email from a few days ago, brought to his attention by his Vienna computer security official. He leafed through the others with similar, recognizable threats. The last page was a list of theories, the first part typed, the last ones in Rivka's slanted handwriting.

A gathering of atheists produced a thunderstorm

UFO linked to 30 missing children

Y2K bugs will shut down power grids and banks – will occur in 2016, 2038

Oil spill in Virginia cleaned the river

World Economic Forum declares all babies must be grown in labs by 2030

President filed to overturn First Amendment

Doctors are euthanizing elders to save the planet

Erase Civil Rights history to protect our youth

K-Mart sells satanic merchandise

Borax is cure for dementia

Vaccines cause strokes

Jews' secret plan to replace European Americans with Muslim non-whites

Police microchip children to prevent trafficking

Group of Black Alabama women used witchcraft to start brawl.

Federal Government planned SARS outbreak

Proposal to add vaccines to water supply in New York

Law will require DNA test before any father can sign birth certificate

Thousands of scientists collude to sign false evidence that we are at fault for changing climate

Holocaust denier is human rights activist

Government orchestrated Ebola outbreak in Texas.

US president secretly flies African illegals into the country on Air Force One.

"Mulilo, would you call Zolt up here, please?" Archie said.

"Is something wrong? Did Mom do something wrong?" Logan said.

Archie looked at the silver walls and considered the haze that was Logan's life. Yet he had not been taken in by this. It seemed like a miracle that Logan saw past it.

Someday, Archie could tell Logan about his mother and her illness, that the beliefs people have sometimes work against them. Fear and nihilism ate at her thinking. Their search for a more significant concept to justify or affirm false beliefs came at a cost. He couldn't say he should have been there to save his sister from herself. But he would remind Logan that it's possible to keep two opposing ideas together in our minds. His mother loved him beyond measure.

"These emails may have gone to the wrong people. Zoli can fix it. Did you read any of these?"

"She never said not to, but I have enough reading from school. I figured it was work stuff," Logan said.

Archie kept his voice calm. "Layla, Elida, could you keep the boys downstairs? There's the game *Othello* in the cabinet by the sofa."

Mulilo returned with Zolt. "I need you to review these emails," Archie said. "We may need to send some messages of – clarification." He pointed to a covert address with links that referenced an international hitman. "Our office in Vienna has steps they can take to – secure things here, and they need to know who they're up against."

Mulilo found Logan at the bottom of the stairs. He walked down to join him. "Let's go back to your room," Mulilo said.

Logan learned which old stair treads creaked and practiced going up and down without a sound. He told Mulilo how to do it. "Follow me."

"Why would I want to birdwalk all over the steps?"

"In case you want to be quiet," Logan said.

"Again, why?"

"I didn't want to be found when I ran away. Then, after, I did it to listen to my dad and mom talking. I tried to figure out Dad's moods so he wouldn't be so mad at me, but it didn't work," Logan said.

"There were times I had to be quiet from the terrorists," Mulilo said.

Together, they made their way up in a silent crisscross to the top of the stairs. Logan felt relief that his uncle knew about the closet, a burden he no longer had to keep to himself.

In his room, he led Mulilo to a shelf by his bed where he pointed out a collection of rocks from hiking trips.

"What's that?" asked Mulilo looking up.

Logan took a crude clay figure from a high shelf and handed it to Mulilo. "*Dod* Archie says it's from Jewish folklore. He gave it to me when I had my appendix out. See?" He raised his shirt to show Mulilo the scar.

"See this word? He pointed to the word carved into the clay, *Emet*. "Emet means truth. It's just pretend, but it's supposed to come to life in times of great trouble, and this is one of those times. When the time is over, it loses its power again."

Mulilo turned the weighty figure over in his hands and gave it back. "It's like a goblin, then. Special powers, not real," he said.

Mulilo reached into the bottom of his pocket and pulled out the compass Archie had given him after their soccer game. "When things get hard, I hold the compass in my hand." He handed it to Logan. "I held it when I left my village and again on the plane to New York. It reminds me to point myself in the direction I need to go."

He handed it to Logan. Together they watched the needle sway and rotate. "Maybe the compass pointed me here," Mulilo said.

Logan turned it around in his hand and asked Mulilo what Africa was like.

"It is very hot. Here it is cool. I have a joke. Why do fish live in saltwater? Because pepper makes them sneeze."

Logan smiled and the boys sat on the floor. "For my people the word life is *l'chaim,* We celebrate being alive."

"My father was a farmer and miner," Mulilo said. "He wrote music, made speeches, and led our village until the violence came. They killed him because of his speeches. Aunty Elida's home is – was a square of metal at the end of a street, not solid like this. Your house will stand up to bad weather."

"It has a few leaks, but *Dod* Archie will fix them." Logan returned the compass to Mulilo. "We could go to Coney Island and ride the Cyclone. Do you have rollercoasters in Kenya?"

"We have cyclones during monsoon season, but we don't name rollercoasters after them. Aunty Elida took me to an amusement park in Nairobi last year, and I was tall enough for one rollercoaster." He put the compass back in his pocket. "What about this Cyclone?"

In the living room, Archie and Zolt joined Elida and Layla, who had found a few games for the boys to play. "You need to spend time with the boys," Zolt told Archie. "Something normal. *The Goonies* is playing at The Roxy on 6th Avenue. I can secure it. Take them."

Archie slapped Zolt's back in a gesture of thanks."I spoke with the CIA yesterday. They asked for any information, and I didn't know where to start until now." He thought about the baskets of papers. "But first, the boys. That movie is the best idea I've heard in a long time," he said. "Popcorn and Twizzlers for everyone."

Archie looked at Elida and then at Layla, for confirmation.

"What is a Twizzler?" asked Elida.

After the *Goonies* movie and Twizzlers, it was pizza at Grimaldi's, Archie drove everyone back to the brownstone drained and ready for bed. Zolt had put Elida's bags in Rivka's room and Mulilo's bags in a spare bedroom with a window that overlooked the back yard. Archie took Layla's bag up the stairs himself, making sure it didn't end up anywhere else but his room.

She opened her suitcase and took out a suit to hang up. Opening the closet door, she wasn't surprised to see only three changes of clothing in Archie's closet. "I'm so tired, I'm going to bed," she said. "I can unpack tomorrow."

She shed her clothes and slipped into bed. Archie did the same. They soon found that they weren't quite as tired as they thought.

CHAPTER 65

2000 New York

Archie's bare feet tramped into the kitchen early on the second morning after Elida had arrived. He found her bustling around the kitchen in her brightly colored robe, hair tied up atop her head, and the scent of coffee filling the room.

Archie looked at her, and a wave of home washed over him. He pushed the sentiment out of his mind, the nostalgia, remembering the kerfuffles he had with Layla about the value of this feeling. "Elida, I hope you know how important you are to this family. You sacrificed your community life to come here, and I can't tell you – "

"No need," Elida said with a wave of her hand. "Mulilo will benefit, so it is what is best for us, too. I heard the boys talking in Logan's room last night. I think in time, they will each fill an empty spot in the other." She was about to say more but turned to pour the coffee before she spoke. "We all suffer losses." She placed a cup on the counter in front of him, and he warmed his hands around it.

Archie looked at his laptop on the counter and fired it up before sorting through Rivka's mail, stacked on the kitchen table. Past the bills, he saw a handwritten envelope with a familiar name and a Syrian return address, postmarked the week before. He ripped open the letter – although it was addressed to Rivka – something he would have to do more of now. The note inside was addressed to him, and he was sure that if Rivka had ever opened the envelope, he would never have known that Bibi had sent him the message.

Rafiq Archie,

I heard you were on your way to the States, so I'll try to reach you this way. I continue working with lawyers archiving reports of repression from the new regime. There is talk of a new Truth and Reconciliation Commission to get victims and their antagonizers face to face, work through the problems, and live in peace again. Layla suggested that in collaboration with deposition lawyers, your journalists could work together, writing and archiving crime evidence for social justice, letting the villages know they have a choice. Would your new university in Tartu, Estonia, help with this? Let me know what you think.

The two lawyers we trained to continue Layla's work have allowed us to expand our plan. We have decided to publish a book about our work. Of course, the book cannot be published in Syria. Beirut will publish for us. In my dreams, the world takes notice, and Syria accepts human rights justice.

Best wishes,

Bibi

He finished his coffee and wondered about Bibi and Layla's plan. In their long conversations since her arrival, she hadn't mentioned anything in the letter. Bibi and Layla were laying the groundwork for the kind of world he wanted to leave for his nephew and Mulilo. He returned the message to the envelope to show Layla later, and found something he had missed — the photograph of Layla and himself on Marek's barge. On the back, Bibi had written that she had just found the photo at the bottom of a box of papers from Layla's desk when she was away for rehabilitation. How young they looked. He consumed every detail, holding the corners as if he'd never let go.

Next to the mail, the *New York News* headline punched a hole in his morning. "Jail Death Ruled Suicide" brought to mind his call with Rivka pleading for money. He read that the man died in his cell, hanging from bed sheets. Guards had not checked on him as they were supposed to, but his death was still ruled a suicide. Rivka had wanted this man to die before he could tell what he knew.

Rivka's death left Archie with a staggering sense of responsibility. He had failed in his promise to protect her. It could have been a distraction from the coup to overthrow Havel, or a coverup. He should have tried harder to convince her that she was misled. All the wild stories she told, and those Logan talked about – she was tricked. He could have reminded her that Logan needed her. Why didn't he try to get her to realize that her sources clouded her sense of reason? Surely, she wouldn't have gone through with the plot to kill him. Somewhere there had to be evidence that she tried to stop it. Where along the way did this unquestioning, ridiculous loyalty overtake her that she would conspire to destroy the freedom she prized so much? Maybe she felt she was in so deep that there was no going back.

This feeling of loss triggered a cascade of past events when the world became meaningless and overwhelming. He stared at the words on the page. His hands rubbed the sides of his aching head. An examined life, on scrutiny, always came up short, but he pushed that out of his mind. Time to focus on protecting those he could and exposing those who forced the need for protection. Now, he would do what he always did after a great loss: get to work.

His phone lit up. "Zolt, when is my flight?" Archie traipsed the kitchen at his peripatetic lecturer's pace and listened.

Tia Gabriella had called him the night before. The story had made the national news of Europe. Archie told her about a small column on the front page of the American news. As he flipped through the front section, he was encouraged to see four pages and five articles dedicated to the conspiracy. One of the articles was a translation of his students' work that he'd read on the plane to New York. Their journalism had made the leap from village news to the national New York paper. At this point, it would be impossible for Chertok to carry out his plan to remove Havel.

Gabriella's words were sharp and coherent when she'd called him in the middle of the night. This time, it wasn't about her health. One of Zorica's special friends visited, and he had important information about Rivka's contact, Andrei Orlov. Zorica would tell no one but Archie in person, and it had to be done soon.

There he was, Andrei Orlov, the man from Dominion Directive who tried to manipulate Rivka. Archie was eager to question Zorica, to discover everything that she had learned. Did Orlov have connections to Turla? To *Bratva*? Kristof and Nicoletta's article mentioned Koslov as well. It read, "The work of village journalists was instrumental in exposing corruption." To weaken Archie's support, Dominion Directive had killed his sister. The evidence of propaganda and the takedown of Chertok's disinformation empire spread to the BBC and Germany's *Die Zeit* before the Kremlin could produce *kompromat* to counteract it. Archie recalled his last conversation with the communications operative Chertok, how he had labeled the university journalists as coddled and delicate. His *kompromat* warp and distortion fueled the poisonings and disappearances, eliminating any clear-eyed worldview.

Messages from Zolt and Havel, as well as the probable move of his university to Estonia, were arriving on his laptop. In a breathtaking display of support for the rule of law, thousands of news sources, local and regional, carried Kristof's and Nicoletta's story – even the *Yomiori Shimbun*, the newspaper of record in Japan. No source of propaganda in the world had that reach – not even Chertok.

Breaking news of a prisoner exchange shared the page with

Nicoletta and Kristof's story. The Russians traded an assassin for an American journalist, a *Times* reporter. The American President and NATO leaders flexed their statecraft muscles, forcing a camel through the eye of a needle to get the journalist home. The life cycle of news was short, but Nicoletta and Kristof's story was just unfolding, and their continued reporting would make new headlines going forward.

The moment had presented itself. Now, with undeniable evidence, the quiet rebellion of his journalists would follow Chertok to the Hague's International Criminal Court. The small actions of village news had reverberating consequences. A stone in a pond made ripples that spread in every direction.

Zolt gave Archie the flight time only a few hours away, and Layla's flight back to Syria was shortly after. He had enough time to talk to Logan before they left for the airport. Zolt confirmed that security was set for his meeting in London with the European Society of News Editors and the Society of Professional Journalists. Archie made a mental note to include student representatives, think tanks, and humanitarian groups in the network.

"The Quiet Crush: How Trust in Village News Exposed a Strongman Dictator." Archie wanted to read the article below the headline, but first, he would contact Kristof and Nicoletta and arrange for them to wait in a safe space in Madrid. Zorica had a contact for Nicoletta, inside the detention house. She would provide disguises, an Orthodox priest's robe for Kristof, and an aged woman's dress and scarf for Nicoletta. Together, they would free Nicoletta's friend, Tonya.

He could put it all on hold for a while, release the inner howl, and stop to feel his no-longer-solitary existence, but the menacing unease to get back to work clawed and scratched at him. He could almost hear Layla's remonstrations: *Take time to heal*. But for him, work was the only way through the loss.

CHAPTER 66

2000 Hungary/New York

Kristof and Nicoletta stood outside the door of Kristof's local town hall meeting. "Are you going to tell me to remove my black lipstick and piercings before we meet your local people?" she asked.

"No. You are beautiful as you are," he told her. "Mr. Hoffman has a contact in Spain who may have information about your friend Tonya. We'll meet him and his contact in a few days. There's more to investigate."

"You are right with the investigating. I need to make the obvious possible. No more *is not possible.* When this is over, I'm going for the myths – dissect why people fear and believe the fakery that does nothing but hurt them." She unbuttoned the top two buttons of his shirt. "You are a stud," she said. Together, they walked into the village community center to answer questions about the local man-turned-traitor.

After a second coffee, Archie recalled the warmth of the bed where Layla still slept, and the tiny scar over her left eyebrow. "Now we both have scars," she told him before they fell asleep. The memory of her was no longer an imagined fiction. In the midst of so much tragedy, was it wrong that his soul could be filled with such joy? He looked through the window at the overcast sky and smelled coconut. Elida was warming *Mandazi* in the microwave. She had found an African bakery yesterday and brought the triangular donut pillows home for the boys' breakfast.

For some reason, his focus shifted to something Zolt had mentioned about his coming trip to Spain. Kristof and Nicoletta had found a few slips of paper with the Russian Cyrillic for NYSTINEHZLOS. When they met in Spain, Archie was curious to know if they could be part of Zorica's lost notes. The notes were only scraps, but releasing information might encourage those with the rest of the stolen evidence to make a move and expose more information.

But now the visit to Spain would be expanded – a reunion with *Tia* Gabriella and Layla. He decided to arrange for a pitcher of Sangria on her patio, and to play the tango music she loved. Why not? Havel would call it a delight of the heart. Time measured in loss when he saw the wreckage of his sister's SUV, was now ticking toward love.

He turned to see the boys in their pajamas and slippers scuffling into the kitchen, safe from the world. After everything they had been through, he relished their fidgety restlessness and innocent chatter, inching out the soreness in his heart. They pulled out chairs that scraped the floor and sat: neither looked like he had slept much.

"That smells great, Elida," Logan said. "*Dod* Archie, you have to leave again, don't you?"

Archie pulled an imaginary thread from his robe.

"I know." Logan picked up a *Mandazi* and watched Mulilo dip one in a big bowl of coconut cream before popping it into his mouth.

Logan grabbed a spoon. "I want gobs of cream." He dipped his *Mandazi* and mentioned that he'd like these again some time. They didn't get stuck in his braces like Twizzlers did.

Archie said, "The word 'gobs' is a Middle English word from the 1300s, and it means a mouthful."

"You have to get used to that," Logan said. "*Dod* Archie always tells me where words come from."

"Gobs?" Mulilo said.

"You don't have to use that word, Mulilo. You have new things to learn here, but that word doesn't matter."

"I like it." Mulilo dipped the spoon and covered a *Mandazi*. "It has gobs of coconut."

Logan swallowed. "Mulilo and I decided last night that you're getting old, *Dod* Archie."

Archie frowned at them. Two bright-eyed young men looked back.

"I mean, you still have some good years left, but when we grow up, we can take over for you," Logan said. "Don't worry. We'll take care of your business, and we'll take care of you."

Elida's hand rushed to her mouth to hide her smile.

AFTERWORD

- Most events and conspiracies are based on real events, with details fictionalized.
- Arnold Schwarzenegger was governor of California in 2003, not 1989.
- Havel's poem to his wife was written in 1989.
- Brychtova's glass obelisk is on display at the Flint Institute of Arts in Michigan.
- The Czech flood was real. Over 30,000 citizens became homeless. But the flood occurred in 2002, after the end of this book.
- The Alchemy Museum was not discovered until after the flood had receded, rather than in the 1990s as the book would suggest.
- The CIA's Operation Eris is fiction.
- "Come Away With Me," Nora Jones's song referenced in CHAPTER 31, was not written until 2002.
- The closing words of Zolt's letter, "No legacy is so rich as honesty" are from Shakespeare.
- The *Samizdat Network* took place in the 1970s, not the 1960s.
- Havel's first wife Olga actually died in 1996 from cancer.
- The FBI's Operation Intering was real.

ABOUT GRATITUDE AND THE AUTHOR

Much gratitude and appreciation goes to the encouragement and fine-tuned editing skills of my writing group member and friend, Susan Sage. I am also indebted to the dedicated work of Penny Silva, Jan Worth, and Theodosia Robertson.

Patty Duffy is curious about history, world markets, and the effects of leadership. The Compass Point is her third novel. She is the mother of three amazing children, and lives in Michigan. She can be found on many spring and summer days hiking and cycling with her partner, Ralph.

READERS' GUIDE QUESTIONS FOR THE COMPASS POINT

In the beginning, Archie is torn between his commitments to the university and his concern that his nephew Logan will run away. How could he have handled it differently?

Much of Archie's life is spent trying to atone for Rivka's injury and the British Pound debacle. How does this guilt work to his disadvantage?

Archie and Layla have periods of trust and distrust in one another. What character traits do they share?

What happens to change Layla's mind concerning her Jewish/Palestinian conflict with Archie?

What is it about Kristof that makes Archie set up the meeting with Havel?

Is it realistic that a letter about one African boy, Juma, would motivate Archie to continue his work with providing low-cost loans?

What is typical about Archie and Rivka's sibling rivalry?

Layla's deposition work makes her feel numb, so she climbs mountains to recapture her ability to feel. What would it be like to lose your ability to experience emotions?

At what point do Logan's childhood complaints seem to be about more than rebellion?

What is Chertok's power that makes him a challenging adversary?

How do you feel about Nicoletta's Russian ambivilance and her behavior?

In the end, Archie can't locate Logan's dad. What do you think this means for Archie and Logan's lives going forward?

What is the flaw in Archie's reasoning throughout his life, to take care of those he loves?

BOOKS THAT INSPIRED ARCHIE'S CHARACTER

The Power of Myth – Joseph Campbell with Bill Moyer

Humanly Possible – Sarah Bakewell

Age of Revolutions – Fareed Zakaria

Open Society – Reforming Global Capitalism – George Soros